T0145779

Also by Austin Williams

Rusty Diamond Mysteries
Misdirection
Blind Shuffle

The Platinum Loop
Crimson Orgy
Straight Whisky (with Erik Quisling)

Diversion Books
A Division of Diversion Publishing Corp.
443 Park Avenue South, Suite 1008
New York, New York 10016
www.DiversionBooks.com

For more information, email info@diversionbooks.com

First Diversion Books edition May 2017.
Print ISBN: 978-1-68230-311-5
eBook ISBN: 978-1-68230-310-8

Connect with Austin Williams on Twitter **@awilliams_books**

TORN &
RESTORED

A
RUSTY DIAMOND
MYSTERY

AUSTIN WILLIAMS

DIVERSIONBOOKS

1.

The box contained a sheet of textbook paper, three human teeth, an adult index finger severed just above the second knuckle, and a greeting card. Made of lightweight cardboard and roughly a foot square in size, it begged for destruction.

Rusty wanted to yank the box from its perch on his kitchen table and throw it into the fireplace. Douse it with lighter fluid and toss a match. The box leered at him like some kind of foul rebuke. It offended his eyes. He wanted to take a hammer and smash the thing to dust. Drop it in a landfill hundreds of miles away and bury every last fiber so deep it was beyond any chance of salvation.

Those were not realistic options. Rusty had no choice but to deal with this box on its own terms. The first step was finding out who the hell had sent it to him.

"Still there?" he asked into the cell phone. Over the course of this long-distance conversation, Dr. Lima had shown a propensity for silences.

"Still here, Mr. Diamond," she eventually answered. "Sit tight, I haven't forgotten you."

"Take your time," Rusty said, careful not to sound impatient. It had required some digging to obtain a direct line for Dr. Estrella Lima of the Anthropology Department at the University of Nevada, Las Vegas. If she took offense at his tone and decided to terminate the call, he'd be back at square one.

The box had appeared on his doorstep in Ocean Pines this morning. It was the third one he'd received in the past six days, each arriving via parcel post. The contents found inside each box had grown progressively more alarming, and the prospect of what a fourth box might contain terrified him.

A call to UNLV's Anthropology Department wasn't much to allay his fears, but it was a start. Dr. Lima just might be able to impart some tiny fragment of knowledge to propel him in the right direction.

If she ever comes back on the damn line, Rusty thought as he paced the kitchen floor.

He'd almost tripped over the first box last Thursday, emerging from the house shortly after dawn for his daily six-mile run. He couldn't account for its unexpected appearance. Rusty had managed to live for more than two years effectively off the grid; the postman rarely brought him anything other than junk mail. His initial response was to assume it had been delivered to the wrong address.

He was wrong. The package had most definitely been intended for him, as were the others. All three boxes were identical, at least on the outside. Same size, same lightweight cardboard. Someone had scrawled his name and address on one side and affixed a dozen stamps. A handwritten return address didn't offer him much in the way of trackable information:

Nossa Morte
The Underworld
NV 89109

Compared to what followed, the first package had seemed almost innocuous. The sole aspect of its arrival that disturbed Rusty was knowing someone in Nevada had discovered his whereabouts. The box contained only a 32 MB flash drive. Curiosity overrode his fear of malware. Plugging it into his laptop, he'd found a single item on the drive, an MP4 video file. He'd played it, at first astonished and then dismayed by what he saw.

It was a low-resolution piece of video, just under four minutes long, showing a performance of some kind. No audio. A young woman in a stained t-shirt and jeans lay strapped to a table in murky lighting. Behind the table stood a tall, broad-shouldered man in a sleeveless black robe. He clutched a small hatchet in one hand and walked around the table, gesticulating to someone out of frame.

Rusty recognized the movements, the specific body positioning of the man circling the table. He'd performed the exact same motions, hundreds of times, on the stage at Caesars Palace. The accuracy of this pantomime was so strong it made him almost dizzy.

But that wasn't the most disconcerting element of the video.

The man looked exactly like Rusty. Long black hair, tapered goatee, snaking vines of tattoos covering both sinewy arms. The resemblance was so strong, Rusty needed multiple viewings to confirm he wasn't looking at some moment from the past captured without his recollection.

Dead ringer. No other word for it.

The video ended abruptly, just as the robed man started lowering the hatchet toward the woman's neck. The implication of what happened after the camera stopped rolling was clear enough.

Rusty tried to dismiss the video as a prank, or possibly a misguided attempt at flattery via sick imitation. Someone must have seen one of his performances from his run at Caesars (YouTube was loaded with such fan-made clips) and decided to recreate it. Creepy, but not worth freaking out over.

He'd returned the flash drive to the box and deposited the box in his hall closet. Then he'd almost managed to forget about it, until two days later when the second package arrived.

No flash drive in that one, just a small, cubical object. Rusty recognized it even as he teased away a protective wad of bubble wrap.

It was one half of a pair of dice, but not the standard casino variety. This was a magician's die, pure black onyx, eight sided and marked with various arcane symbols. Again, Rusty recoiled with a sense of personal violation. He'd used dice of exactly this type in countless illusions back in his early days as an unlicensed performance artist on Fremont Street.

It took several minutes of examination to notice a detail that made him almost physically sick. The die had a small nick on the side containing an omega symbol. Rusty still remembered when he'd dropped his onyx cube on a sidewalk and scratched it like that.

Six…seven years ago? Longer?

The date was irrelevant. What mattered was the realization that this die wasn't merely similar to one he'd used in an ill-remembered past. It was *his* property, an artifact of a former life he'd lost track of long ago. Inexplicably mailed to him from some phantom address in the Mojave Desert. And it was covered with what looked like dried blood.

A handwritten note had accompanied the die:

> *Looks like you've been up to some dirty business, Raven. Your fingerprints and someone else's blood all over this thing, as well as its companion (which is safe in our possession—for now). Could find yourself in some hot water if you're not careful. You'd better come back home before things get really nasty.*

After reading that note enough times to memorize it, Rusty had deposited the second package in the hallway next to its precursor. He'd spent much of the following two days in a state of reeling speculation, trying to figure out what the deliveries could mean.

Then, today, the third package had arrived, its contents so gruesome Rusty couldn't stand to examine them closely for more than a minute or two.

The extracted teeth were all molars. About the roots they were dotted with dried blood of the same dark hue as that covering the die. These teeth had not come from a mouth treated to regular dental hygiene, and they hadn't been pulled gently. The finger was unquestionably male. A thatch of dark hair sprouted from the third knuckle. The jagged rim of flesh around the severed edge and the short protuberance of yellowing bone suggested the work of a hacksaw or a similarly serrated implement.

All day, Rusty's mental focus had ping-ponged in two directions, seeking answers to a pair of unanswerable questions:

What in God's name is Nossa Morte, and whose fingers and teeth am I looking at?

The latter question was buzzing around his mind when Dr. Lima's voice interrupted it.

"Sorry about that," she said. "My computer's running like it has a hangover for some reason."

"No problem. We were talking about Nossa Morte."

"Indeed. You have quite a keen interest in that subject."

"Can you spare another minute?"

"I've been generous with my time already. We're in the middle of finals; it's a very busy—"

"I really appreciate your help. Just one last question?"

"Suppose I ask *you* a question, Mr. Diamond. What made you think to direct your inquiry to my office?"

Rusty glanced down at the sheet of textbook paper spread out next to the bloodied teeth. A faint stamp in one corner of the page indicated it had been torn from a book belonging to the UNLV library.

"I came across some intriguing material in a textbook checked out from the library on your campus. It's an incomplete fragment, unfortunately. I was hoping to assemble a fuller picture of its contents."

"I see. And rather than call the library, you consulted the Department of Anthropology. Latching onto the first tenured professor you could reach, I'm guessing."

"If there's someone else at the university more qualified to help me…"

He let the sentence dangle unfinished.

"Your interest, Mr. Diamond. It's academic in nature?"

"You could say that," he lied. "I'm a documentary filmmaker, preparing a project on indigenous tribes of the Amazon. The Payocu in particular. This seems like an interesting angle."

Rusty heard an exasperated sigh.

"First of all," Dr. Lima began, "the focal point of your interest is of little relevance to the Payocu. It represents only a small fraction of their culture. There's considerable doubt about whether the phrase is legitimate, or maliciously implanted upon the tribe as a means of justifying their eradication. I tend to support the latter theory."

"But what does it mean?"

"The words 'nossa morte' are Portuguese. They translate to English as 'our death.' I'm sure you could have discovered as much on your own."

"Yes, but how do those words relate to the Payocu tribe? Some kind of ritual, I gather."

"That's not completely inaccurate."

Rusty waited but heard no further reply.

"Doctor Lima, you sound a little hesitant to answer my questions. Can I ask why?"

"I resent this conversation, frankly. I resent being chosen to assist with your project, which strikes me as dubious in merit."

"This is your field, isn't it? Anthropology, with a focus on indigenous people of subequatorial regions."

"Indeed. As someone with twenty years of research to my

credit, I'm fed up with the insulting ways these cultures have been represented even in so-called respectable publications."

"Look, I'm not trying to—"

"You say you're planning a scholarly film project on the Payocu. Yet all you want to discuss is some sensationalistic legend, the reality of which has been called into question by many academics."

"OK, I hear what you're saying. Nossa morte is a fraud, contrived to make a peaceful tribe look like savages. Probably by someone with an interest in grabbing their land, if I had to guess."

"Quite right," Doctor Lima answered, her tone a few degrees less hostile. "None of that's been proven. It's just a viewpoint I happen to endorse."

"I'm willing to buy it. Trust me, I have no agenda other than gathering information."

"In that case, let me conclude our discussion with one critical point. Just because tribes like the Payocu lack what we might call sophistication, that hardly means they maintain some grossly atavistic lifestyle."

"Like practicing death rituals, for instance? Rituals that involve dismemberment and mutilation?"

A moment of cold silence greeted those words.

"I have to go, Mr. Diamond. Good luck with your—"

"Maybe we could meet in person," he said quickly. "At the university, any time that works for you."

"You didn't mention being in Las Vegas."

"I'm not, at the moment. Catching a plane to McCarran tonight."

"My schedule is insane right now," she sighed. "Give me a number where I can reach you. If anything opens up, I'll be in touch."

Figuring that was the best he could hope for, Rusty recited

his mobile number. Dr. Lima terminated the call before he could finish thanking her.

An oppressive silence filled the kitchen. Reaching out to Dr. Lima had been a long shot at best, but there was nothing else he could do from here in coastal Maryland. More direct action would have to wait until his arrival in Vegas. He'd be there in less than twelve hours, a prospect that made him shudder with fear and a kind of perverse anticipation.

He pulled the greeting card from that day's delivery and once again tried to make sense of the handwritten message inside. It was longer than the note in the previous package, and more cryptic.

When is a trick not a trick?
When does the rubber knife turn to steel?
When do the suckers get what they came to see?
When Nossa Morte takes the stage.

Come out of hiding, Raven.
Drag yourself home where you belong.
Bring this tribute or you can expect more.
Come find us, and come alone.

Fail to show, and your local police
department will receive a package containing
more than enough evidence to burn you.

Don't lose your nerve.
The next performance will start
before you can stop it.

There it was. A veiled yet overt threat to frame him for some unknown crime if he didn't cooperate. The pattern of escalation was obvious, the need to respond impossible to ignore. Rusty was ready to do that, but first his appearance needed some more work.

He walked upstairs and stepped into the master bathroom. The sink was filled with a scattering of dark hair—remnants of the pointed goatee that had adorned his face for the last ten years before he'd shaved it off that morning.

Rusty gazed into the mirror, assessing the alteration to his visage.

Not enough. Not for Vegas.

He picked up a Braun electric shaver and flicked it on, aiming the blades at a tangle of dark hair over his brow.

A knock on the door downstairs froze his hand in place.

"Mr. Diamond, this is the police!"

Rusty turned off the razor and walked into the bedroom. Pushing aside a window sash, he peered down at the driveway.

An Ocean City Police Department cruiser was parked next to his Lexus. The cruiser sat empty, the driver's door open. Rusty couldn't see who was standing on the doorstep—or how many—as another thunderous barrage of knocks rose from below.

"We have a warrant, Mr. Diamond. Open up or we'll be forced to break down this door!"

Rusty quickly moved to the stairs. His mind churned with unsettling scenarios. Was it possible Nossa Morte had already sent a package to the OCPD, as the handwritten note had threatened?

Why bother tipping me off if that was the plan? he thought as he reached the bottom of the stairs. More to the point: *Why the hell didn't I just go to the cops myself?*

Rusty had considered doing that ever since the second box arrived, but something stopped him each time he reached for the phone. Fear. He'd let the fear of being unable to account for his whereabouts in recent weeks stop him from making what anyone would recognize as the most sensible move.

The door shook with renewed pounding. He could see the knob jerk violently.

"This is your last warning, Mr. Diamond. Open up!"

Rusty squinted into the peephole. He saw nothing but the fleshy obstruction of a thumb pressed over it.

"Hold on, goddamnit!"

He removed the safety latch and reached for the knob. The door flew inward, slamming hard into his chest. The impact stole Rusty's breath and he fell to one knee.

The door kept swinging open, knocking him to the floor. Lieutenant Jim Biddison—all 280 pounds of him—stood on the other side, one hand planted on the door and holding it open.

Rusty braced himself for a rush of officers, but Biddison was alone in his doorway, wearing civilian clothing.

"What the hell," Rusty wheezed, struggling to stand and refill his lungs with oxygen.

"You were warned," Biddison said. He took an aggressive step into the house, whipping a pair of cuffs from his belt.

2.

"Turn around and show me those—"

Lieutenant Biddison didn't finish the command. It disintegrated into hoarse laughter.

"Jesus," he guffawed. "The look on your face."

Another spasm doubled him over, and Rusty finally understood what was happening. He stepped around the hulking lieutenant and kicked the front door closed.

Rusty stood there watching the hysterics, feeling as annoyed with himself as with his cop friend. The fact that he hadn't recognized this as some asinine prank was a stark indication of how badly his powers of cognition had been jarred over the course of the last six days.

Biddison regained some composure as Rusty brushed past him toward the kitchen.

"You're an asshole, Jim. Want a beer?"

"What'd you expect?" Biddison asked, accepting a bottle of Dogfish Head Indian Brown Ale from the refrigerator. "Had to get your attention somehow, didn't I?"

"You must love pulling stunts like that." Rusty handed him a bottle opener. "Do it all the time. Hell, you're probably one of those pricks who pulls over women for bogus moving violations, just to see what they'll do to get out of it."

Jim flipped him the finger. Rusty smiled, but the unannounced visit still had him on edge.

"Why didn't you just call?"

Biddison almost choked on a swallow of beer.

"Seriously? You've been ducking me for, like, *weeks*. You were never the most communicative guy to begin with, but lately you've been a goddamned ghost. What gives?"

"Nothing. Just busy."

"Right. The schedule of a retired magician living like a hermit has got to be brutal. Do you even leave the house to buy groceries, or do you have them delivered?"

"Look, Jim—"

"I mean, it gets to be more than just annoying after a while. I start to take this personally, understand? Must've left you a dozen messages since Memorial Day."

"I know—"

"I just want to hang out once in a while, shoot the shit. That's what people who call themselves friends do. Normal people, anyway."

"You're right. I've been a little elusive lately."

Biddison took another swig and gave Rusty an appraising look.

"Finally got rid of the goat, huh? Good move. Trim that mop and you might actually look like a respectable citizen."

Rusty changed his mind about it being too early for alcohol. He was more of a scotch man, but made a sociable gesture by matching Biddison with a beer. He raised a cold Dogfish and Jim clinked his half-empty bottle against it.

"Anyway, I didn't just stop by to bust your balls. Guess who's got a hall pass all week long?"

"No wonder you're so keyed up. Where's Kim?"

"Virginia, to see her mother. Took the baby with her, so it's bachelor time for your old pal Jim. Even better, I'm off duty. Racked up so much unused vacation, they fucking ordered me away from the station until next Monday."

"And yet you're allowed to drive around in a patrol car."

"No choice; Kim took the wagon. Being a senior officer has some perks."

Rusty saw the pent-up excitement in his friend's eyes, and noticed how Biddison was bouncing on the balls of his feet. A shard of memory stabbed him from the distant past. Jim used to act like this back in high school before a big game. He'd made All-State Linebacker in his junior year. They were pretty close at the time, but Rusty felt like the distance separating them now could be measured in more than decades.

"How come you didn't make the trip to Virginia?"

"Me and Kim's mom don't exactly see eye to eye. She's a mean old bitch, to be more direct about it. I think she's never adjusted to the fact that her daughter married a civil servant instead of some Wall Street schmuck."

"So you did the noble thing. Told Kim to enjoy the trip while you guard the homestead."

Biddison shrugged. "She didn't argue. More enjoyable visit for her without me and the old lady sparring all the time. It's one of those win-wins that bless every marriage now and then."

Jim drained his beer and set it on the table, inches from the cardboard box. He gave it a curious glance, leaning closer to inspect the return address. Rusty reclaimed his attention with a fresh bottle from the fridge.

"Let's sit in the front room. It's cooler in there."

He immediately wished he'd suggested relocating to the back porch instead. As Jim lowered himself into a leather couch, his eyes flashed onto a pile of luggage by the door.

"Taking a trip yourself, I see."

Rusty came within a hair of saying he'd just gotten back from a trip and had been too lazy to unpack.

Bad idea, he thought, canceling the lie. A bloodhound to the core, Jim would notice the absence of check-in tags on the luggage and would start asking pointed questions. It was his nature, had been even before he'd become a cop.

"Yeah," Rusty replied. "Some stupid thing I can't get out of. That's part of why I've been unreachable."

"Where you headed?"

Again, the urge to lie beckoned. Providing Jim with the most boring destination imaginable struck him as an appealing form of misdirection, but caution intervened. He didn't feel prepared to dole out a bulletproof fabrication right now, so he opted for the truth.

"Vegas. Just a couple days."

Biddison leaned forward on the couch, almost spilling his beer.

"That's perfect! I'm off the chain all week, no reason for me to stay home. I can get the neighbors to water the lawn. Other than that, I'm scot-free!"

"OK, hold on."

"Fucking Vegas," Biddison sprang to his feet. "And with Rusty Diamond as my wing man. Hell, you must have that town wired better than anyone."

"Not really. Haven't set foot there in almost three years, and I didn't exactly leave on a high note. Wouldn't be going unless I absolutely had to."

"Look, I know it was a shitty prank, busting in like this. Chalk it up to boredom. I'm suffocating, man. Need a getaway like nobody's business."

"Jim, listen to—"

"It's not the family; it's the goddamn job. Desk work's gonna kill me faster than a heart attack. You know I'm made for the field."

"Under any other circumstances I'd say yes. This just isn't the right time. I've got some fairly heavy shit to deal with and I'd make a lousy traveling companion."

Biddison seemed not to hear him, his mind running fast down an alternate track.

"You got no idea how tedious it is. When they tapped me

for squad captain, I figured at least half my rotations would be in a prowler. Christ, I haven't seen the outside of the station since New Year's. Paperwork and staff meetings all fucking day."

Rusty rose to his feet. He could see this was not going to be a pleasant exchange and wanted to get it over with as rapidly as possible.

"Listen to what I'm saying. I don't want you tagging along."

Biddison gave him a hard look, then set down his bottle on the coffee table. Ignoring a coaster within easy reach, he placed it on the table's oak surface.

"You know something—I don't get offended all that much. I like to think of myself as easy come, easy go. Hear what I'm saying?"

Rusty found that to be a staggeringly myopic self-assessment, but kept his mouth shut.

"I've made a real effort to be your friend since you moved back here," Jim continued. "We've got history, and that's something I respect. *Most* people respect that kind of thing. Now here we are, with a perfectly reasonable opportunity to spend a little time together, and you're giving me the brush-off. Again."

Biddison stepped forward. The hostility of his movement was thinly veiled at best. Rusty tensed and forced a measured breath into his lungs. It suddenly felt like years' worth of unvoiced resentment was coming to a head, a long-overdue confrontation that had been avoided only by a flimsy strand of former friendship. That strand was breaking, and there was nothing he could do to stop it.

He matched Biddison with a forward step, not to escalate the moment but to hold his ground.

"I respect you, OK? And I do value your friendship, even though I may not show it much. The reason I don't want you coming on this trip has nothing to do with you. This is something I need to do alone. Can you live with that, or do we have it out right here?"

A moment of silence passed. Rusty felt the odds were at least fifty-fifty that Biddison would take a swing at him. If it happened, he'd protect himself but he wouldn't fight back.

Jim finally looked away and reached for his beer. He frowned at the watery ring he'd left on the coffee table.

"Sorry about that."

"Forget it."

Then Rusty surprised himself by adding, "Truth is, I'm moving out of this place."

"Is that right?"

"Yeah, soon as I get back from Vegas. I'm leaving Ocean City, for good. Been hiding out in the house for too long. Not from you, from a whole bunch of shit."

Biddison gave a blank stare and Rusty felt a return of the tension that filled the room moments before. But the stare gave way to an amiable nod.

"Where you moving?"

"New Orleans. Got some people down there. I reconnected with them on a visit a few months back. That's where I first lived after high school, you may recall. I think it's where I belong, if I belong anywhere."

"Ocean City was never really home for you, was it? Even back then, you were always looking to get out. Looking for something better."

Rusty almost replied but no meaningful words came.

"What the fuck," Jim said with a grin. "At least you're telling me this time. Instead of just skipping town without a word."

Rusty met his smile, feeling with relief a dissipation of any conflict waiting to erupt.

"Can I ask you a favor? It would mean a hell of a lot."

Jim shrugged. He clearly wasn't going to give a blank check to any unasked favors.

"My flight leaves from BWI tonight at seven thirty. That

gives us a few hours to shoot the shit and grab a bite, if you feel like driving me to the airport."

Lieutenant Biddison appeared to give the request serious consideration. He lifted the bottle and drained it.

"One more beer and I'll probably say yes."

3.

Twilight was falling over the Strip, but people all across town were just waking up. Towering monuments of neon and glass reached out to tap the same gargantuan power grid, sending eight thousand megawatts of juice to millions of circuits. In less than an hour full dark would envelop the Mojave Desert, but this small section kept pulsating brighter than the midday sun.

Rusty piloted a silver 2017 Dodge Barracuda, recently acquired from the Hertz desk at McCarran, along the grooved blacktop of Tropicana Avenue. Traffic was heavy, drivers assuming a territorial approach to their lanes.

He pulled to a stop at the corner of Tropicana and Las Vegas Boulevard. To his right, the Strip traced a northeastern course, eventually petering out into no-man's-land before reaching Old Downtown a mile beyond.

An SUV behind him needlessly flicked on its highbeams. Rusty glanced up at the rearview and suppressed a flinch. A stranger stared back from the mirror.

His head, which for the past fifteen years had been covered with black shoulder-length hair, now looked like it belonged to a Paris Island recruit. He'd shaved it all off in a men's room at BWI shortly before takeoff, wielding the electric razor in a stall and dumping thick handfuls of hair into a trash can. Hours later, it still felt like he was carrying around someone else's head on his shoulders.

22

Relax, for Christ's sake. It grows back.

A desert breeze came in through the open window, cooling his cranium as if to drive home the sensation of being naked. Unprotected.

The light changed and Rusty banged a hard right onto the Strip. A city block later he pulled into the lot of the MGM Grand. A valet approached and opened the driver's door.

"I'm checking into a loft," Rusty said.

"Just keep going and veer right. There's a separate entrance."

Rusty thanked him and wheeled the Barracuda into a smaller valet lot hidden behind a cluster of palms. When booking his room here online, he'd decided to blow some extra cash on a suite in the exclusive Skylofts section of the hotel.

He began to question that decision during the check-in process. The price tag didn't deter him, even with monstrous resort fees tacked on, but the ostentatious luxury of the place gave him pause. The concierge, Gustave, told him his own private butler would be on call as needed. Rusty insisted he had no use for that. Standard housekeeping once a day would be fine.

"But sir," the concierge protested, "butler service is part and parcel of the Skyloft experience. We already have an excellent man appointed for your stay. If it's privacy you're concerned with, I can assure you he's the model of discretion."

"I'm happy to cover his salary, Gustave," Rusty said, "if he loses any hours on my account. And of course a healthy gratuity, when I check out. Five hundred sound about right?"

"Well, yes, that's in line with—"

"Great, so you can assign him to another loft or tell him to take the week off. Either way, he won't be missing a paycheck." Rusty stifled another complaint by leaning hard against the terrazzo reception desk. "A butler's just not my style. Got it?"

Two minutes later, he walked away with a pair of access keys to Skyloft 1418. He stepped into a glass elevator built on the outside of the Grand's western flank and gave the operator his floor number.

The view as they ascended skyward almost made Rusty weak in the knees. Not from a sense of vertigo, or simple astonishment at the vast landscape of blinking neon that stretched wider with each floor they passed.

Memory. That's what's making me so goddamn seasick.

The past came flooding over him. Not just the bad memories he'd buried, but a lot of good ones too. All that time he'd devoted to mastering every aspect of magic, mentalism, and escapism—and the rise to something like fame that had eventually followed.

Seeing the Strip laid out below, a view he hadn't partaken of in three years, felt like a hammer blow to the kidneys. A kaleidoscopic whirl of lost moments made him clutch the elevator's brass rail with sweaty palms.

He didn't want to be here. His body was rebelling on a cellular lever at finding itself back in these coordinates.

What choice do I have, he thought as the glass box continued its ascent. *Destroy the packages and hope I never get another? Go to the cops and hope for the best?*

Neither of those options held water. Nossa Morte had laid their hook perfectly. Rusty had no way of proving he wasn't the man in that flash drive video. That he himself hadn't been the one to liberate those fingers and teeth from their presumably deceased owner. If Nossa Morte had taken possession of his old dice, who knew what other artifacts laced with his DNA might be available to close the net around him.

Gotta fly solo. It's the only way, for now.

Two days, max. He'd already set that as an ironclad timeframe. If he failed to dig up anything that might safely exonerate him from any connection to the contents of the boxes, he'd go to the Vegas police and hope for the best.

The elevator operator cleared his throat, startling Rusty out of his reverie. They'd reached the fourteenth floor. He handed the operator a tip and stepped out. Thirty paces brought him to the door of 1418. He swiped his key and stepped inside, and any hesitation he'd felt at the concierge desk evaporated. This was Vegas the way it should be done, for those with the means.

The loft consumed three thousand square feet, split into two levels. It reminded Rusty of his former residence at Caesars Palace, the scene of so many freewheeling good times in the bad old days. Floor-to-ceiling windows faced the Strip, one of which slid open to provide access to a private balcony with a plunge pool. He'd never had a plunge pool at Caesars, despite continual lobbying with the entertainment brass to supply him with one.

Rusty slowly canvassed the kitchen, his boots scuffling along the limestone floor. It was laid out in a checkerboard pattern, similar to a suite at the Rio where he'd once spent a delirious weekend celebrating his runner-up award as *Vegas Entertainer of the Year* in 2012. Rusty winced as he recalled the way he and a band of revelers had demolished that suite over the course of seventy-two unhinged hours.

He stepped through the kitchen into a spacious living area. A vintage pool table with red felt brought another hazy jolt of remembrance; he'd once split an eight-ball with a salesmodel from Agent Provocateur on just such a table.

Where was that? The Mesa Club? The Sky Palace?

The memory didn't come to him. He gave up and checked out the rest of his digs. A loft-wide soundsystem was controlled by an all-in-one remote, along with the TV, drapes, and pretty much anything else that moved. The gleaming bathroom featured a walk-in sauna and a six-jet shower that looked like it belonged in a science fiction movie.

I think I can stand this for awhile, Rusty thought with the first grin to part his face in several days.

He plucked a strawberry from a sterling bowl of fresh fruit

and poured three fingers of Glenlivet 18 from the bar into a crystal tumbler. Picking up the remote, he flicked on a seventy-inch flatscreen TV and settled into a comfortable chair. Barely a minute passed before he turned it off again.

The Skyloft's novelty factor was already fading. What had first impressed him as opulent rapidly grew oppressive. He hadn't flown all the way out here to feel pampered.

Rusty rose and grabbed his access key. Any wariness about being back in Las Vegas had been numbed by the drink, and he was ready to get out and resume his place in the action.

• • •

The Strip thrummed with an unruly flow of foot traffic. Rusty wove between clusters of sunburned tourists clutching go-cups and street vendors hawking pamphlets for escorts and private dancers. He narrowly missed trampling a homeless person sprawled on the cement walkway in front of the Cosmopolitan. The near mishap jolted Rusty, spurring him to keep his gaze low and adopt a more measured pace.

The thought that someone might recognize him would not dislodge itself from his mind. A stupid notion, but a stubborn one. He rubbed a hand over his clean-shaven chin to remind himself of how different he appeared now than when his face had filled billboards on this boulevard. It didn't do much to dispel his nerves.

Waiting for the light to change at Flamingo Road, he steeled himself. Across the street, the aqua towers of Caesars Palace rose into the twilight, set back from the sidewalk by a maze of gardens. Rusty held his breath as he stepped onto the property.

Carried by a moving walkway toward the entrance, he glanced up at the Palace Tower. His eyes counted floors until reaching the seventeenth. He settled on the corner window overlooking the pool. Suite 1720. A thousand square feet of luxury that once represented everything that mattered to him.

Home sweet home. Should've burned the fucking place down before I left. Wonder who's in it right now?

The moving walkway deposited him onto a broad concourse. Rusty stepped into the gilded entry plaza. He circled a burbling fountain that had three marble nymphs as a centerpiece, then turned right to skirt the line of impatient guests at check-in.

Making a lap around the casino floor, he paused near an oval side room devoted to poker. A tall man with a flattop haircut leaned casually against a Corinthian column. Too casually. A velvet dinner jacket did little to hide his muscled dimensions. The wireless mic tucked behind his left earlobe was hard to spot, unless you were looking for it.

Bingo. He'll do.

Rusty moved in slowly. The flattopped man took a swig from a bottle of Heineken, pretending not to notice his approach.

"I need to speak with Charlotte Raines."

Mr. Flattop didn't look at him, just muttered: "Beat it."

"I'll say it again. I need to speak with—"

"Can't help you."

"Sure you can. You can escort me to the security office. Right below where we're standing, down two flights and through three doors with digital passcodes. Piece of cake for me to get there with your say-so. Left to my own devices, it's more of a challenge."

That yielded a quick, curious glance.

"Who'd you say you wanted to see?"

"Charlotte Raines. Your boss."

"See, that's where you're mistaken. My boss is an asshole named Chuck who owns three carwashes in Phoenix."

"Cut the shit. I'm talking about the head of security for

the Palace Tower. Real ballbuster. Makes you report in three times an hour, doesn't she? And submit a written debrief at the end of each shift, even if nothing interesting goes down."

"Gee whiz. You sure know a lot about this place."

"Used to live here. Had a suite in the Palace Tower."

The security guard shrugged with disinterest and took another swig. Rusty laughed.

"Who's that supposed to fool? Not even any foam in there."

Flattop glanced down at the green bottle reflexively.

"Tap water instead of O'Doul's?" Rusty goaded him. "Don't tell me they're cutting corners."

"Enjoy your night, sir. That means start walking."

"You're not listening. This is urgent. I have some information Charlotte will want to hear."

The security guard turned to face him, accentuating his size advantage.

"I've been patient. Do we have a problem?"

"Just tell her Rusty needs a minute. That'll get her attention."

"One last time before this gets ugly. Walk."

Rusty smiled as Flattop tilted his head, straining to hear something in the ear mic.

"Negative. No backup needed."

He reached out with one hand, moving with impressive speed for a man his size. Two fingers pinched the tendons above Rusty's clavicle. Not hard enough to cause pain, but telegraphing that capability.

"Ms. Raines no longer works here. She took a leave of absence last fall, if you must know."

"So where—"

The fingers pinched tighter, stopping Rusty's question.

"She left for medical reasons, and that's as much information as you're getting. I'm doing you a favor, mainly to spare

myself a lot of bullshit paperwork. If you're too stupid to cooperate, it's gonna be a long night for both of us."

He spun Rusty around and started walking him toward
the rear entrance. Rusty felt an opening to slip free but knew
better than to initiate action that would bring a phalanx of
other guards into the mix.

"Get Charlotte on the phone," he said calmly as they
crossed the casino floor. "She'll confirm she's a friend of mine."

"Such a good friend you didn't know about her condition."

The guard pushed harder, forcing Rusty to pick up the
pace. In another ten steps they'd be in the rear entrance foyer.

"We haven't talked in a while, OK? I've got some vital
news to give her."

"You tried that already. And you see where it's gotten you."

They were almost to the rear doors. Once outside, this
would only get more difficult.

Time to mix it up.

Rusty planted one foot on the tile and wheeled around.
His movement was untelegraphed, catching the bigger man
off-guard. Rusty squared up, steadying himself with a low
center of gravity. One hand rose to a defensive position while
the other slipped into his hip pocket.

"OK, let's try something else."

4.

It was dark in the performance area. Without question the darkest place in all of Vegas. No neon, no sunlight, no moonglow. The arrival of another night was little more than an abstraction down here, where it was always night. This darkness was tactile. It breathed, and sometimes it screamed.

Trent was ready to make the darkness scream again. Just a few more moments to draw out the collective anticipation as tightly as it could go before snapping. The blade would fall, and the trick that was no trick would be complete.

Nossa Morte would claim another triumph in the name of the Raven.

Trent worked better in the darkness. It gave him heightened control over not only tonight's participant squirming against his binds on the table, but over the audience. Everyone inside this sepulchral space was under his control. Even Soren, though Soren would never admit it.

The pervading gloom in the Underworld created a sense of temporal disorientation more profound than in the casinos with their universal lack of windows. Time was so impossible to track it lost all meaning. The only source of light was a string of forty-watt bulbs hung over the stage by baling wire. Just enough to let everyone see what was about to happen.

Trent knew what time it was. The screen of his iPhone read 7:56 P.M. He gave it a brief glance from his position on the stage and then quickly returned the phone to the folds of his heavy black cloak. The time check was done with such an expert deployment of misdirection that no one in the audience saw it happen.

That was important. Trent was a stickler for details. Creating a performance flawless from beginning to end was something that occupied his mind greatly.

Not much of a crowd tonight, but that was alright. Even one live witness was enough to consecrate the ritual, along with the lens of the video camera pointed at the sacrificial table. Besides, the performance area couldn't accommodate a large group.

It was roughly fifty feet square, covered by a low ceiling riddled with piping. Drippage was always a factor, but not for Trent. When setting up for the first performance three months ago, he had instructed Soren to ensure all the pipes directly above the stage were leak-proof. If a member of the audience happened to catch a stray droplet of runoff, they should consider themselves lucky. At least it wasn't blood, though that was sometimes a possibility for those in the front row.

Above all else, anyone occupying the rows of wooden benches facing the stage should consider themselves lucky not to be up there on the performance table right now.

The hood on Trent's head limited visibility, but he could see well enough through a pair of narrow eye slits. He didn't need to have a good view of the audience to know they were out there. Their presence announced itself audibly with impatient coughs and hushed mutterings.

Trent didn't have a precise head count for tonight's performance. He guessed less than a dozen, as per usual. Any bigger and the possibility of containment became too chancy. Trent trusted himself and Soren with the task of instilling sufficient fear to prevent any loose lips. Who would believe the testimony of a tunnel rat anyway?

Such was Trent's calculated gamble. It didn't really matter. The wheels were in motion; the bait was set. Just two more performances—the tenth and final being the only one of any consequence—and Nossa Morte could dissolve into the mists of urban legend. Trent would have his closure and be ready to move on.

He raised the knife in his left hand, ready for tonight's crescendo.

"Behold the ancient illusion of the Willful Dagger. First used to entertain debauched royalty in the palace of Nebuchadnezzar II, if legends are to be believed."

Trent paused here in his scripted recitation, having stumbled over the pronunciation of the ancient king. He felt his face go hot with embarrassed fury beneath the scratchy false goatee. It happened every goddamned time, no matter how much rehearsal he'd done! Christ, he'd spent well over an hour practicing in front of a mirror this morning until he felt certain he could utter that five-syllable name without error! Only to blow it when the spotlight was on him.

Some small rustling arose from the audience, a sense of waxing impatience filling the tight space. Trent forced a note of composure into his voice and continued:

"This illusion was adopted and altered over the centuries. Until it finally morphed into the craven sham performed nightly in the Etruscan Room at Caesars Palace, not far from where you sit. A cowardly lie, pulled off with the cheap skill and fakery with which the Raven so distinguished himself during a career cut too short. Fear not, friends. Tonight, we pay tribute to the Raven—not what he was but what he failed to become—by performing this sacred illusion in its purest form."

Trent gestured toward the slight young man in unwashed clothes trussed to the table.

"Show some appreciation for tonight's participant. Without him, we are practitioners of a fruitless art."

A few hoarse cheers burbled up from the audience, sounding less than enthralled. That's what happened when the crowd was at least partially comprised of newbies. They didn't know what they were in for. Fine. They'd be reacting differently soon enough.

The participant spoke to Trent, careful to keep his voice low as he'd been instructed.

"Uh…we're almost done, right? Then the party starts?"

Trent gave a slight nod of his hooded head and waved a silencing hand. He didn't want any distractions right now.

How many times had he watched Rusty perform this trick, hiding like a scared child in a darkened corner of the Etruscan Room's balcony? All those clueless rubes filling the premium seats, what appreciation did *they* have for the work being done onstage? What did they know of the conjuring arts, and of the dark demigod who entertained them with such brazen talent?

Night after night Trent had crouched there, mouthing the words of Rusty's opening spiel as if he'd written them himself. Always keeping an eye over his shoulder for a security guard's approach. Feeling self-conscious in that fucking custodian's uniform but never taking the time to change into street clothes at the end of his shift for fear he might miss a minute of the show.

Trent had memorized every aspect. When Rusty made some minor alteration to the sequence—swapping the order of the Willful Dagger and the Sunken Coffin, for example—Trent alone took notice, and spent hours afterward wondering what trail of thoughts had inspired the Raven to make the change.

Well, now Trent had his own stage on which to perform. Not as glamorous as the Etruscan Room, but a much realer place. And that was the point. Nossa Morte might honor the Raven but it would never repeat his cardinal sin. The sin of false promises. Of miracles undelivered.

Down here, so far removed from the glitter and the easy

money, the audience got the one thing Vegas could never give them. The one thing this entire filthy town strove to distort and eradicate.

Nossa Morte gave them the truth.

Trent glanced down at the participant's anxious face, feeling a mix of pity and admiration. Being so blind to the inevitable was almost a state of grace, granting some unearned dignity to the final moments of an otherwise worthless life.

The blade dropped another inch toward the participant's bare neck. Trent felt himself stiffen beneath his robe.

This was the best part, even better than the climax. That fleeting moment when the participant thought that maybe— surely—it was all just an act.

Trent always stretched out this interval of false hope as long as he could. The tension filling the room took on a hive-like quality, a large rustling force. Someone in the audience bellowed for him to finish the trick.

The participant's eyes darted upward, directly into the hooded face above. Seeking deliverance.

Trent waited for that last miniscule shift telling him it was time for the resolution.

There it was. An almost imperceptible flicker in the participant's gaze as a deeper dread washed away the nascent hope that had appeared just moments earlier. And with the dread, a kind of fatalistic certainty.

Yes, Trent communicated wordlessly. *You knew this was how it would end. Everyone down here knew it.*

The scream never had time to leave the participant's gaping mouth before the knife struck. Tearing through the larynx, its tip embedded in the fifth cervical vertebra at the back of the throat.

Trent barely heard the responses from the audience. His ears were tuned solely to the final escape of trapped oxygen from the participant's deflating lungs. He could detect it over the growling chorus of lustful approval, disbelief and outrage—a sibilant hiss, the fading sound of a spent life.

Trent raised his head to face the audience. A hush fell over the enclosed space.

"Once again, truth emerges from the Raven's lie. Where he deceived, Nossa Morte delivers. And he will do the same, in time."

5.

Darkness finally claimed the valley a few minutes past eight thirty. A handful of miles south of the Strip, all those blinding lights faded to a mellow glow. Few lamps burned in the residential community of Henderson, though countless lay ready to provide illumination if only someone were there to hit the switch.

Rusty kept one eye on his phone's GPS system as he steered the Barracuda down desolate residential streets. House after house, street after street, a flat landscape of carefully planned suburban sprawl. All of it virtually lifeless.

Feels like one of those Old West ghost towns, he thought, turning right at a prompt from the GPS. *Except this place was alive and kicking less than ten years ago.*

Henderson was where the great housing wave that swept over Vegas came to a crest and then crashed. Nine out of ten houses Rusty passed stood dark and empty. Most had fallen into a state of disrepair after months or years of abandonment. Few vehicles were parked in driveways covered with windswept debris.

Rusty had just barely managed to avoid ejection from Caesars. *Good thing I had that much on me. Almost surprised he was willing to play ball for a lousy grand.*

Vegas, home of the greased palm. The flat-topped security guard had glanced at the roll of cash Rusty pressed in his hand, gave it a riffle to confirm *all* the bills were hundreds, then told him not to move.

Less than five minutes later the guard reappeared, passed Rusty a folded note, and turned away without a word. On the note was written what Rusty prayed was an accurate home address for Charlotte Raines.

The Barracuda's GPS system now told him he'd reached that address. He slowed to a crawl and surveyed the property.

It was a ranch-style hacienda set back from the road on a slight incline, in better condition than most of its neighbors. A window adjacent to the front door leaked dim light from behind closed drapes. With the garage door lowered, Rusty couldn't tell if any vehicles sat inside.

He parked across the street and stepped out, chilled by a blast of desert night wind.

The quavering cry of a coyote from some distant ridge rang in his ears like a feral lament.

As he approached the house, Rusty saw a sign planted in the front yard. WARNING: LOOTERS SHOT ON SIGHT!

A reasonable precaution in post-crash Henderson. Vast quantities of copper pipes and aluminum siding lay within reach, begging to be stripped. Thousands of appliances, bought on layaway back when easy credit flowed like water from a busted hydrant. A king's ransom of medicine cabinets filled with pharmaceuticals left behind in the hysteria of mass evictions. All of it laid bare and defenseless to plunder.

Rusty felt a crunch under his heel. Kneeling, he picked up a spent shotgun shell from the driveway. He held it to his nose and detected a whiff of spent gunpowder.

Scare tactics? he wondered, recalling the flair for suggestive intimidation Charlotte had displayed during her tenure with the security staff at Caesars. The shell emitted no heat.

Maybe it's for dramatic effect. Or maybe she's not kidding with that sign.

Dropping the shell, he rose to his feet and stepped onto the hacienda's stoop.

No knocker on the front door. Rusty raised a fist to give it a heavy rap. A sound caught his ear, stopping him.

The window next to the door slid open with a click. Two barrels of a pump-action shotgun emerged from the gap, hovering within an inch of Rusty's left temple.

"Turn around and walk," a voice he recognized commanded. "I'm no crack shot, but I hardly need to be at this range."

"Charlotte, it's Rusty Diamond."

Another click came from within. Louder than the window opening, its source impossible to mistake.

"That's the sound of a Remington 870 ready to let its payload fly. You won't hear the next sound, but it'll deafen me for days. And I'll be on the right side of the law."

"Don't shoot, please. Let me—"

"Maybe you're not familiar with Nevada Statute 200.160 regarding victims' rights in the event of a home invasion. It states that a citizen legally in possession of a firearm may discharge that firearm in self-defense in any case involving threat to his or her safety, with added leeway when said threat appears from persons unknown."

"Listen to my voice. You know me. It's really—"

"I'm a sick woman, living alone, unable to defend myself. The fucking statute was written *expressly* for people like me. I'd advise you to get the hell out of here before I have time to take another breath."

"You *know* me, Charlotte. It's Rusty."

"Bullshit. I may be in poor health but I've yet to meet a walking dead man."

"Alive and well, as you can see. Contrary to what may pass for popular opinion in this town."

In the pause that followed, the shotgun receded a few inches.

"If Rusty Diamond's not dead, he should know better than to darken this door."

"I need your help. What else is new, right?"

"You still haven't convinced me."

"I was your favorite headache for eighteen months. Crowd control, stage-door security at the Etruscan Room, around-the-clock surveillance of suite 1720. I relied on you, and I infuriated you half the time, but you couldn't help loving me just a little."

Rusty thought he detected a sigh from the darkness.

"Christ, Charlotte. We were friends, or something like it. I got you a Rolex for your fortieth birthday."

More silence. Just as Rusty was about to try a different tack, he heard the bolt sliding off a chain. The door opened.

A woman stood before him, barely visible in the interior gloom. She flicked on the outside lamp, casting a curtain of amber light onto the stoop.

"I'll be damned," she uttered.

A moment of mutual assessment passed. As different as Rusty knew he must appear from Charlotte's memory of him, he barely recognized her at all.

The last time he'd seen Charlotte Raines, she was a commanding presence. More handsome than beautiful, with bobbed chestnut hair and a leggy frame invariably clad in a chic business suit, she'd overcome any gender disadvantage as head of a department comprised almost entirely of men by sheer force of personality. *Nobody* gave her shit—not even Rusty when he was equipped with the license for bad behavior that accompanied the peak of his fame.

The woman now in front of him, posture stooped as she used the shotgun as a crutch, was a spectral shell of the Charlotte Raines he remembered.

"Don't stare, for God's sake. I know I look like hell."

"Sorry," he said, failing to keep a note of dismay from his voice. "I heard you were on sick leave, but—"

"Who told you? I'll have the cocksucker canned with one phone call."

"Some floor guy, I didn't get his name. It doesn't matter."

"The hell it doesn't. Whole fucking unit must be falling apart if they let you bribe your way to my door."

She stepped aside, allowing him entry. Rusty saw her wince as she lowered herself into a leather recliner. He sat on the arm of a tattered couch.

"What's ailing you?"

"Early onset osteoarthritis," she replied with a disgusted frown. "Is that a kick in the ass or what? Not even fifty, and an old-person's disease takes me out of the game."

"That's manageable, isn't it?"

"Yeah, manageable. Nice word; it covers everything from mildly annoying to chronically debilitating. Most mornings I need an hour just to get out of bed. Knees, ankles, shoulders, they're all shot."

"Jesus. I'm sorry."

She batted away his sympathy with a wave of the hand.

"You don't look so hot yourself."

"Better than a walking corpse, I hope."

"I never really believed you were dead. Too simple, and nothing was ever simple with you. Just because you vanished in the middle of an engagement that most entertainers would kill for, not leaving so much as a fucking note for someone who might give a damn about your well-being…"

"It was a shitty thing to do. Try to believe me when I tell you I *had* to bolt. Things went bad, worse than anything you might have heard about."

Charlotte reached for a pack of cigarettes and lit up. She exhaled a funnel of smoke in his direction.

"Doctor recommended?" Rusty asked.

"My lungs happen to be in excellent shape, but let's talk about you. Why are you here? To clean up the mess you left? A little late for that, not that my opinion counts for much with the casino brass."

"I do hope to clean up a thing or two, but not with Caesars. They seem to have done alright in my absence, even if I left them in the lurch."

"So I'll ask again. Why are you here?"

Rusty stood, grateful to get down to cases.

"There's something I want to show you."

He stopped, not sure how to proceed.

"Always with the dramatic flair, this one," Charlotte said as if speaking to an invisible companion. "Are you going to tease it out some more, or show me what you've got?"

"It's in the car. Just a second."

He let himself out of the house, grateful for the release from its dreary confines. As he descended the driveway toward the street, he listened with one ear for the sound of the front door slamming shut. Locking him out for now and ever.

He popped the Barracuda's trunk and retrieved the cardboard box. Charlotte's door was still open for him when he made it back to the house.

6.

Thirty minutes later, Charlotte was hunched over the box, examining its contents with a sharp eye. Rusty's presentation of it had seemed to enliven her, like a bolt of fresh air blown into a hermetically sealed enclosure.

He'd removed the finger and the teeth—using surgical gloves to secure them in a Ziploc bag back at the loft—providing Charlotte with the flash drive, eight-sided die, greeting card and textbook sheet to examine. He wanted her attention and her acumen, but he didn't want to tip her off to the criminal gravity of the situation. If she suspected that a possible homicide or act of mutilation was connected to the deliveries, her first move would be to call the police and nothing Rusty could say would stop her.

He watched as she set aside the greeting card and picked up the textbook paper for another glance.

"Ask you a question?" Rusty said.

"Not yet. Hold your horses."

"Not about the package, about this place. How can you stand to live here? It's like a subprime cemetery."

"Let me explain something to you. It took me five years of careful saving to afford this place. Unlike all the other idiots who grabbed zero-down mortgages, I waited until I could actually afford it. When the market went tits up, I paid the price for their folly."

"OK, but it's been years now. Why hang on?"

"For one thing, I'm not exactly in the pink of health. Relocation is more than I'm prepared to handle at the present time. But more importantly, this place is coming back."

"Henderson?"

"Correct. Vegas is the most cyclical town in the western world. There's so much prime real estate within a five-mile radius, most of it built in the last decade. Trust me, as soon as the pendulum swings back, this'll be the hottest residential zone in Nevada. That's when I sell."

Rusty thought she'd just described a wildly delusional prospect, but he didn't have the heart to challenge her.

"What about that?" he asked, pointing to the box.

"So impatient," she sighed. "Entertainers are all the same, and magicians are the worst. Expect things to just materialize like a fucking rabbit from a hat."

"Charlotte, please. I came here for help."

She sat back in the chair and lit a cigarette.

"Two possibilities. Number one: blackmail. Someone wants to shake you down. Figure they need a dramatic gesture to grab your attention, and I'd say it worked."

Rusty shook his head.

"Doesn't add up."

"Really? You're positive no one's got anything on you? All that time you were living like a maniac, burning the candle at both ends. You never gave *anyone* the means for extortion?"

Rusty couldn't hold her gaze. "What's the second option?"

"Deranged fan. The handwriting calls it a tribute, right? Pretty sick tribute, but then you did some pretty fucked-up shit onstage. All nice and safe behind the tawdry trappings of the Raven, of course."

"That was just entertainment."

"To you, maybe. I dealt with those kids who lined up outside the stage door every night. It was my responsibility to keep them away from you, and I saw plenty of damaged goods in that crowd. Every time you pushed the whole death trip a little farther…Christ, how juvenile. Like when you got in that coffin and set it on fire, remember?"

Rusty grinned. "The Six-Foot Inferno. One of my better effects."

"Yeah, well every time you went closer to the edge, letting people think you might actually take the eternal dirt nap onstage, that crowd got a little bigger and a little crazier."

She tapped her finger against the box.

"This might just be your number one fan. Trying to raise you from the afterlife, or wherever you've been hiding yourself."

Rusty didn't reply. He felt a sheen of sweat forming on the back of his neck. There was a twisted truth in her words.

"Any idea how they got the dice?" Charlotte asked.

"None. There's plenty of my memorabilia for sale on eBay, some bogus but not all. Some guy in Seattle is selling a pair of monogrammed leather gloves that look legit. How these bastards got the dice is beyond me but—"

"Not as worrisome as if that's really blood, right? Easy enough to find out, but it wouldn't necessarily point to a crime. Some nut could have pricked his own finger and applied a few drops, just to freak you out. Hell, it could be a squirrel's blood or red dye number two for all we know."

Rusty felt a brief impulse to tell her about the fingers and teeth, but he curbed it.

"Want my advice?" Charlotte continued, pointing to the box. "Burn the fucking thing. Go home and forget about it. If another one arrives, take it to the cops. It's harassment at the very least."

"Can't do that. The card said to bring it with me."

"And do what, exactly? Am I missing out on some master plan here?"

"I'm gonna find whoever sent it. Have a word with 'em, or whatever it takes to stop this shit cold."

"Rusty, this could be a prank. A warped one, but still. Or it could potentially be a criminal matter. Either way, it's not something for you to handle."

"I've made up my mind. I won't leave Vegas till I get some answers."

She picked up her cell phone from the coffee table.

"Just because I failed to prevent some of your crazier stunts back in the day doesn't mean I'm gonna let you do something this stupid."

"What are you doing?"

"Calling a buddy of mine at Metro. This is a job for the police, not a goddamned magician."

"Don't!" Rusty shouted. He took an step toward her, so aggressive she flinched.

"Listen to me," he said, forcing calmness on himself. "I can't go to the cops until I find out how these fuckers tracked me down. Whoever they are, they've got leverage."

"What kind of leverage?"

"Using my name, my legacy. Twisting everything I created into some sick…whatever the hell this is. I need to find out what they want."

That empty rationalization felt lame leaving his mouth, and Charlotte seemed to pick up on it.

"Who gives a shit about your legacy? You did a pretty decent job of destroying that, remember?"

"Forty-eight hours. Give me that much to see what I can find. If I come up empty, I'll either walk away or go to the cops, whatever you want."

Charlotte warily set down the phone, checking the time.

"Forty-eight hours to the minute," she grumbled, then reached for the textbook page stamped from the UNLV library. "There's something else here."

"What?"

"Hold it," she grumbled, rising with a wheeze and shambling into another room. Rusty heard rummaging, followed by a small crash. Charlotte reappeared moments later, holding a silver box the size of a loaf of bread.

"One of my favorite toys from the salad days," she said with a crooked grin. "Nothing like it for finding traces people don't even know they leave behind. Prints, cocaine granules, microscopic blood flakes, whatever."

"Sounds like a pretty good blackmail machine."

"Never used it against *you*, did I?"

Rusty poker faced that well-aimed barb.

"Not that I didn't have ample opportunity," she added, sitting. "I swept your dressing room a bunch of times. You'd never believe what I picked up."

"I'd rather not hear about it."

"Don't worry. It wasn't half as incriminating as the shit I found in your suite."

"Wait a minute," Rusty said sharply. "You searched my living space with a goddamn crime scene lamp, and I didn't know about it?"

"My job was to protect you, as much from yourself as any obsessed fan or asshole paparazzo. You didn't really think Caesars gave you a West Tower suite, rent free, without some kind of surveillance?"

"Christ. Next you'll tell me my phone was tapped and there were cameras in the bedroom."

Charlotte deadpanned him with a raised brow. Rusty waved a hand to say he didn't want to know.

She plugged the lamp into a wall outlet and flicked it on. A dull wave of bluish light seeped out from the narrow bulb. She picked up the textbook page and ran the lamp across it slowly, stopping to focus on the right margin.

"That's what I thought. There's a watermark here. Looks

like it was burned into the paper with high frequency radiation. Some kind of a synthetic resin…probably methacrylic acid."

Rusty shot to his feet.

"What's it say?"

"It's a URL address. With a dot onion domain, no less."

"What the hell's dot onion?"

Charlotte glanced up at him.

"You never heard of the deep web?"

"Sure. That's where all the illegal shit happens online, right?"

"You're about half right. Most of what's out there is actually pretty innocuous. But, yeah, there's plenty of nasty stuff too. Illegal porn, narcotics, hacking codes, military-grade weaponry. It's pretty much all available. Stuff you'd never use Google to look for, if you've got half a brain."

"Can you read the whole URL?"

Charlotte squinted at the page. She recited a web address one letter at a time: "www.sacredfire.nossamorte/members onion."

Tapping the address into the web browser on his phone, Rusty felt his fingertips vibrate with nervous energy.

Nossa Morte. One step closer.

Charlotte gave him a disgusted look.

"You're not trying to access this, are you?"

"Not right now. Just saving the URL in my browser."

"Jesus. You don't know shit about the deep web, do you?"

Rusty resumed his seat on the couch for the lecture he knew was coming.

"First of all, you can't use a normal browser to access any deep web sites. That's what the dot onion domain is for. It hides the page from a standard search engine's capability."

"So how do I—"

"Secondly," Charlotte said, cutting off the question. "You need to be *extremely* cautious about accessing any site with a dot onion address. Theoretically, the deep web offers invisibility to its users, so people can go hunting for whatever kind of deviant shit they're looking for without leaving any digital footprints. The feds allow that perception to exist, but in truth they have all kinds of ways to track deep web users. Unless you know *exactly* what you'll find at that address, I suggest you stay the fuck away."

"OK, I got it. Thanks for the intel."

Charlotte made a noise acknowledging that everything she'd just said had fallen on deaf ears. Rusty stood again.

"Can I be of assistance in some way? Anything you might need that I can bring you?"

"I've managed to hang on this long without your help."

Rusty laid a card with his phone number on the coffee table.

"Open offer."

Charlotte didn't respond, gazing into a corner as if he were no longer in the room. He turned for the door.

"Leave the box, if you want. I'll take another look in the morning. It'll give me something to do other than ignore the sorry state of neglect around here."

Rusty gazed at the visible layer of dust on the coffee table.

Must be dust bunnies the size of footballs in this place, he thought sadly.

"How about I send over a cleaning crew? Top to bottom job, my treat."

"Just go. This surprise visit has tired me."

"One last thing," Rusty said, his hand on the door knob. "That return address on the box, 'The Underworld.' Mean anything to you?"

Charlotte shook her head, then turned with a glint of recognition in her eye.

"There's this club I remember hearing about. Some goth-metal dive in no man's land. It's called Unterwelt. That's German for 'underworld,' isn't it?"

"Sounds right," Rusty answered.

"I don't know much about the place. Supposed to attract a rough crowd, so I've heard. Motor psychos, death metal freaks, whatever. Sounds like the kind of place a sensible person would avoid, but look who I'm talking to."

7.

Unterwelt had no sign. It wasn't that kind of club, not that Rusty could tell *what* kind of club it was from across the street. Sitting in the Barracuda with the headlamps dark, he checked the Yelp page on his phone to confirm he'd come to the right address, then glanced at the building again.

It was a dilapidated three-floor pile, long abandoned from the looks of it, replete with obligatory busted windows and artless graffiti. Some faded paint on the brick facade indicated a former life as an auto parts manufacturing center.

Five blocks from the north end of the Strip, in a zone of grimy urban squalor, the building sprouted from the street like a malignant tumor.

A ragged trio stumbled onto the sidewalk from a darkened alley along the building's west flank. Two hulks with matching mohawks each had an arm around a willowy blonde girl in a leather miniskirt who could barely remain upright.

Rusty watched as the mohawk twins steered their wobbly companion into a van parked on the far corner. Whatever was about to go down looked ugly, and Rusty fought off an impulse to intervene.

None of my business. Might not be as bad as it looks anyway.

The van pulled a hard U-turn and rumbled away. As soon as it rounded the corner, Rusty got out of the Barracuda. He crossed the street.

A low thumping bassline emanated through ancient brick walls, growing louder. The building loomed over him, looking ready to collapse even without the assistance of a wrecking ball.

Rusty tried the only door in sight. Locked. Glancing down, he noticed an arrow spray-painted on the sidewalk, pointing toward the alley from which the mohawks twins and their companion had emerged.

He followed the arrow, arriving at a chain-link fence. Someone had cut a slit into the meshed wire, easy enough to miss if you weren't looking but just the right size for a determined person to slip through. On the other side of the fence, Rusty assessed the rear of the building.

A single red bulb drew him towards another unmarked door. The door was slightly ajar, an acrid whiff of body odor and cigarette smoke escaping the partition.

He reached out and pushed on the door. It opened to reveal a broader swath of reddish haze. He stepped through and down a low-lit hallway.

The noise soared to a level beyond deafening. It couldn't quite be classified as music, rather an aural assault designed to cause serious damage. During his stint at Caesars, Rusty had consulted a sound tech who'd worked for Slayer to construct a system that would blast orchestral music at key moments in each performance.

And I thought that *was loud*, he thought, wincing, as he walked into a room filled with thrashing bodies. Strobe lights mounted at various angles offered scant illumination as he navigated through the scrum. It was a blur of shaved skulls, pierced flesh, and unhinged motion. Rusty fended off some stray elbows and a few fists, staying upright only because there was no free space in which to fall.

He eventually staggered from the mosh pit into another hallway lit with black lights. The hallway terminated in a smaller room with a bar and some tattered leather couches.

The sound level was marginally lower in here, allowing him to hear the ringing in his ears and wonder if it was permanent.

Two people were grappling in what looked like an amorous clutch on a couch, watched with an amused eye by a young woman working the bar. Small and lithe, with spiky hair the same deep black as her lipstick and eyeliner, Rusty couldn't help but notice she was a stunner even in the room's sepulchral light.

"Scotch, whatever you got."

The bartender poured three fingers of J&B in a plastic cup. Rusty laid a twenty on the bar, waving away any change.

"What are we listening to? Grindcore?"

"Deathcore," she replied with a smirk, like the question was childishly obtuse.

"Can't say I recognize the difference. But I'm pretty much out of the loop these days."

"Broken Flesh wouldn't be caught dead playing grindcore. That's totally not their ethos."

"This place is kinda tough to find," Rusty said after a pause.

"Most worthwhile things are."

"I wasn't even sure Unterwelt existed till just now. Heard some things, but nothing too concrete."

"And you had to see for yourself."

"Curiosity's my Achilles' heel. I figured this was some kind of urban myth bullshit. Like that black market organ donor club supposedly operating out of the Silver Sevens. Or the Nazi bunker at the base of Mount Charleston. Or Nossa Morte."

The bartender's left eyelid fluttered slightly. A fairly common tell Rusty had come to recognize from his years of training in mentalism—often indicating a lie was about to be spoken. But the bartender said nothing.

"You can probably tell I spend too much time poking around the deep web. Bound to get myself in trouble someday."

The eyelid flutter came on again, more pronounced than

before. Rusty had an odd feeling that she was doing it intentionally. A warning? Or just an involuntary reaction that had nothing to do with this conversation?

"Maybe someday soon," she said.

"Touché. If this wasn't such a friendly place, I might take that as a threat."

The bartender gave a bored roll of the eyes, looking over Rusty's shoulder at the couple grappling on the couch.

"Even if someone found Nossa Morte on the deep web," she said just barely loud enough to be heard, "it wouldn't be the real thing. Would it?"

"Can't say. I'm what you'd call a member of the uninitiated."

"Could've fooled me."

Rusty drained his scotch and set the cup down with a nod for a refill. He placed a hundred-dollar bill on the bar when it arrived.

"So where would someone look for the real thing, if they were curious?"

The bartender glanced at the bill.

"I can't break that just now."

"Keep it. I was asking where someone might look for Nossa Morte."

She grabbed the bill and folded it under the strap of her tanktop.

"Where do you start anything?"

"Is that a riddle?"

"It's a question. If you're going on a trip, or reading a story, or solving a mystery, where do you start?"

"At the beginning?"

"See, he can learn. If I was looking for Nossa Morte, I guess I'd start where it all began."

Both eyelids were quivering like hummingbirds. Rusty wasn't sure if she nervous, high, or off her meds. Quite possibly all three.

"Where *what* began? I think a ninety-dollar tip should buy me something more specific."

"Where are we right now?"

Rusty thought about it, aiding the process with two swallows of scotch.

"Some shithole bar that smells like bleach and bad plumbing."

"Not the bar, moron. You're right, by the way; this place needs an industrial-strength power cleaning. But try again."

"We're in Vegas."

"Correct. So think about where Las Vegas began. That's where you want to go, if you're sure you want to go there."

"OK, I'll bite. Where exactly did Vegas begin?"

He sensed a presence behind him before the hand landed on his shoulder. Without adequate time to anchor himself, Rusty felt his whole body being swiveled around with a hard jerk. The behemoth's face staring down at him sported a scar on each cheek, descending from temple to jaw with a kind of rough symmetry that looked deliberate.

"This is a private club," the scarred man said. "Get out."

"Door guy let me in," Rusty replied.

"Nice try. There's no door guy here."

"I was gonna ask about that. Kind of unusual for a club, private or not."

Scarface jabbed him in the sternum with a finger that felt like a piston.

"You're trespassing, fucknut. Walk out or get carried out."

"Think I'll finish my drink first."

Rusty turned around, not waiting for a reply. It was a calculated move. A mirror mounted behind the bar offered him a clear view of the scarred man. If he'd been less involved in his conversation with the bartender, the big fucker wouldn't have caught him by surprise.

"Where were we?"

"Forget it," she said. "You should probably—"

Rusty never heard her advice in its entirety. The mirror showed two brawny hands reaching for the base of his neck. Scarface moved much faster than he'd anticipated from such a large man. Not just fast, but with a quiver of misdirectional body language that concealed his movement.

How the hell did he pull that off?

Both of Rusty's feet left the floor. The scarred man grabbed him by the collar and the back of his belt, then hoisted him across the room.

Rusty barely managed to lower his head before it smashed into the club's back door. Half a second later and his nose would have cracked like a peanut shell.

Stars filled his vision but a rush of adrenaline swept them away. He felt a melon-sized knee ram into the small of his back. Rusty managed to remain vertical and spun around with a high right fist. He caught his assailant just behind the ear. A solid hit, more lucky than skillful. Its impact bought him just enough time to bury an elbow in the man's solar plexus.

Even as he saw that scarred face grimace with pain, Rusty knew he was in trouble. A wild flurry of blows followed. For each one Rusty landed, he received three. A jab to his right temple induced vertigo and he knew this would be over soon.

He never felt the impact of his left cheek against the gravel, but his departure from consciousness couldn't have lasted more then a few seconds. He was awake and alert enough to see Scarface retreating into the club through the back door.

The big man turned, one hand on the knob, and looked down at Rusty. His expression conveyed more amusement than anger.

"You won't find what you're looking for here," he growled.

"What I am looking for?"

Scarface smiled at the question, two rows of blood-smeared teeth gleaming in the light of a street lamp.

"Tell me," Rusty said, regaining his footing. He felt badly depleted by the fight but prepared to continue if that was what was needed to get some information.

"You heard it already. You've got to look where it all began."

With that, the big man stepped back into the club and yanked the door shut.

8.

Paul Ponti winced and cursed softly under his breath. A spot on his left shin hummed with a fresh stab of pain. The pain died quickly, his irritation less so. The old son of a bitch had done it to him again.

"I definitely felt that one, Cy."

Kneeling next to the stool on which Ponti stood, the white-haired tailor held a two-inch straight pin in one quaking hand. Exhibit A, the weapon in question. His other hand clutched the left cuff of a pair of gabardine trousers worn by Ponti. The tailor looked up with an expression of horror on his face.

"I…I don't know…"

"Really hope you didn't draw blood, Cy. That's some expensive fabric, and it stains real easy."

"I'm so sorry, Mr. Ponti. For the life of me, I don't know what's wrong with my hands today."

"There's also my health to consider. You *do* sterilize those things before each fitting, don't you?"

The tailor flinched, keeping the errant pin at arm's length like it might in fact be contaminated.

"It's perfectly clean, Mr. Ponti. I assure you there's no worry of infection."

"Easy for you to say. You're holding the dull end."

Ponti wasn't feeling particularly sadistic this morning, but he couldn't resist ribbing the old man. Not that he'd ever do

57

anything serious to Cy Goldstein for such a minor offense. Good tailors were hard to find. And Ponti nursed a sentimental streak that even his closest friends would be surprised to know of in its totality. Cy had been altering his clothes for going on thirty years, and Ponti was content to withstand a few needle jabs in exchange for keeping him on the payroll.

But that didn't preclude busting his balls a little.

"You're starting to worry me, fella. Maybe you need a new eyeglass prescription. Or maybe tailoring is a young man's game after all."

Fuming silently, Cy used both hands to push up the pant leg. He rolled down a sock of pure organzino silk, exposing Ponti's muscled calf.

Ponti caught some small movement in his peripheral vision and turned his head. He made eye contact with a striking redhead in a charcoal business suit, seated on a sectional sofa. It was the only piece of furniture in the whole office, other than Ponti's massive oak desk and padded leather chair.

The redhead gave him a cautioning glance: *Don't tease him too hard.*

Ponti shot her a wink, not failing to notice the amusement in her eyes. She was enjoying this as much as he was.

The tailor picked up another pin and returned his attention to the cuff. For a few moments silence filled the spacious office, located on the thirty-seventh floor of the Veer Towers in City Center Complex. Paul Ponti leased this entire floor for a mix of personal and business use.

"Can we continue?" the woman on the sofa asked.

"By all means. Where were we, Jeanette?"

She flicked the screen of an iPad with a glossy fingernail.

"Next week's social engagements. Fairly light, for a change."

Ponti nodded absently, gazing through a broad window behind the sofa. Just past Jeanette's slender shoulders, a panoramic view of Mount Charleston stretched into the western horizon. He found himself pausing to drink in this view a dozen times daily. The changing of the light across the bleached landscape caused dramatic alterations in shadow and hue that consistently fascinated him.

Unlike most with the means to occupy topflight real estate in this town, Ponti eschewed a view of the Strip. Too cliché for his taste, too lowbrow. Despite having lived in Vegas his whole life, and made a literal fortune here, he had no affection for neon. The quiet vista of the desert with low peaks in the distance gave him far more pleasure.

"Top priority," Jeanette looked up from the iPad. "Benefit for the Wounded Veterans Fund at Mandalay Bay. May 17, that's Wednesday."

"We've already donated, correct?"

"Fifteen thousand. Terry Charles with the fund wants to know if you plan to attend. That's worth a lot more to him than the check."

"What else is on my plate?"

Jeanette scanned the iPad again.

"Not a whole lot, actually. You told me to clear just about everything to get ready for the party. There's dinner with Monty Lewis on the twelfth."

"Don't tell me. Piero's again?"

Jeanette favored her boss with a wry grin.

"Where else? You know he insists it's the only place in town to get a decent eggplant parmesan."

Ponti sighed. "The man's an implacable creature of habit. At his age, a little variety would be healthy. Keeps the blood flowing."

"You want to cancel?"

"Of course not," Ponti snapped. "And I don't want to suggest another restaurant either." In a softer tone, he added, "Certain people are due respect, Jeanette. Even if it means eating the same dull food and hearing the same dull stories for the hundredth time."

"I'll confirm with Monty."

Ponti glared down with fresh annoyance as the tailor fussed with the hemline.

"Don't fidget, Cy. Just finish the fucking thing."

The tailor made one last adjustment and backed away from the stool in a low crouch. From Ponti's perspective he looked like an ancient fiddler crab scuttling across the sand.

"Got it the way I like it, did you?"

"See for yourself, Mr. Ponti. A slight break, six centimeters above the shoe."

Ponti stepped down and walked toward a three-paneled floor-length mirror. He moved with unusual grace for such a solidly built man; his waxed alligator wingtips barely made an impression in the thick wool carpeting. He stood before the mirror, making a precise appraisal of the alterations.

"Tell me where we are again, Jeanette."

"Mandalay, the seventeenth. Yes or no?"

"Entertainment?"

"Lance Burton's headlining. They haven't confirmed the opening acts yet."

Ponti stepped out of the trousers and handed them to Cy Goldstein. He grabbed a pair of twill slacks from the sofa and slid into them.

"All right, I'll make an appearance. Just make sure I'm not at a table with any of those city hall twits."

"Will Vanessa be joining you?"

The question lingered unanswered, filling the sunlit room. Any unprompted reference to Paul Ponti's wife tended to yield this type of pregnant pause, tenterhooks settling beneath whoever happened to be within earshot.

"I'll see how she feels."

Ponti brought both hands together in a brisk clap. Loud as a firecracker, it startled Cy Goldstein.

"Come on. What else, what else?"

"One more thing," Jeanette said with a small tremor of caution, "speaking of Vanessa. You haven't confirmed the guest list for the party. She calls me about it roughly every two hours."

"Why doesn't she ask me direct, for Christ's sake?"

"Says that's not the best way to get your attention."

Another sigh from Ponti. As wearisome as he found the prospect of another fundraiser with the same stale crowd of Vegas functionaries and B-listers, it felt like a vacation when contrasted with the looming specter of his fiftieth birthday party. Only three days away.

His house had morphed into a construction zone recently as preparations unfolded. Ponti was firm with his wife about the number of invited guests: fifty, no more. One per year, neat as a hatpin. She'd sullenly agreed, only after insisting it was his responsibility to decide who made the cut. That meant roughly 10 percent of those expecting to receive an invitation would elude disappointment.

The inevitability of putting noses out of joint all over town didn't provide much cheer. Even a man as respected as Paul Ponti didn't relish the idea of offending a large swath of the Vegas power structure. But then again, fuck 'em. He was the one turning fifty, the party was at his house, and he could invite exactly who the hell he wanted.

Still, he'd avoided the task of completing the guest list for weeks. The calendar no longer allowed for dithering.

Ponti sunk into the leather chair behind his desk with an annoyed grumble. A blue light lit up on the console. From across the room, Jeanette saw a visible change come over her boss, a kind of subtle full-body stiffening she'd witnessed before. She rose and started moving for the door before he spoke to dismiss her.

"E-mail me the guest list," he said absently, barely noticing her leave. His eyes took on a glassy, drunken sheen—he was only half in the room. That soft blue light transfixed him as surely as a hypnotist's swinging pocket watch.

Poor old Cy Goldstein failed to pick up on what was happening. He was too busy folding the six pairs of trousers and four shirts he'd marked with pins and chalk. Jeanette had to step back into the office and lead him out by the arm. She shut the door softly.

Ponti reached out and stabbed a button on the console. He heard the hiss of a door hidden in the wall behind him slide open and felt his twill slacks tighten. Cy Goldstein had left ample room in the crotch, just the way the way Ponti insisted. He didn't like to be cramped in his power zone.

The hidden door hissed shut. Ponti didn't turn around right away. He liked to listen to the soft padding of her feet on the carpet as she approached unseen. It took a Herculean imposition of self-control not to swivel the chair around and tackle her. He resisted the urge, waiting until he felt the soft pressure of her hands on his shoulders.

Then he spun the chair slowly, looking up into the face that never failed to steal his breath.

She looked different in the light of day. More wholesome. In some ways more human. Her short hair was soft instead of spiky—her lips bare of the black goth gloss. Removed from Unterwelt's murky barlight, she could be anyone's daughter.

She could even be Ponti's daughter, and wasn't that a big part of what this was about?

"You're early," he said, moving toward her like some jungle cat preparing to pounce. The image amused him, because in the thick of their amorous bouts he often felt more like prey than predator. It was a complete inversion of the normal order of things, one that he enjoyed greatly.

"Should I come back later?" she said, the natural huskiness

of her voice adding steel to his erection. "You're not happy to see me?"

"What kind of question is that? I told my day planner and my tailor to scram the minute I saw that little blue light. Would've dismissed the fucking governor if his sorry ass was in here."

Ponti's thick arms wrapped around her slender waist. It struck him, coming as a revelatory shock as it always did, that she was barely more than child. At least that was how she felt when clutched this tightly.

"Just a little slip of a thing," he whispered. "I could carry you over to that sofa using two fingers."

"Don't get filthy," she said, going on her tiptoes to bite his earlobe almost hard enough to draw blood. "I'll let you know when I'm ready for that."

"I'm yours to command."

That was true, at least for the next hour or so. For a man who wielded Paul Ponti's kind of influence, it was sweet release to discard every last vestige of power for short intervals. As long as he remained in her private company, he gleefully relinquished all control.

He did whatever she told him. Gave whatever she asked, within reason. He savored these moments of supplication, and she could be a cruelly demanding mistress. After decades of rampant philandering with companions of every conceivable stripe, nothing compared to Luna's pitiless dominance. It was the biggest turn on of his life.

He picked her up, using both hands, and carried her to the sectional sofa. Sunlight came pouring in through the large tinted window, giving his office the feel of a movie set.

"You want to talk about him?" she asked as he set her down.

"Maybe later," he answered, lowering himself to a kneeling position. He grabbed the heel of one leather boot but didn't pull it free. Better to await her instruction; everything was better that way.

"Nothing before we get started?" she asked. "Not even some fantasy talk about all the different ways he could die?"

Ponti felt his lower back stiffen with annoyance. Why was she pushing him? Why now, when he offered no welcoming signals? That wasn't like her. She was usually more attuned to his rhythms, knowing when to probe his soft tissue and when to back off.

"I'm not in the mood. Fuck him, it's just you and me this time. Nobody else on the fucking planet, as far as I want to know."

"Maybe you don't need him to get the blood flowing any-more," Luna continued, her manicured fingertips finding the zipper on Ponti's slacks. "A psychologist would probably say that's a healthy sign. But I'm not so sure…"

The taunting smile on her face grew a shade more sadistic. Ponti lay a heavy hand on her left thigh.

"Don't push me, girl. Not too far."

"It's just…I have a weird intuition you want to talk about him. Now, more than ever. With your big night coming up, it must gnaw at you to—"

Ponti squeezed brutally on her thigh, his nails digging deep. Luna gasped with surprise and pain.

"I said it can fucking wait!" he said through gritted teeth.

As quickly as it came, his anger passed. He relaxed his grip on her leg, raising his hand to reveal five red patches on the pale skin. She looked at him differently. Less in control, but determined to maintain the illusion.

He slid off one boot and softly kissed her foot. A wave of woozy repentance washed over him, even as his rage simmered beneath the surface. He didn't need any mention of that cock-roach Diamond to fuel his lust right now. Not today. And the way Luna seemed to be goading him on the subject only made him mad.

Ponti didn't like the idea of hurting this girl, or even scaring her. It didn't jive with their carefully crafted power equation. His spooky little witch was supposed to be the one in control; that was the most fundamental rule of their game.

But even as he prepared to sink into the bliss of Luna's torrid domination for the next hour, Paul Ponti needed her to know on some core level that he was still the boss.

Reaching for her other boot, he didn't see the look in her eyes. Had he noticed, the calculating sheen that stole over them might have prompted him to ask a few pointed questions before they progressed any further.

9.

Halfway down the Strip, a beam of sunlight awoke Rusty at the exact same moment that Paul Ponti removed Luna's other boot. It was the kind of sunbeam only the Mojave Desert could produce at half past nine on a clear morning, blazing directly onto his face through the east window.

He'd been hovering on the rim of consciousness for several minutes, navigating a hazy dreamscape of scarred flesh, kohl-rimmed eyes, and atonal deathcore as the sunbeam grew hotter on his bruised cheek. Some survival impulse cautioned him from emerging into consciousness, sensing this new day would bring nothing good.

But the sun would not be ignored.

When his eyes fluttered open, they were instantly blinded. He rolled over and opened then again. A moment of confusion passed before he identified his whereabouts. The Skyloft's bedroom was surreally bright thanks to the blackout drapes he'd neglected to draw last night.

Rusty stumbled to his feet with a muttered curse and pulled the drapes shut.

He'd returned to the loft a little after two o'clock and promptly collapsed onto the bed, too tired to fully disrobe. His clothes now stuck to his skin, redolent with dried sweat and the Unterwelt's general funk. He shook them off and lurched into the shower for ten scalding minutes beneath all six jets.

A look in the bathroom mirror confirmed he'd suffered minimal damage at the hands of his scarred attacker. His knuckles had lost more skin than his face, a cheering discovery. It was nice to know he'd dished out at least a bit of damage in those frenzied moments behind the club.

And I got something out of it, he thought, remembering the twice-spoken reference to "where Vegas began."

Now I just have to figure out what the hell it means.

Rusty descended into the loft's kitchen and navigated the cutting-edge system of a Technivorm coffee maker to brew a pot. Swallowing five Advil, he resisted the urge to add a shot of scotch to his first mug. Not a good idea. He'd need all his faculties today.

Rusty opened his MacBook and fired up Google Chrome. It took him less than ten minutes to locate, download, and install the Tor browser required to access the deep web. A welcome screen congratulated him, but cautioned that additional steps were required to guarantee browsing that left no digital footprints.

He didn't bother with those additional steps, remembering Charlotte's admonition that there was no such thing as true online anonymity. He opened the text message on his phone where he'd entered the dot onion URL address watermarked on the textbook sheet. One letter at a time, he typed the address into the Tor browser's search window.

Rusty's finger hovered over the Enter key, reluctant to press it. His instinctual protection mode kicked in once more, telling him that this may well be a rabbit hole impossible to climb out of once entered.

Maybe. But that's why I came here in the first place.

Rusty tapped Enter and his Mac's screen went black. Three seconds passed and nothing happened. Five, then fifteen.

Mind reeling with all the sensitive personal data that could be mined from the laptop, he ripped the power cord free. The screen stayed lit, reminding him he had at least five hours of battery juice stored. He fumbled in his pants for a coin to use in twisting open the battery lock, but a ping from the laptop's speaker halted him.

A new window opened in the Tor browser, filled with a jumble of vibrating text. A spool of letters and mathematic symbols faded up in concentric circles, changing and replicating so fast he couldn't track them with his eyes.

Before he could decipher any of it, the Mac's screen went black again. It stayed that way almost a full minute.

Then a line of red text faded up in the center of the screen, one letter at a time:

> *It can only cut when its elemental substance*
> *changes from* _ _ _ _ _ _ *to* _ _ _ _ _.

A cursor blinked at the left side of the first blank space. These were clearly password prompts. Instinctively, Rusty sensed he'd have only one chance to make the proper alphanumeric entries. If he got even a single digit wrong, the page would likely shut down and deny him another attempt. It might even unleash the kind of virus onto his hard drive he'd been fearful of a moment earlier.

Rusty sat there, drinking his coffee and impatiently waiting for the Advil to kick in. He stared at the screen, feeling a sense of vague recognition that shimmied away whenever he tried to bring it into focus.

Something about the question struck him as familiar. Rising to pour a second cup, he flashed on something: the message in the greeting card. It had made some reference to a knife, but what was it? Rusty almost ran to the closet to retrieve the cardboard box before remembering he'd left it with Charlotte. It was too early to call without risking the chance of waking her.

Think, asshole! What did it say…something about when a trick isn't a trick. When the suckers see what they came for…

It hit him. The sentence from the greeting card appeared in his mind's eye and his fingers started typing of their own accord.

*It can only cut when its elemental substance
changes from <u>rubber</u> to <u>steel</u>.*

The text box disappeared as the entire screen went red. The red started folding in on itself with a series of looping pixilated swirls. Then nothing but black.

Rusty clutched the forgotten mug as his coffee went cold, staring at the screen. Willing it to tell him he'd successfully navigated past the prompt.

Instead, another line of text appeared, one character at a time.

*Congratulations. You made it past the first barrier.
One more and you're in. Have fun with this one.*

And that was it. Nothing changed for more than ten minutes. Rusty got up to take a piss, do some stretches, grab a pear from the sterling bowl. When he checked the computer again, the same words taunted him.

He couldn't quite believe that was it. What was the point of creating an obstacle that led to nothing once surpassed?

As if in answer, the screen went black and a new sentence started typing itself across the screen.

*A chegada de que mês informa o Payuco
há apenas dois meses no período chuvoso?*

And then, with a flashing cursor, room for nine characters to be entered:

_ _ _ _ _ _ _ _ _

"That's helpful," Rusty muttered to himself.

He recognized the language at least, or thought he did. Portuguese, same tongue as Nossa Morte itself. It would be easy enough to find an English translation online, but how much would that help in figuring out what to enter in the box?

Rusty sat there for a few minutes, reading the line over and over. Only one word popped out at him.

Payocu.

That was the name of the tribe contained in the sheet of textbook paper, the same tribe he'd asked Dr. Estrella Lima about on the phone yesterday. Felt like it could have been a week ago.

Now he had two reasons to call Charlotte and have her verify something from inside the box. He checked his watch. Still too early, most likely. He didn't want to wake her and interrupt what may be the only pain-free moments she enjoyed these days.

Rusty paced the room, amped and frustrated.

His mobile phone started vibrating. The screen showed a number he didn't recognize with a 702 area code. Local call. Not Charlotte's number. Rusty felt a suspicious dread take root. He couldn't justify it, but couldn't quite shake it off either.

Answer it, for Christ's sake.

He was both relieved and annoyed at his own paranoia to hear Dr. Estrella Lima announce herself. She sounded no more friendly than during their previous call.

"Impeccable timing, Doctor. Still have a window to see me?"

"You remain convinced meeting in person would prove helpful for your film?"

"Absolutely. More than ever."

Rusty poured himself another cup of coffee, listening to silence over the fiber-optic line and wondering if she'd hung up on him.

"Tomorrow. Twelve thirty."

"Perfect."

"During my lunch hour," she added in a tone that emphasized the inconvenience.

"I really appreciate—"

"Twenty minutes, Mr. Diamond. No more. I've got a stack of papers to review by the end of the week."

"Whatever you can spare. I'm grateful."

"Come to 105-A at Wright Hall. Twelve thirty sharp. Use the Harmon Avenue entrance and ask the guard for directions."

Rusty started to ask if she'd mind translating some Portuguese but she'd already terminated the call.

He put the phone down and took another look at the laptop. No change to the screen. Just that same taunting line and the blinking cursor. Rusty knew he could waste a whole day sitting here waiting for something new to pop up. That clearly wasn't a good use of his time, but he didn't have a better idea handy.

His cell phone rang again. It was Charlotte. Things were looking up all of a sudden.

"Morning," he said brightly. "Couldn't wait very long to hear my voice again, could you?"

"This may shock you, but these days I've got plenty of time to burn. So much so that I can even spare a few minutes for the likes of you."

Showing off her trademark ability to read him, she asked, "What kind of trouble did you get into last night?"

"No trouble. Stopped by Unterwelt for a nightcap. Charming spot. I'll have to take you sometime."

"That sounds like half the story at best, but I guess you'll volunteer more if you feel like it."

"Got a question for you, actually. Where did Vegas begin?"

"What?"

"It's like a riddle or something. I don't know if it's connected to the box, but I heard it twice last night. Felt like it was planted. Like something I was supposed to hear."

Rusty waited as the metallic snap of a Zippo came from the other end of the line.

"Goddamnit, Charlotte. That can't be recommended for someone in your condition, can it?"

"I've cut way back; fewer than ten a day."

"And your doctor says that's acceptable."

"I tell him what I think he needs to know. The rest is none of his business."

"Sensible approach. So, any insight you can share?"

"About where Vegas began? Depends who you ask. Most rubes would probably say Bugsy but that's just a lot of Hollywood BS."

"Yeah, I don't think that's what she was getting at."

"Who?"

"Young lady who posed me the question. Seemed like she had something more—I don't know—*mystical* in mind."

"Well, that's what they say about the Old Mormon Fort. It's even on the postcards they sell, if memory serves."

"Come again? Mormon Fort?"

"What, you didn't realize this town was originally established as a spiritual retreat for Mormons?"

"That factoid somehow managed to escape my notice."

"It's the straight truth. A bunch of polygamous Bible-thumpers from Utah built a fort in the 1800s. They were aiming to convert the Mojave Paiutes. You know, show those godless heathens the one true faith."

"This fort," he asked. "Where is it, exactly?"

10.

Soren parked his van at a corner on the two hundred block of Paradise. As always, the street name struck him as hilariously inapt. Laid out in the '50s as a sparkling thoroughfare of high-end housing and entertainment structures, it was now little more than a two-lane ghetto, at least this far away from the Strip.

Soren never parked too close to the Charleston Arms, employing a level of stealth he realized to be unnecessary. His near-daily comings and goings to this place were all recorded by a dozen surveillance cameras, but at least he could prevent any of them from reading the van's plate number by parking out of sight.

Not that the van was hard to identify. The large blue logo for Superior Pool Cleaning painted on the side panels was easily readable from a block away. No such company existed. Soren would be cold in the dirt before he ever cleaned a goddamn pool, but he felt a business designation gave the vehicle a certain sheen of anonymity that came in handy when he was carrying a load that would not pass even the most cursory inspection during a traffic stop.

Soren glanced in the rearview mirror, taking a fresh look at the bruise under his left eye. As a mark of recent combat it failed to impress, certainly not in comparison to the three-inch vertical scars running down both cheeks. But then, last night's scuffle in the lot behind Unterwelt hardly qualified as a battle.

Trent would probably get a kick out of it anyway.

Soren got out of the van and walked. He passed a debt-collection agency, a 24-7 marriage chapel whose display window featured a soiled heart-shaped pillow on a stand, and a Western Union office said to do the biggest money order business on the planet. All these establishments built to near-identical prefab standards: flaking stucco and cracks at the window joints were the most common design flourishes.

Climbing a set of stairs to the Charleston Arms's double-doored entrance, Soren resisted the urge to groin-kick an emaciated man slumbering in a crouched posture on the stoop. He punched in 706 at the callbox and waited. Trent wasn't in the habit of answering the door in a timely fashion, especially if he was in the middle of an online transaction.

The door buzzed open. Neat trick Trent had pulled off, wiring the building's security camera to his own desktop computer. Given Trent's day job, to say nothing of his other pursuits, there was no telling who might come looking for him.

Soren rode the elevator to the seventh floor and strode down the hallway to the rear corner unit. The door clicked open after three knocks—another automated refurbishment Trent had installed upon moving in last year.

Soren walked through the darkened living room, blinds drawn and only some sputtering candles offering illumination. He entered the master bedroom, which was even darker, save for the glow of five computer monitors.

"Hold on," Trent said without turning around in his chair. It was a superfluous order; Soren knew better than to speak before getting clearance. Just another cog in the superiority apparatus Trent needed to keep his ego intact. Soren found it tiresome, but he'd grown used to it by now. Despite his flaws, Trent was clearly possessed of a certain slant of warped genius.

The chair's back was so tall Soren could only see the tip of Trent's head, stringy reddish hair standing up like he'd stuck his finger in a live outlet. He eyed the left monitor, which showed a transaction web page for Amazingattractions.com.

"It never ceases to amaze," Trent muttered, typing with speed and precision.

"What's that?" Soren asked blandly, knowing the answer.

"The gullibility. The sheer, mindless gullibility. It's bad enough no matter where you find them, but in this town it's like any last shred of cautionary instinct fades away."

Trent kept typing a series of digits into a box on the monitor. Soren could tell it was an American Express number. He'd come to recognize the plastic issued by various banks from their four-digit prefixes. Looked like some sucker was breaking out the Gold Card to secure phantom tickets to some over-hyped Strip extravaganza.

"That's not quite right," Trent added. "It doesn't fade away, they willfully dispose of it. Just begging to be fleeced, all of them."

Soren grunted something that sounded like agreement. He'd heard this observation more than a few times before.

"Do you think," Trent asked, "these rubes really believe they're getting valid front row seats to Mystère, five hours before curtain? It boggles the mind. At least some little corner of their brain must be screaming: 'Stop, this isn't legit!' But what do they do to that little voice? Snuff it out and click *Pay Now*."

An alert box popped up on the computer screen reading: *Transaction completed: $875.00 verified from Amex Gold business account #29845722179.*

"Another satisfied customer. My only regret is not being able to catch their reactions. Thought about doing that, actually. Just hang around will call and soak up the futile outrage as Joe Fuckhead, desperate to impress the wife or some clients, finds out he's been burned."

"So what's stopping you?"

"I suspect the actual event wouldn't live up to my mental image. You know I don't handle disappointment well."

Trent spun around in the chair. He looked totally different out of the Raven getup. In place of the long black mane, a tangle of stringy auburn hair shot out in all directions. A pointed chin shone almost ivory white without the paste-on goatee. His cobalt eyes, the left noticeably darker than the right, seldom failed to make Soren feel like a zoo animal under review by its keeper.

"Give me the whole story. Don't leave out any details even if they strike you as meaningless."

Soren started talking. After describing how Rusty's entrance to Unterwelt was picked up on the infrared monitor at 11:14 P.M., he went on to describe his appearance in the back bar six minutes later.

"He looks different. Definitely him though."

"Different how?"

"Shaved his dome. Lost the goatee. Put on some weight too, I'd say." Soren pulled a zip drive from his pants pocket. "Footage from all three cameras. Door, mosh pit, and the bar. Don't expect much; the quality's shit. Infrared lenses are useless with all that dry ice."

"Describe his interaction with Luna."

"Pretty sad. Buys a drink and asks straight out. All the subtlety of a jackhammer."

"Tell me what he *said*. Be specific."

"Ask her for specifics. I can't pick up audio in there."

"Oh, I will. Just tell me what she told you so I can see where your accounts might diverge."

Soren recounted what Luna had related to him about her conversation with Rusty, then went on to tell Trent how he'd entered the picture as planned. Trent leaned forward in the chair, taking visibly greater interest as Soren described ejecting Rusty from the bar and the brief skirmish that followed.

"And you're positive," Trent said slowly, "you didn't intervene too soon?"

"No way. I dropped the Fort intel on him, just to make sure it stuck."

Trent's eyes narrowed.

"Even though that was part of Luna's script?"

Soren shrugged, trying to disguise his unease at having broken protocol last night. And compounding the error by revealing it now.

"Wanted to make sure it landed. Lot quieter outside, better chance he'd hear it right."

"Were you instructed to offer any repetition?"

"Jesus. I can make a few calls on the fly, can't I? What's the point of getting him here if we don't forward the action?"

"Did it occur to you that drawing overt attention through repetition is likely to reveal it as a lure? That you might impart the impression he's being guided down a prelaid path?"

The interrogative tone in Trent's voice was growing a sharper edge. Soren could feel himself losing ground.

"Trust me, that's not what he's thinking. Not after the beatdown I gave him."

"Took a few shots yourself," Trent said wryly.

Soren's fingers rose to the bruise on his face before he could stop them. Bad giveaway. Trent's smile grew wider.

"Dude's a shadow of himself," Soren said dismissively. "This will be too easy, if anything."

"Perhaps, but we can't make it *too* easy. We have to let him think he's getting past some resistance. I thought I'd explained all this."

"OK, OK. I got it."

A *ping* came from one of the monitors. Trent spun around

in his chair. Another order appeared on the spreadsheet: six loge tickets for Blue Man Group.

"Enough about last night. Let's get to the bellman."

"All lined up," Soren said, glad to be on a new topic. "Clocks in at four. I'm ready."

"Where will you make contact?"

"Staff parking lot, three blocks south. He uses the elevated walkway to cross Tropicana. Stairs at the bottom should work, otherwise I'll do it in the alley. After that, it's all you."

Trent nodded slowly, conveying marginal approval.

"Sounds workable, barring any unnecessary mistakes. What about recruitment for tonight?"

Soren rubbed his palms together with relish.

"We're all set. Got just the right lamb picked out. You're gonna love this one, can't be a day over sevente—"

"Don't tell me now."

"No details?"

"I trust you with this part of the process, Soren. If you'd start embracing that fact, you'd be less tempted to prove yourself by going rogue."

"What about the other end? You trust her to deliver?"

"Don't worry about Luna. Her hooks are in plenty deep; it's just a matter of time."

"So she tells you. Not that she'd have any reason to lie."

A slight grin formed on Trent's face, something Soren rarely witnessed.

"Worried she might suffer from a case of split loyalties? Don't. If this all goes as scripted—and I have every reason to think it will—there's nothing but upside for everyone involved. Plenty of real estate in the Homeless Corridor to go around."

"Maybe so. But I'd guess Ponti's in the habit of *choosing* his fucking tenants, not the other way around."

"No one's ever come to the table with what I have. It's

called flipping the script, and you can stop worrying about aspects of the plan that don't concern you."

Trent rotated his chair back toward the desk and started processing the new order. Another annoying habit of his, bringing a meeting to an end so abruptly.

Soren rose and made for the door.

"Remember," Trent said without turning around. "Rubber gloves. Details are everything from here on out."

Soren almost flipped him the finger but stopped himself. He didn't really believe Trent had eyes in the back of his head, but didn't see any sense in risking it.

11.

Rusty parked on Washington Avenue, not far from the wrought iron entrance to Cashman Park. The view through the Barracuda's tinted windshield was one of pure shimmering heat, and the park appeared to offer little relief. Three or four wilted palms threw slivers of shade onto some brown grass. Directly across from the park stood a modest collection of mud and adobe structures approachable via a stone walkway.

He'd reached his destination. It didn't look too promising.

Rusty stepped from the car and took in his surroundings. This was not a part of town with which he had much familiarity. To tourists and a good portion of locals alike, it was a virtual wasteland that occupied ten dreary blocks connecting the billion-dollar resorts of the Strip with their downmarket counterparts in Old Downtown.

Rusty took a quick look at the dry expanse of Cashman Park. He held some vague recollection of this place serving as a locus for LV's homeless population, which had grown at an alarming rate in the wake of the '08 housing crash.

That recollection was borne out by the sight greeting his eyes. A sizable population of transients was sleeping on or milling about the sun-scorched grass. Near the park's entrance, a young woman in a long black robe was setting up a picnic table, assisted by two Latino youths.

She's got to be burning up in that thing, Rusty thought.

He turned away and crossed Washington to the entrance of the Old Mormon Fort. At the ticket booth he shelled out twelve bucks for an all-day pass. A placard behind the booth read: WELCOME TO THE HISTORIC MORMON FORT—WHERE LAS VEGAS BEGAN!

The elderly woman who sold him the ticket said a guided tour was just about to start. Rusty joined a cluster of people fanning themselves with brochures beneath a cheesecloth awning. A church group from Salt Lake City, in matching t-shirts.

Their guide appeared, an oddly energetic young man whose name was illegibly scrawled on a tag pinned to his shirt. He seemed thrilled to have a live audience this morning.

Rusty spent most of the next hour learning more than he'd ever wanted to know about the founding of this fair metropolis. The tour group shuffled dutifully across the grounds from stable to ranch house, avidly described by their guide as the oldest standing building in Nevada. They beheld wonders of bygone times including a corn separator and a spinning wheel.

Then, the main event—a sojourn into the fort itself, constructed of adobe in 1855. The tour guide seemed to approach orgasmic release as he described (and acted out) some of the trials and setbacks endured by hardy Mormon settlers as they toiled to erect this monument to preservation and piety.

Rusty slipped away from the group before the tour was finished. He trudged past the ticket booth toward the entrance, rivulets of sweat pouring down the back of his neck.

Clearly, his mission had proved a dead end.

He'd seen nothing that bore even a tenuous relation to Nossa Morte. What did two centuries' worth of dusty rock have in common with the bizarre threat that had beckoned him out to this desert? Was it possible he'd misinterpreted the bartender's words, or simply misheard them in Unterwelt's din?

No, because they'd been repeated with a kind of rehearsed fidelity by Scarface at the back of the club.

As Rusty activated the Barracuda's keyless entry, a commotion inside Cashman Park caught his eye. The group of transients he'd noticed before was clustered around the picnic table. Three LV Metro Police prowlers had assembled near the park's entrance, cherry tops rotating pointlessly in the blinding sun.

Rusty watched as a half-dozen cops worked to organize the gathering of homeless in a single-file line. It looked like an efficient operation, carried out with a whiff of excessive force. No billy clubs drawn, but plenty of prodding and shoving. The picnic table got knocked over, spilling food, plastic utensils, paper plates, and water bottles all over the ground.

Away from the table, a scruffy, underfed young man was arguing loudly with a cop. He waved one hand over his head while the other clutched a half-eaten sandwich, refusing to be corralled. The officer nodded calmly a few times, then suddenly reached out and threw him up against a palm tree.

The woman in black Rusty had noticed earlier saw it happen. She dropped a case of bottled water and started running across the grass. Only now did Rusty apprehend she wore a nun's habit. She vehemently berated the cop for his rough treatment. He ignored her as he handcuffed the youth and marched him toward the park's exit.

Three minutes later it was all over. The cruisers rolled away down Washington, having collared a half dozen of the less cooperative transients. The ones who'd avoided arrest wandered away from the table, leaving only the nun to clean up the mess. Even her two assistants had made themselves scarce.

Rusty stepped into the park.

A gust of hot wind blew a stack of plastic cups across the grass. Rusty picked them up and dropped them in a box of other picnic items. The nun glanced at him curiously.

"Thank you," she said.

"What was the commotion all about?"

"Oh, just another roust. They're a little early today. Usually they let us serve the food before storming in."

"Looked like overkill, at least from my vantage point."

"In that, we agree."

She kneeled down to flip the picnic table over and folded its metal legs.

"Need a hand? Looks like your helpers bailed on you."

"You're very kind. My truck's just outside."

They carried the table to the street and laid it in the bed of a Dodge pickup. Emblazoned on the driver's door was a logo for the Sisters of Mercy Halfway Home.

"You do this often, Sister..."

"Irene," she said with a wan smile. "Twice a week. I'd be out here every day if we had enough food to offer. Donations have been on a downslide for quite some time."

He followed her back into the park and they gathered up the debris. A few transients waved goodbye to Sister Irene as they ambled out through the gates. She told them to come back for another meal in three days.

"The police don't give these people any public space to get fed except this park," she said to Rusty. "Then when they decide too many have congregated, they lock up a few. For appearances, mainly."

"Didn't look like they were causing any trouble," Rusty commented. "Why the heavy hand?"

"You must not follow local politics. The mayor and city council have established a zero-tolerance policy toward homelessness in any part of the city designated as a tourist draw."

"And this qualifies?" Rusty asked with a glance around the park. His dubious expression elicited a smile from Sister Irene.

"It's a moving target. A citywide game of whack-a-mole. If LV Metro spent all its time booting people from public areas they'd have no one left to handle real crime. Of course, the casinos have private security to deal with the issue when it crosses onto their property, but that doesn't happen often."

"Aren't there any shelters around?"

"Sure, but that's not realistic. In a desert climate with median temperatures in the eighties, you're not going to entice the average person without a home to hunker indoors."

"Lot of 'em looked like kids."

"Many are. Runaways, from broken homes more often than not."

Rusty watched as the last few transients exited the park.

"Where do they go now?"

"To the nearest shelter, I'd like to think. Maybe some will. Others will hit the corners downtown, panhandling. That's the most direct route to a jail cell, but I can't seem to dissuade them."

Sister Irene paused, looking reluctant to continue.

"Some of the more desperate ones…I hate to think of it, but they'll go where even the police don't dare patrol. God help them."

Rusty dumped some debris into a trash can. The area appeared clean, like no one had ever been here.

"I try to talk them out of it," Sister Irene continued, her voice strained. "Few listen, not that I can blame them. The temptation must be strong to seek a haven down there."

"Where?" Rusty asked, hearing a silent alarm somewhere in the back of his brain.

"You know about the flood tunnels underneath the city? Two hundred miles worth. Some choose to seek shelter in them, despite the obvious dangers."

"Yeah, that got quite a bit of coverage a while back. Some pretty big encampments down there, huh?"

"I wouldn't know from personal experience. I tend to suspect a certain amount of exaggeration from the media."

"Well, I hope things go a little easier next time."

Sister Irene looked at him curiously. Rusty got the impression she was searching for an explanation for his presence.

"Thanks again for your help. We can certainly use it."

He nodded and stepped away, turning at the sound of her voice.

"Not what the city planners had in mind when they built the tunnels back in the '40s, I'd wager. It was quite an engineering feat at the time, with a fittingly grandiose name. The Clark County Subterranean Aqueduct System. They have a different name for it now."

The alarm grew louder.

"What name?" Rusty asked, knowing the answer before it took shape on Sister Irene's lips.

"The Underworld."

12.

The Strip vanished from Rusty's vision as he dropped feetfirst into the plunge pool on his loft's patio. A bracing funnel of water consumed him as he sank downward. It felt good. He curled into a ball and expelled all the oxygen from his lungs, letting gravity pin him to the pool's marble floor.

He'd used a digital thermostat to chill the water temperature to its lowest setting. With several more hours till sundown, the desert heat was still roaring full blast. Rusty was feeling edgy, ill at ease. He needed a rejuvenating jolt to his system.

The pool did the trick, and he emerged energized. Pulling on a plush terry cloth robe, he leaned against the chrome safety railing and let the sun dry him. In the patio directly below, a bronzed couple was frolicking *au natural* in a clam-shaped Jacuzzi. Rusty stepped back into the loft to give them some privacy.

A digital chirp issued from the in-room phone. He picked it up.

"Front desk, Mr. Diamond. A Ms. Raines is here to see you."

"No shit. Send her up."

Rusty hung up and quickly threw on some clothes. A minute later he answered a knock at the door. Charlotte stood in the hallway with the cardboard box in her hands.

"This is a surprise," Rusty said with a smile.

"I'm not interrupting anything too depraved, am I?"

"See for yourself."

She shoved the box into his hands and stepped past him.

"I was curious to get at look at these lofts. Not as nice as the villas at Caesars, but not bad."

Rusty set the box down on the kitchen counter. He was about to tell Charlotte to make herself at home but she'd already lowered herself onto the couch.

"You seem to be moving well today. Without any support."

"Appearances can be deceiving, as you know better than anyone. Half a dozen aspirin make walking for a few minutes almost tolerable."

Looking to change the subject, Rusty pointed to the box.

"Find anything else?"

"Zilch. Got sick of staring at the damn thing and didn't want it in my house anymore."

"Can't say I blame you."

"Do what I said, Rusty. Get rid of it and go back home. If another box shows up on your doorstep, and it contains something that points to a serious crime, notify the police and go about your life."

"I can't do that. Sounds like I'm on my own from here, but I appreciate the help."

Charlotte gave him a sardonic roll of the eyes and pulled a pack of Kools from her pocket. Rusty walked over and opened the balcony's sliding glass door a crack.

"Christ, performers," she said, exhaling a long plume. "Always playing the 'poor little me' card. I didn't say I was done."

"Come up with another angle?"

"Your description of Unterwelt grabbed my curiosity. Got me thinking."

"And?"

"I did some digging, cashed in a few favors. Found something kind of interesting."

"Me too, actually. Up by the old Mormon Fort, thanks to your tip."

Charlotte shot him an annoyed look.

"Go ahead," Rusty said. "You first."

"The building that houses Unterwelt, it used to be an auto parts plant. Shut down a couple years ago, along with a whole swath of manufacturing facilities in that part of town. You know what they call it? The Homeless Corridor. That whole section northwest of the Stratosphere. I'm serious, you can even find it printed on some maps around town."

"Hmm," Rusty said. "I suppose Cashman Park would be included in the Homeless Corridor too."

"I checked with a contact at the Department of Public Records," she continued. "Someone in the Assessor's Reporting Unit owes me a favor. The property was purchased last year by a holding company called Allied Interests. This same company owns a string of properties in and around the so-called Homeless Corridor, all purchased within the last year. Couple of D-grade strip clubs off Industrial. A cell phone reseller on Paradise. An all-night laundromat that doubles as a massage parlor, so I'm told. Definitely not what you'd call high-end real estate, but all very pricey. I saw the figures. Struck me as odd that someone with those kind of resources would invest in the Unterwelt building. And after making the acquisition, all they've done with it is open some dive metal-head bar?"

"They might be leasing the space to another party. Probably on a short-term basis, hence the lack of signage and advertising. Some of these new club promoters like to open a place for a few weeks and cash out."

Charlotte shook her head dubiously.

"Doesn't make much sense either way. Especially when you consider who's behind these acquisitions. My Public Records contact didn't go so far as calling Allied Interests a shadow holding company, but he said the owner's taken all possible steps to keep his name off any deeds associated with this recent buying spree."

Charlotte's eyes searched the room for an ashtray. Rusty slid an empty mug across the table and she dunked her smoke in it. He had the feeling some kind of bombshell was coming, but he wasn't prepared for what she said next:

"Does the name Paul Ponti mean anything to you?"

The walls of the loft seemed to tighten, all the air in the room compressing.

Jesus fucking Christ.

Rusty hadn't been expecting Charlotte to throw out any name he was familiar with in more than a passing way. But the one she *did* throw out…there was more than a little bit of personal history at stake. Forcing his mind to focus so as not to set off her radar, it occurred to him he really shouldn't be surprised to learn Paul Ponti was tied up in this mess.

Makes all the sense in the world. Kinda crazy I never thought of it myself.

"Sure," he answered casually. "Anyone hip to the Vegas power structure knows that name. Last of the old-time hoods, right?"

Charlotte made an expression of mock outrage.

"Bite your tongue! Mr. Ponti's a respected pillar of the community. Just ask the good people at the Clark County Cancer Center. They added a wing with his name on it last year. Sure, you might hear some scuttlebutt about a past loaded with more criminal contacts than El Chapo, but that doesn't prevent Paul Ponti from playing golf with the governor twice a month."

"So an all-around good guy, huh?"

"Oh, I wouldn't say that. I've heard Ponti's more danger-ous now than when he was a straight-up crook. He's got the imprimatur of official sanction to cover up any messy work."

"OK," Rusty said, suppressing an urge to forcibly usher

Charlotte from the loft. "Ponti owns the building that houses Unterwelt. Along with a sizable chunk of the Homeless Corridor. What's that tell us?"

"Let's say these Nossa Morte characters are operating out of that building, which means they're paying rent to Paul Ponti. The question that comes to mind is this: How deep does their connection with this man run? Because if he's the muscle backing their sick little operation, this whole thing becomes a lot dicier than it already looks."

Rusty couldn't stand to sit in the crosshairs of her inquisitive gaze any longer. He grabbed the mug and carried it into the kitchen. Charlotte followed him.

"You're pretty twitchy all of a sudden. More than usual, I mean."

"Too much java," he said lamely.

"OK, I'll ask the question so obvious it shouldn't require asking. Do you have any dealings with Paul Ponti that I don't know about? The kind that might involve him wanting to see harm come your way?"

"Never met the man," Rusty said in an even voice. It was as good an acting performance as he'd ever been able to muster. And he was pretty sure Charlotte bought it.

13.

The VIP lounge of the Neon Garter overlooked the club's main floor, offering a wide-angle view of both the main stage and the two side cages. The glass wall facing the club was smoked on one side, offering total privacy to anyone partaking of the action from the lounge's exclusive confines.

There wasn't much to see at 10:37 on a Tuesday morning. Both side cages remained dark until the lunch shift started, and the sole topless dancer working the main stage did not represent the apex of talent on display during peak periods. The clientele at this hour matched the quality of the performance—just a smattering of hardcore loners hunched over their drinks, tossing bills onto the stage with zombielike detachment at the end of each song.

Paul Ponti gazed through the smoked glass from a leather chair in the VIP lounge. It bored and slightly depressed him to be here. The Neon Garter easily ranked as the weakest link in the chain of gentlemen's clubs he owned around town. More accurately, he held these establishments under the shadow banner of Allied Interests. There was nothing shameful or even mildly untoward about owning a strip club in Vegas, but Ponti preferred a judicious approach in selecting properties to which he attached his name.

He hadn't set foot in the Neon Garter in years, but it was a good place for this particular meeting. The odds of being spotted by anyone whose opinion mattered while entering and leaving the joint were pretty much nil.

Ponti watched Trent emerge from the men's room and cross the carpet, taking a leather chair opposite him.

"Sorry for the wait," Trent said. "My stomach's a little touchy this morning."

Ponti didn't offer a reply to that odd opener. He'd decided to sit quietly and let this brief meeting officially start so it could end. Already, he could tell it had been a waste of time if not an outright mistake to come here—no matter what Luna may have whispered to the contrary.

Unbelievable, the power of suggestion that little witch held over him. She'd insisted that Trent merited a sit-down, and in a moment blurred by passion he'd allowed himself to be convinced. An error of judgment not to be repeated.

He disliked this gangly red-haired kid upon first sight. Even in the VIP lounge's black-lit gloom, a twitchy quality stole over Trent that betrayed something more than a little *off*. Ponti suspected his prolonged visit to the men's room had been spent packing his nose.

"Nice place," Trent said, taking a look around. "Not the classiest destination of its type on Industrial, but I've seen worse."

"You're saying it's a shithole," Ponti replied. "And that's OK, don't think I'm gonna take offense. This town still needs a few shitholes. Like the place you've been renting out, for example."

"That's a harsh assessment, Paul. I can call you Paul, right? The building has worked quite well for our needs. Unterwelt attracts a certain breed of patron, and we couldn't ask for a better fit."

"I could care less. Had no idea whose name was on the lease. I don't involve myself on that level. Whole block's gonna be dust soon enough."

"So I gather. Big plans in the making."

"Let's cut the shit. A common acquaintance tells me you're worth five minutes of my time."

Trent reached out and picked up a glass of ice water from the table between them. He took a deliberative sip, refusing to appear rushed.

Ponti couldn't help but study him with a kind of repulsed fascination. Despite the sharp angularity of his features, his face held a childish aspect that was offset by the wired intensity of his eyes.

"First of all," Trent said, "I really appreciate you making time in your schedule. Luna's endorsement aside, I know there are people all over town who draw a lot more water than I'll ever hope to, who'd gladly give their eyeteeth for a private audience."

"This isn't an audience, for fuck's sake. It's a favor to a friend I'm already starting to regret."

"Favors come in handy. I like to do nice things for my friends too."

"So what do you want?"

Trent shook his head.

"Oh no, you've got it all wrong. I'm here to give. To offer you something of tremendous value."

Trent reached into his pocket and produced a 4 × 5 piece of glossy photo paper. He held it to his chest like a gambler concealing his hole cards. "How much is it worth to raise a man from the dead, just so you can kill him again properly?"

"Is that a fucking riddle?"

"Not at all, it's a straightforward proposition. If you were given the chance to scratch an itch that's been bugging you for a long, long time…what would it be worth to you?"

"I'm losing my patience."

Trent laid the photo down and slid it across the table.

Ponti's curiosity overrode his annoyance after a protracted pause, and he picked it up.

The image was dark and grainy, tinted with the green blur of a surveillance camera's lens. It showed the back room of Unterwelt where the bar was located. Ponti recognized Luna's slim figure toward the right edge of the frame. She appeared to be engaged in conversation with a tall man with a shaved head.

"He looks different," Trent uttered, "I'll grant you that. But that's him alright."

"Who?"

"The Raven. He's alive, and he's in town."

Ponti set down the photograph, then immediately picked it up again. He brought it close to his face and squinted.

No," he said in a half whisper. But he kept looking.

"Luna told you I wasn't going to waste your time."

"No," Ponti repeated, louder. "I don't buy it. Doesn't look anything like—"

"Ignore the superficial changes. Hair, a goatee…that's nothing. Simple stagecraft, but it makes a big difference, especially from a distance."

Trent pointed to the photo.

"You can't really make out the tattoo on his right hand, but it was verified as being identical to the symbol any follower of the Raven would recognize. The person who verified it is someone you should have reason to trust. Ask her, if you don't believe me."

"A tattoo doesn't prove a goddamned thing."

"Paul…" Trent began, pausing at a fierce glance from the larger man. "You know, it's strange," he continued. "I feel almost akin to you in some way, if you'll pardon the liberty. We're bonded on some level, undeniably. You can believe me when I tell you that the man you're looking at is Rusty Diamond."

Ponti flinched slightly at the name he'd refused to allow be spoken within his hearing for more than two years. The name that still rung in his ears in his darkest moments.

"Let's say I believe it. How'd you find him?"

Trent smiled, settling back into his chair.

"That's the wrong question, or at least not the central one. It's almost impossible to stay hidden in this day and age; you know that. I'm sure you could have tracked him down yourself, if you'd given the matter sufficient effort." He paused, cocking his head as if piecing together an equation. "Why didn't you? I think I know the answer. A man in your position, with so much at stake, can't risk dirtying his hands with this kind of work. No matter how justified you might be in wanting it."

Ponti lay the photo down on the table. "Pick your next words carefully, kid. I've tolerated about as much of your lip as I care to."

"No offense intended. All I mean to suggest is that *finding* him wasn't the notable task. Luring him out here, right into your backyard...that took some doing. It took the mind of someone who knows how the Raven thinks, how he responds. I've done it, Paul. I've brought him here, less than a mile from where we're sitting. And I'm prepared to deliver him to you."

"In return for what?"

Trent finished. "Nothing you'll even notice. A tiny crumb of an expanding empire. Sounds like a reasonable trade, doesn't it?"

"Specifics. Now."

"You must take a dozen meetings a day from people with the same objective. Getting a piece of the action, their own little corner of the next big thing. That's what I want. A lease of my own—at a discount of course. Three thousand square feet, with zoning clearances for public gatherings of up to five hundred at a time."

"A stage. Some kind of performance space?"

"A theater. The Nossa Morte Playhouse. The premiere

venue for serious illusion off the Strip, nestled right in the midst of your new development in the Homeless Corridor."

"And you got the pockets for that?"

"Like I said, we'll work out a reasonable sum. I'll deliver something better than the market rate. Diamond's head. Or I can keep him intact and let you do the honors personally. Whatever suits you."

"Why the fuck do I need him at my back door, or even in my goddamn zip code? How does that help me?"

Trent started to reply but Ponti kept speaking.

"You've overplayed your hand. Whole lot of assumptions you've made here. Think I couldn't have Diamond popped back east, or wherever he's been holed up? Give me an address and it's done in less than twelve hours. All at a nice, safe distance. You think I want to be anywhere nearby this piece of shit when he gets his?"

"Actually, I do. I don't think you'd receive proper satisfaction from taking him out with a long-distance hit. I don't claim to know why you hate him, only that you do. And it's personal, which I can relate to. We share a vested interest, Paul. Let's both benefit from getting what we want."

A glance at his watch told Ponti it was almost eleven. He'd given this freak far more time than he ever intended. And he still didn't know what to make of what Trent had presented him.

He stood, suppressing an urge to reach for the photograph.

"I'll think about it."

14.

Rusty didn't make the decision to drive out to Paul Ponti's house immediately. It took several hours for the temptation to prove stronger than his ability to resist it. Not until Charlotte had finally taken leave of the Skyloft and he'd lubricated himself with one too many stiff drinks did his resolve crumble.

There was absolutely no logical reason to do it. Why on Earth would he choose to visit the house of a man he knew had every reason to want him dead?

Hell, I've spent the last three years trying to erase all memories of that house from my mind. If I had any sense I'd catch the next plane out of town and spend the rest of my life in hiding.

He knew that cowardly impulse wouldn't hold weight. He'd been leaning on it for too long now. If the debt he owed Paul Ponti proved to be the driving force that had brought him back out to Vegas, better to face it head on.

This part of the desert always got to him at night. Out here in Summerlin, he felt like he was in an inverted version of Henderson. Roughly the same distance from the throbbing heart of the Strip, but in this elevated planned community the housing boom had never crashed. The properties, McMansions all, were fewer in number and spaced much farther apart. Lights burned in almost every window; luxury cars filled every driveway.

Ponti's house was the grandest of the entire community,

and the most isolated. Rusty made four wrong turns trying to find it by memory. He didn't have the address so the GPS was worthless. But he wouldn't need it. He'd only driven to this house once, half stoned at the time, but that was enough to sear the place into his memory.

What if I'd just said no? he thought, turning the Barracuda around at a cul-de-sac and starting down another narrow street he thought might be the right one.

What if I'd told Ponti to go fuck himself, find someone else to play dancing monkey at his little girl's bash? What's the worst he could have done to me? Could it have possibly compared to the wreckage I brought into my life by accepting his invitation?

No easy answers arose in his mind. Rusty had already wasted considerable time asking himself these same questions. First in those desperate early weeks after abandoning Las Vegas and the career he'd worked so hard to build. Then later, during the long months of solitude in Ocean Pines. Hour by hour, the questions would haunt, torment, and infuriate him. Thousands of miles away in coastal Maryland, with the passage of time, they came to seem mere abstractions.

Driving slowly up a curved incline, he recognized Ponti's gate. Predictably ostentatious—gleaming brass bars, a giant *p* on a plaque in the center. Rusty pulled a three-point turn and parked far enough from the gate not to activate any motion-sensor lights.

He got out, dressed for covert work. Black turtleneck, pants, and gloves. A pair of tactical shoes he'd worn onstage for any number of dangerous stunts, complete with integrated climbing lugs for extra traction and a high-density collar to promote heel lock. He was glad to have them on his feet.

Some premonition back east had told him to pack a sheer black nylon mask to pull down over his head with two narrow eye slits. A pair of fold-up binoculars slid easily into his pants pocket.

He walked across the street before heading farther up the hill. Two surveillance cameras were perched on opposite ends of Ponti's gate. He doubted their lenses could capture anything from this distance.

Rusty knew the entire property lay protected by an alarm-activated fence, forming an unbroken perimeter around all three acres. His only way over the fence was from a position of greater altitude on the hillside above the back face of the house.

It wasn't the easiest terrain to navigate in darkness, and he didn't dare use his phone for guidance. The sunbaked soil disintegrated under his heels no matter how gently he moved, inviting him to twist an ankle with each upward step. Bristly bunches of chaparral sprouted up at odd intervals, forcing him to take a circuitous path.

He was fairly winded by the time he reached a small crest overlooking the back of the property. He took a knee, regaining his breath.

There were lighted windows on both floors of the main house, but no manmade noises found his ear. A long rectangular pool surrounded by a larger square of tiles lay between his position and the main house. Off to the right, a smaller guest house sat dark.

It's all coming back. I can almost see myself, standing out there by the pool as the guests crowded in. Getting ready to blow my whole life to smithereens and too ripped to know it.

Rusty detected a flicker of movement on the second floor of the main house. Someone had walked past a lighted window covered only by thin drapes. He lifted his binoculars for a closer look, but the person had stepped away. A gap in the drapes was wide enough to offer a clear view inside, but it revealed nothing.

He had to get closer, and that meant jumping the fence—a move that would carry this expedition from the realm of misguided to moronically dangerous.

Rusty raised the binoculars higher and did a lateral pan across the roof. He spotted four objects planted at irregular intervals, two of them identical in shape to the surveillance cameras mounted on the driveway gate. Though he couldn't pick up much visual detail on the other two objects, he felt more than reasonably certain about what they were.

Motion sensors. And if I can see two of them from here, there are probably another dozen installed around the place.

For most would-be intruders, this would qualify as an insurmountable obstruction. But not for Rusty. He'd antici-pated the sensors, and had a plan to counter them.

The Invisible Veil, all over again. Except this time it's not an act, and I'm not exactly in peak form.

During Rusty's stint performing in the Etruscan Room at Caesars, the Invisible Veil had been one of his most reliable numbers. Far simpler than many of his tricks, requiring vir-tually nothing in the way of prep. He'd randomly select six audience members to join him onstage—never confederates, always legit strangers—and would hand them earplugs.

Once they'd muffled their hearing, he positioned them into two rows facing away from each other. He'd then walk a wide circle around both rows, allowing them to see him clearly, before stepping into the gap between them. From there, he spent the next ten minutes moving from one to the next while never being seen.

It was such a well-rendered trick some audience members habitually complained it was a setup. How could the six people onstage fail to see him when he was literally standing right next to them, picking their pockets? When the trick was complete and all the pilfered items returned to the astonished guests, Rusty would invite anyone who doubted the trick's legitimacy to come onstage. There were always a few takers—and he did the same thing to them, generating huge gales of laughter and applause.

The key lay in monitoring his breath, slowing the pace so

that a single exhalation lasted as long as a minute. Exquisite control of all major muscle groups and a sense of corporeal balance were the two other main components of his training.

He'd studied a host of practices in order to attain that level of bodily control—yogic breathing with a Zen monk in Palo Alto, balance and footwork with a former Olympic gymnast, visual acuity enhancement with a holistic ophthalmologist in Reno. One by one, over the process of countless months, these disciplines congealed to grant him the level of combined mental and physical control needed to pull off the Invisible Veil twelve times a week.

He hadn't even thought about the trick—much less performed it—since his last performance at Caesars almost three years before. But he knew the muscle memory was there, if only he could narrow his mental focus properly tonight.

Rusty closed his eyes and began slowing his heart rate, one breath at a time. He visualized the oxygen traveling though his bloodstream, nourishing tissues from the soles of his feet to the center of his optic nerve. He was almost surprised at how quickly that long-ignored sensation of heightened capability washed over him. After less than ten minutes of meditative silence, he was ready to move.

The fence was his first obstacle. He'd have to suspend himself from the limb of a ragged cottonwood a few feet up the hill, swinging back and forth until he'd gained sufficient momentum to launch himself over the top metal rail. The jump in itself was manageable; it was the landing that worried him. Maintaining his lightness of detectability would become much harder during the second or two he'd be airborne.

Rusty's gloved hands clutched the cottonwood's limb and he started to crank his legs. Soon his whole body was swinging like a pendulum. He'd already selected his ideal landing spot, a shady patch of grass just opposite the fence.

Now!

His fingers released the limb at the moment his feet reached the apex of their forward swing. The momentum carried him easily over the top rail. He cleared it by a healthy six inches, then jackknifed his legs down for a feetfirst landing.

The manicured grass was less forgiving than he'd anticipated. The impact made him stagger but he managed to remain upright. Receding back toward the fence with a soft tread, he stood motionless.

No sound emanated from the house. No security light blinded him. After a full minute of silent observation, it seemed clear he'd entered the property without setting off any alarms.

Rusty took a few tentative steps toward the house, then froze.

He heard it before he saw any indication of danger. An innocuous sound, just a light metallic tinkle like coins in someone's pocket. The sound came from a darkened hollow in the hillside behind the pool's perimeter.

Dog collar. Shit.

A guttural growl drowned out the metallic sound of the collar's jiggling. Deep, almost mellow, like it was emerging from slumber. Not yet angry or alarmed, perhaps just curious about an unknown scent carried on the night wind.

A thin cloud bank dimmed the moonglow, granting Rusty some small edge toward invisibility. It would pass by quickly, leaving him exposed in a lunar floodlight.

He turned and sought shelter from the closest obstacle he could see, a thick rosebush flanking the main house.

The collar shook again, louder. Rusty tracked the sound and identified the source.

Directly across the pool from where he crouched, a low structure squatted behind a row of sun chairs. No ordinary dog house, its terra-cotta tiles and arched entrance matched the architectural stylings of the larger residence.

Another growl rumbled across the pool's placid surface. Its

depth and timbre indicated a large canine. Pitbull, maybe. Or a Shepherd. Or a Rott.

No shit, Rusty thought grimly. *Ponti's not exactly a terrier kind of guy.*

The dog's next grumble spoke to him like a human voice, berating him for his stupidity in coming out to this house. Rusty knew it was a mission as futile as it was perilous. What did he hope to accomplish—just to catch a glimpse of the girl? Verify with his own eyes that she still lived? That he hadn't doomed her to a life of grotesque disfigurement?

No. I came here because I just had to set foot on this property one more time, and fuck the risk.

Rusty turned slowly and started retracing his path back to the car. He hadn't measured the distance, but he figured no less than fifty steps would bring him to the alarm-activated fence. There was no worry about setting it off now. He just had to get the hell out of here.

To occupy his mind and keep calm, he counted his paces.

On his sixteenth step, the dog started barking. The sound of its claws scuffing across the tiles was accompanied by a blinding wash of overhead lights. Rusty didn't know if it was his movement or the dog's that had triggered the switch, and he didn't pause to think about it.

He broke into a sprint, still keeping the count in his head.

Just get to fifty, he commanded himself, refusing to acknowledge that the number was no more than a hopeful guess.

And don't look back, the oft-quoted words of Satchel Paige rang in his ears. *Something might be gaining on you.*

The barking grew louder, more frenzied. It carried a fever of bloodlust impossible to mistake, any trace of fear erased from the canine register.

Rusty reached the fence sooner than he'd anticipated. He clutched the wire mesh with both hands. Another alarm sounded but that didn't matter. The fence was shorter than he'd estimated from the other side, a small break in his favor. He climbed up and cleared the top rail with a two-handed vault, barely breaking stride.

He whipped his head around, unable to resist a look at his four-legged pursuer.

From a momentary glimpse, Rusty determined his initial estimation was right. Too lean for a Pitbull, too dark and muscular for a Shepherd.

Rottweiler. Gotta be.

Rusty knew from firsthand experience the vertical leaping capacity of that breed. It didn't bode well. He cursed the shortness of the fence, which just moments ago had seemed like a blessing. Then he kept scrambling up toward the car.

The fence shuddered with the impact of the dog's muscled body. Rusty caught a blurred glimpse of two front paws embedded in the wire mesh, clawing upward. He didn't wait to see how high it went.

He scrambled up the hill, boots failing to maintain traction in the crumbly soil. Small avalanches of dusty pebbles fell with every panicked step.

The dog made it over the fence. Hidden from the curtain of overhead lights, it was charging up the hill in the darkness straight at him.

A clump of chaparral loomed directly in front of Rusty, causing him to alter his path several steps to the right.

It proved to be a decisive delay.

He could feel the dog's charging presence for a protracted moment before its teeth sunk into his right calf. The pain was instantaneous, a crescent of fire ripping deep through his musculature. Tearing tendon and ligament, sending a torrent of blood into his sock.

Rusty barely heard the scream that traveled along the breeze-swept valley, nor would he have recognized it as his own. Every fiber of his being directed itself toward freeing his leg from the dog's foaming maw.

It was impossible. No bear trap had ever been built with a firmer grip.

He lost his balance, the pain overwhelming. Before he knew it he was on his back, coughing up dust. He rolled over, both arms extending to scrabble up the hill as he kicked wildly at the dog's head with his free foot.

The heel of his tactical shoe grazed the Rott's left eye. He heard a whelp, more surprised that pained, and felt the briefest release of pressure from his inflamed calf. He used the momentary freedom to stagger upright, backing toward the Barracuda.

The dog hunched on its hind legs. Time slowed as Rusty saw the strength gathering in its sinewy lower body as it prepared to launch itself forward. The dog had cleared the fence easily, and this was a much narrower gap.

Rusty flailed for the driver's door handle even as one corner of his eye caught a blurred shape flying at him. Jerking it open with both hands, he dropped into a crouch behind the door, using it as both shield and weapon.

The dog's hefty body collided with the door like a sledgehammer. The impact knocked Rusty to the ground. He regained his footing and dove into the car.

Shaking off its momentary daze, the dog lunged again. Rusty had barely swung the door shut before another bruising concussion shook the car's entire carriage. He gunned the keyless ignition and slammed the Barracuda into reverse.

Fishtailing around in a full turn, he floored it down the narrow canyon road.

His eyes darted to the rearview mirror, barely seeing the Rottweiler silhouetted in a reddish cloud of dust. It was up on all four paws, brutish head thrown back, baying into the night with what sounded to Rusty's ears like triumph.

15.

It took him just under thirty minutes to reach Dr. Fred's house. The drive passed in a high-speed blur. Rusty steered the Barracuda on autopilot, aware of little beyond the screaming pain in his leg and the blood congealing in his expensive tactical shoe.

He was almost grateful for the pain. It kept him focused on the road, rather than incessantly berating himself for the reckless thing he'd just done.

What the fuck was that supposed to prove? What did you think, that by setting foot on the property you could erase what happened there?

He forced those thoughts from his mind and tried to consider more practical questions. Primarily: Was there was any better option for treating his injury than the one to which he now drove at breakneck speed?

Sure, I've got other options. They all suck.

A 24-hour walk-in clinic, for example. Plenty of those in LV, but Rusty didn't want to wait around in some overcrowded lobby and answer a lot of prying questions. He needed a very specific kind of medical attention—the kind that came with no questions and entailed no documentation. Private consultation, in the most literal sense.

He knew where to find it, but that knowledge offered scant comfort. The idea of facing Dr. Frederick Schneider disturbed

Rusty more than the dog bite. To go knocking on the door of the one person he'd most resolutely intended to avoid in Vegas made him feel slightly ill. But he saw no other course.

A zippered lip was one of Dr. Fred's prime assets to recommend him to those with the means and inclination for his services. That, and a medicine cabinet loaded with every stripe of pharmaceutical jolt ever devised by man. It was all so easy. Just pay the good doctor for what you need and never be hassled with explaining why you needed it.

No questions. No ethics. No problem.

In a perverse way, Rusty was looking forward to seeing the surprise on the old charlatan's face. Just for the shock value his appearance might generate. After almost three years of no contact, this definitely qualified as a surprise visit.

He'd deleted Schneider's number from his phone long ago, in those frantic early weeks following his decampment from Vegas. Turning onto Country Club Drive, his fingers now punched ten digits from pure memory. How many times had he dialed the number, back when he was one of the doctor's most frequent visitors? At least four or five times a week, in the darkest days.

Schneider answered Rusty's call on the third ring. Didn't sound the least bit surprised to hear his voice after such a lapse. Like he'd been patiently waiting for this moment with no doubt whatsoever that it would come.

That's the pusher's mentality, Rusty thought after terminating the call by saying he'd be there in ten minutes. *He knows the addict will always come back for another taste, no matter how long it's been.*

Schneider's house sat at the end of a well-tended street several blocks west of the country club. He met Rusty at the door with a liver-spotted hand extended in affable greeting. Rusty ignored the gesture, his nerve wavering at the prospect of entering this house once again.

Schneider chuckled softly at his reluctance and stepped aside to let him in. Rusty took a moment to reconsider the pain in his leg, and wordlessly accepted the invitation.

They walked directly to that familiar room behind Schneider's kitchen. It appeared just as Rusty remembered it. Paper-covered examination table beneath a goosenecked lamp, a floor-length medicine cabinet opposite. More modest than the suite he kept at the Sunrise Medical Center for his daytime patients, but serviceable.

The room's smell hit Rusty hard. An uneasy mix of disinfectant and Polo Sport, it smelled like drugs and money and bad decisions willingly made.

Bottles of peroxide and Betadine stored behind glass. Bleach. Stainless-steel sewing needles. Cotton and gauze. Square bandages lined up like snowdrifts on a silver tray.

"So," Schneider drawled, stepping back to size Rusty up as if confirming his reality. "Lazarus walks. Or should I say limps." He glanced at the torn and blood-spattered pant leg.

"You haven't aged a day, Fred. Business must be good."

Schneider lowered himself onto a chair with wheels to slide closer to where Rusty sat on the examination table. He frowned at the injured leg.

"Looks like you've been up to your old tricks."

"Don't tell me, no pun intended?"

"Usually that's a throwaway phrase. A bit more literal in your case, isn't it?"

"Just so you know, I'm not here for meds. Been clean for almost three years now."

"Impressive. You have my congratulations."

"Don't need that, just a little patch-up job will do."

Rusty reached down and gingerly pulled up his left pant leg to the knee.

Flicking on the gooseneck medical lamp, the doctor shook

his head with a *tsk-tsk*. Two crescent-shaped wounds comprised of eight individual punctures covered Rusty's left calf.

"That looks rather painful."

"Yeah, well…you should see the other guy."

Schneider's bushy brows crawled up his forehead like a pair of albino caterpillars.

"Don't tell me a *man* did this."

"Close enough. Man's best friend."

"Not too friendly in this case, was he?"

"It was my fault. Forgot to pack a chew toy."

"Looks like the pooch in question found you an acceptable alternative. Was it leashed?"

"I don't plan to sue."

"What I mean is, did you encounter a feral canine in some dark alley or did this happen on someone's property?"

Rusty cocked a brow and leaned back on the table.

"That sounds like a question, Fred. Don't tell me you've changed your business practices."

Schneider sighed impatiently.

"I'm just trying to determine if we have to worry about rabies."

"Nah, this mutt came from a good home. I'll wager it's had all the basic shots."

"What about you? When was the last time you had a tetanus booster?"

"Couldn't tell you."

Muttering with gentle disapproval, Schneider stepped over to the floor-length medical cabinet.

"I always hoped you would cultivate a greater interest in your physical well-being."

Sure you did. That's why you sold me as much coke, ecstasy, and Vicodin as I could shovel into my system.

Rusty almost uttered those words but instead just gave a shrug. Why start pointing fingers now?

Schneider rummaged around for a minute and returned with a pair of 25-gauge hypodermic syringes in hand.

"Let's do that tetanus booster, just to be safe."

"What's the other one?"

"Ceftriaxone. Very effective antibiotic. Lie down."

Rusty couldn't suppress a flinch at the sight of the syringes. Despite being someone who'd built a reputation based on borderline suicidal fearlessness, he harbored a lifelong phobia of needles. In retrospect, he'd come to see this inclination as a blessing. It may have been the sole factor that stopped him from experimenting with intravenous narcotics at his debauched nadir.

"This will sting, but not as much as the bite itself."

Rusty kept his gaze glued on the ceiling as Schneider plunged the needle directly into the largest of the bite wounds. The old bastard hadn't lied; it hurt like infernal hell. The tetanus booster was just slightly less painful.

Then came the sutures. It was not a quick procedure: thirty minutes and twelve stitches in total. Rusty hopped off the table gingerly, setting down his good foot first before testing the other. He knew he'd be limping back to the MGM Grand but it didn't feel too incapacitating.

Yeah, terrific. But what about tomorrow?

A narrow grin stretched across Dr. Fred's face, sadistic in the overhead light of the medical lamp. Rusty felt like his thoughts had just been read clear as a sixty-point-font headline.

"You'll want something for the pain," Schneider said, turning toward a glass-faced medicine cabinet.

"Forget it. I'll manage."

"Trust me, a night's sleep will lead to unbearable stiffness. Unless you'll be spending the next week with your foot on a pillow, I suggest you take something."

Rusty felt a rush of hot blood filling his face, combined with bile at the back of his throat. His body was responding viscerally to the prospect of getting some drugs into his system after untold months of abstinence.

"I'm just thinking of your comfort, son."

Rusty spun away, wincing at the pain. He was halfway to the door when Schneider called him back.

"I really think you're going to want this."

As if drawn by a gravitational force, Rusty turned. The doctor was holding a prescription vial in one outstretched hand.

"It's very mild. Low dose oxycodone, only a half dozen. They'll help you sleep, and make movement easier in the next few days. If you're worried about a relapse, don't. I won't let you in here if you come back."

"You're not the only pusher in town, Fred."

"Flush them if you decide they're unnecessary. But do yourself a favor and don't decide until the morning."

Rusty saw his own hand reaching out to grab the vial. Watched the action like it was a movie, unrelated to him in any meaningful way. His fingers closed around the plastic tube and slid it into his pocket like the fabric had been woven solely for the purpose of carrying those six tablets.

Then he turned and left. Through the darkened living room, across the front stoop and out onto the street. Talking to himself all the way.

Nothing to worry about. Just a mindless reaction. Fuck the pain; I don't need drugs. I'll drop them in the first trash can I see.

Those thoughts sounded good in his mind's ear. But he passed a pair of trash cans at the end of Schneider's driveway. And the vial was still in his pocket when he fired up the Barracuda's engine.

• • •

Rusty let himself into the loft and flicked on the entrance light. The throbbing glow of the Strip through the sliding glass door irritated his eyes. He drew the blinds and poured himself a tall glass of water. His calf was still screaming as he set the drugs down on the counter. He stood there for some time, favoring his good leg and wondering how bad it was going to hurt tomorrow.

Focusing so intently on the pain, he didn't notice it right away. But the longer he remained in the kitchen, the more an intuition grew silently within.

Something was wrong. He knew it without knowing how or why. The loft felt different, like the lingering trace of some unseen presence had contaminated the air.

His nose detected a weak fragrance, sickly sweet. Had a member of the housekeeping staff worn some kind of perfume while cleaning the loft hours ago? Unlikely the scent would linger this long.

Bullshit. You're just freaked out, that's all.

No. There was no denying it—something felt off. It was as if the furniture had been subtly rearranged in his absence. Hadn't that leather chair been directly facing the TV when he left this morning, rather than positioned at the angle it currently occupied?

Rusty shook his head, chiding himself for being paranoid.

Then it hit him again, and this time the smell was more complex. Mixed in with the cloying sweetness was the stench of something unwholesome. Rotting.

He froze, struggling to identify the source. Maybe he'd left some uneaten food out in the kitchen? He knew that wasn't the case but went to check anyway. Nothing. Not in the fridge or sink or in the trash. The place was spotless, and he couldn't trace the smell anymore no matter how intensely he inhaled. Either he'd simply gotten used to it or it hadn't been there to begin with.

Fuck this. Time for bed.

He carried the vial from Dr. Schneider upstairs, wincing

every second step, and walked into the bathroom. Swallowing a handful of Advil, he set the vial down next to the sink. Took a long piss. Considered brushing his teeth and decided he didn't have the energy.

Stepping into the bedroom, he failed to register the smell's return immediately. That came a few moments later, after his initial shock started to wane.

His eyes were welded to the bed, neatly made up as the rest of the loft. Nice little mint on the pillow, but there was something else on the bed. And that's where the sickening fragrance came from. A bouquet of rotting black flowers lay on the coverlet, wedged between two pillows. The stench was overpowering.

A dozen long-stemmed blooms were wrapped in silvery paper. The flower's velvety petals were all dead and covered with a slimy residue. A greeting card in an envelope was affixed with a thin black bow. Hand drawn on the envelope, a crude black bird.

The Raven.

Rusty approached the bed, breath stilled in his chest. He reached out with one hand for the envelope. The bouquet rolled over with a sudden lurch. A thick column of cockroaches crawled out from within the silvery folds. They scuttled across the blanket, trailing the black viscous substance covering the flowers.

Rusty jerked the card away and spun around. At the sink downstairs he washed his hands with scalding water and anti-bacterial soap. Then he checked the door to make sure it was bolted. Back in the living room, he scanned every last nook to make sure he was alone. Sitting on the couch and feeling marginally calmer, he opened the envelope.

The greeting card was identical to the one that had been contained in the box sent to Ocean Pines. Ignoring a cautionary urge to handle the card with a tissue rather than his own fingertips, he opened it.

The words inside were scrawled by a hand familiar to him by now.

What happens when the Raven comes home?
Will he show his face for us to see?
Will he fulfill his empty promises at last?
YES, HE WILL.
You've made it this far.
No backing out now.
Keep digging, time runs short.
The next performance is almost here.
You can only stop it
if you're ready to pay your debts.

16.

The Skylofts concierge desk was virtually lifeless at a little past eight in the morning. Rusty drummed his fingers on the smooth terrazzo, watching a flustered Gustave talk in hushed tones into the house phone. Though he hadn't said as much, Rusty suspected he was speaking with someone from the security unit.

The concierge hung up the phone and smoothed his lapel with a frown.

"Well, Mr. Diamond. I can assure you this is a first. In twelve years of operation, with thousands of guests enjoying the premium experience we're proud to offer here at MGM Grand Skylofts, there's never been an incident of this kind. I can't tell you how sorry I am that our spotless track record had a hiccup during your stay."

"'Hiccup' is not exactly the word I'd use."

Rusty rubbed his weary eyes. He'd gotten some patchy sleep at best on the couch. The bouquet's fragrance seemed to gnaw at him every time he was about to drift off. His leg throbbed all night long but the pain was less than he'd feared by the time morning arrived.

"You know," he muttered, "something like this gets out, it's gonna raise a few eyebrows. I'm guessing you can expect some cancellations."

"I appreciate where you're coming from, Mr. Diamond.

All I ask for is a bit of patience while we investigate this matter. Obviously, you'll be comped for last night's room fee."

"I'd think you'd scratch the whole week for me."

"That's not a call I'm authorized to make, but I assure you every effort at adequate compensation will be made."

"I'm not looking to bust your balls, Gustave. Just like to know how this happened."

"That's my top priority as well. The security department is already investigating. They'll report to me and you will be the very next person to learn what they find. In the meantime, I'm happy to relocate you to another loft as soon as one's ready. Three o'clock at the latest."

Rusty saw something in Gustave's gaze, a look that went beyond mere curiosity.

"Mr. Diamond, are we absolutely sure this wasn't some kind of gift? Perhaps left by a friend?"

"I'm a little surprised you have the balls to ask me that."

"Poorly worded. What I meant was, can we rule out completely that anyone else may have access to the loft? You didn't provide your spare access key to another person?"

"Negative."

"I see. And there's no chance that someone you invited into the loft may have left this…perhaps as a kind of, I don't know, prank?"

"I haven't had any guests," Rusty responded, then remembered Charlotte's visit. "Actually, that's not right. I did let someone in yesterday morning, but she had nothing to do with this."

"You're quite sure about that," Gustave ventured, more a question than a statement of concurrence.

"Damn sure."

"Well, I suppose the only explanation is that someone gained unauthorized access to your loft while you were out last evening. What time did you say you came in and discovered the item?"

"Little past two."

"And there's no chance…I'm sure it's unlikely…no chance you may have brought the item in yourself and…forgotten about it."

Seeing Rusty's deadeye stare in response to this suggestion, the concierge continued, "It wouldn't be the first time a guest has brought something back after a night out and been a little fuzzy on the recollection. Just a few weeks ago, a couple on the eleventh floor woke up in a panic when they found about two grand worth of…exotic marital aides scattered about their loft. Seems they'd made a late-night shopping spree at the Bonanza Marketplace and simply forgot about it. All it took was a receipt to clear up the mystery."

Rusty didn't bother replying to that.

"I'm not suggesting that's the case here," Gustave added quickly. "Just trying to exhaust all the options."

"I'll be expecting a report before the day's over," Rusty said. "Any longer, and I might find it hard to keep my mouth shut."

He turned and walked away from the concierge desk, feeling no more satisfied than he had before the conversation started. There was nothing to be gained by making a scene.

Riding the elevator back to the fourteenth floor, he chewed over the primary question that had plagued his attempt to sleep all night.

They know where I am. They want me to know that. How, goddammit?

Rusty stepped into the loft and an idea hit him. He opened the walk-in closet across from the kitchen. The box was stuffed in the far corner, hidden by a hanging garment bag. Rusty carried it over to the living area's pool table. He hadn't looked at the thing since Charlotte returned it yesterday.

He opened the box and methodically removed all of its

contents, lining them up on the green felt. Textbook page. Greeting card. Teeth and finger, housed in a Ziploc baggie. Nothing else.

Rusty ran his fingers along the inside walls of the box, lightly canvassing the cardboard an inch at a time. In the center of the bottom wall, where two flaps were sealed together with glue from the manufacturer, he detected a small lump. Roughly the circumference of a dime, it protruded from the cardboard just a few centimeters. Some faint stitching around the lump indicated someone had opened a small deposit in the cardboard and sealed it back up.

Rusty retrieved a paring knife from the kitchen. With great care he used the tip to slice a small opening just above the lump. Peeling a thin layer of corrugated cardboard away, he uncovered a small black-and-silver object wedged inside.

He knew intuitively what the object was even before removing it for closer examination. A remote GPS tracking device made of black plastic with a narrow metal clip on one side. Smallest such device he'd ever seen—couldn't weigh more than a few ounces. A virtually undetectable way to monitor the package's location ever since it was mailed to his house in Ocean Pines.

That's why the card said to bring this "tribute" with me. Figured if they scare me bad enough I'll follow their instructions to the letter.

Rusty turned the device over and studied the back side. Printed on the panel covering the battery compartment was the manufacturer's name. EverTrac.

He flipped open the panel. Inside was a circular silver oxide battery like the one that powered his wristwatch. Removing the battery, Rusty saw a white sticker inside the compartment. A fifteen-digit code was printed in numbers almost too small to read.

Serial number, if my luck holds up.

On a hunch, Rusty reached for his phone and opened the app store. Typing in EverTrac, he hit paydirt. Described as the world's most sophisticated micro-GPS technology, it cost him $9.99 to download. Once the app was installed, he navigated a few set-up pages until he found a box in which to enter the code of the device to be tracked.

Unaware of how tightly he was clutching the phone, Rusty typed in the fifteen digits. He hit Enter and a map appeared on his phone's screen. It showed a small red dot blinking somewhere in the western half of the United States.

Rusty double tapped to zoom in. Nevada. Another two taps showed Vegas. Then, as he'd hoped, the northern flank of the MGM Grand.

OK, you fuckers. Question number one answered. Now I know how you found me. Next up: How the hell did you get in here?

Even though it was barely past nine thirty Rusty felt he'd earned some kind of reward, preferably one that proved more effective at dulling his pain than the Advil he'd swallowed earlier. He poured two fingers of Glenlivet 18 over a couple of ice cubes. Maybe not the most prudent call, but it was better than opening up Dr. Fred's vial.

The first sip hit him just right. He was feeling pretty good all of a sudden—jazzed up, but also calm.

Goes to show what even a small victory will do for the old confidence.

A text message popped up on his phone. Rusty almost recoiled, impulsively assuming it must be from Nossa Morte. Were they able to monitor any new users of the EverTrac app? Unlikely.

Opening the text, he breathed a sigh of relief. It was from Jim Biddison. The message surprised him.

LOOK WHERE I AM, ASSHOLE. IT'S AN OPEN

CITY AND I CAME WITHOUT YOUR SAY-SO.
HIT ME UP IF YOU WANT TO HANG.

Clicking on the attached photo, Rusty saw Jim's bare feet propped up on a sun chair next to a pool. In the background, he could just make out a corner of the neon sign above Harrah's Hotel and Casino.

Unbelievable. His old friend was just a few blocks down the Strip. Rusty felt a surge of gratitude and a kind of affection for Jim he hadn't experienced in a long time. Just knowing someone he trusted, other than Charlotte, was nearby provided a dose of relief he couldn't have anticipated. And Biddison was as good an ally as he could ask for in a dicey situation.

His fingers started to tap out a response, but he stopped himself.

Rusty set the phone down, determined not to reply at all. What did it matter—Biddison wasn't really expecting him to anyway.

17.

Paul Ponti staggered into his silk boxers, or tried to. The backs of both his legs were covered with red welts from Luna's riding crop. He'd need a fairly thorough application of vanishing cream to dodge any questions from Vanessa. Not that Ponti's wife had gotten a good look at her husband unclothed any time recently.

Luna lay on the bed in only a thong, watching with amusement as Ponti gingerly slid one leg at a time into his expensive gabardine slacks. The smug grin on her face inspired an urge to slap it right off, but Ponti let that pass. Hell, the girl had only done what he'd told her to do.

Room 211 at the Honeydew Inn was their usual meeting place, and not just for anonymity. Out of the entire string of hot-sheet dives Ponti owned around town, this was the only one he'd ever set foot in. Just off Dean Martin Drive, ten minutes from the office. Ideal for nooners.

She'd been harder on him than usual today. That was how he'd demanded it. He needed release, more than ever. It wasn't just the approach of his fiftieth birthday party in two days—with reminders coming in by the hour that the guest list was still not finalized—that had Ponti on edge. No, it was this whole business with Diamond.

The sudden, unexpected proximity was driving Ponti nuts. With each passing hour, he grew more agitated. Couldn't concentrate on work, or fulfill the most basic of social obligations. He needed closure with Diamond *before* the party. No way around it.

That realization perturbed him, but it wasn't going anywhere. And it made sense on a level deeper than the cold logic Ponti applied to the majority of his concerns. For the past three years, he'd held a mental picture of Rusty Diamond's painful death as a cherished fantasy. Something to be savored from the safe vantage point of imaginary projection.

Much as he would love to see Diamond mulched and buried in a hole, Paul Ponti had too much at stake to pursue the kind of hit that once would have been as mundane as blowing his nose. It used to be so simple back then. A thousand times he'd considered putting out a nationwide contract, recruiting as much talent as was needed to track down the errant magician.

Every time, caution intervened. The big picture took priority.

Ponti was about to spread his name across a sizable part of Las Vegas. A twenty-year rise from shady notoriety to the status of full-blown civic leader was on the verge of completion. Respectability came with a price—in this case, the need for restraint in doling out retribution on an eminently deserving target. Thus he'd resigned himself over time to killing off Rusty Diamond in thought only.

And then, twenty-four hours ago, the opportunity to satisfy his thirst arrived from the most unlikely of messengers. His spooky dominatrix not only offered the keys to make it happen, but was in league with someone who'd succeeded in luring Diamond out into the open. It almost felt ordained to Ponti's reluctantly agnostic mind.

Ponti didn't trust Trent any further than he could shove him—and the convenience of his ties to Luna and the property that housed Unterwelt sailed well beyond the bar of happenstance. If the creepy little fuck thought he was actually getting a piece of Ponti's empire, he was even more cracked than he looked. But that didn't matter. What mattered was wiping the ledger clean once and for all.

As for Luna, Ponti would decide whether he could trust keeping her around or not after all this was taken care of. Most likely he'd cut her off and take up with a mistress less inquisitive about his personal past. In moments of delirious submission, he'd revealed far too much to Luna. That was a mistake he wouldn't be repeating.

If only he didn't love the little bitch so damn much.

Ponti turned around, surprised to see Luna was already dressed. Christ, that unnerved him sometimes—the speed with which she regrouped after their couplings while he was still monitoring his pulse. Like it never even happened for her. Like she'd been watching TV or texting one of her idiot friends the whole time.

"OK," he said. "I'm ready now."

"I doubt it," she purred. "You can barely stand, Paul."

"Stop fucking around, you know what I mean. Fill me in."

"Told you everything already. The delivery went through, now it's all about watching the message boards. If he doesn't show movement within the next day, Trent's ready to take more assertive action."

"Fucking delivery," Ponti said irritably. "What's the point? All this goddamned tap dancing."

"Trent knows him. Knows how he thinks, how he responds. It's got to feel like he's the one on the hunt. Come at him too directly, he might bolt."

"Figured all that out yourself, huh?"

"No, I just listen to what Trent tells me. He's pretty smart, you know."

"For a fucking basket case. Don't make the mistake of thinking I trust that little prick. This thing's got a clock on it, understand? You know what happens in two days."

"Yup," Luna said with a playful grin. "You officially become an old man."

Ponti grabbed one of her slender wrists, squeezing hard enough to evoke a yelp.

"This isn't a joke."

Luna held his gaze. "Can I ask you something? What do you need me for?" In reply to Ponti's raised brow, she added, "I don't mean that. I'm talking about your dealings with Trent. After I put you two in contact, I figured you'd take it from there."

Ponti didn't reply, just looped a silk tie around his neck.

"Turn around," Luna said, her last command for this session. "You know I do it better than you can."

He didn't agree with that assessment. Luna tended to make the knot a bit large for his taste, but he indulged her now because this was just another part of the ritual. He'd retie it himself after she left.

"Can I ask you something?" she said.

"Anything."

"You've talked to me about Diamond for, I don't know, the past year. Almost as long as we've been together. Just hating him, getting off on hating him. That's why I put you in touch with Trent, so you could both help each other get what you want."

"I'm not hearing a question."

She finished with the tie and sat on the bed.

"What exactly did he do to you?"

Ponti studied his reflection in the mirror for a long time before answering.

"I invited that piece of shit into my home. My *home*. All he had to do was knock out a few tricks, pose for a couple photos and make my little girl happy on her sweet sixteen. And what does the fucker do? Asks her to assist him with a trick. OK, why not, she's thrilled. A little shy, takes some coaxing to get her up there but you can tell she's dying to do it. Looking at this gothed-out waste product like he's something special. I'm watching, feeling happy I was able to make her birthday wish come true. Way I'd wanted it, Celine would've been there singing. Hell, Carrot Top would've done it for free, just a favor. But Paula wanted Rusty Diamond.

"So we're all there standing by the pool, hundred of us. The band stops playing, all eyes on my baby. I'm expecting a card trick, or maybe he pulls a pair of doves from thin air. Something sweet and simple, you know. Something that would make a girl smile. Instead, he asks her to hold onto something silver and shiny, about the size of a hair comb. Says it's some special kind of magnet. I don't like the sound of that but what the hell.

"Then he pulls this leather sack from his pocket. Tied at the top like maybe it's got some jewelry inside, precious stones. He turns to face us…Christ, I could see how coked up he was from twenty feet away. Eyes all bugged out, jacking his jaw a mile a minute. Fingertips twitching. Should've made me nervous, you're thinking? Maybe I should've stopped it right then? I think about it, but the look in my baby's eyes won't let me. She's expecting the greatest moment of her life to unfold. Hell, it already *is* unfolding, and I'm gonna be the jerk who ruins it? Hell no. Besides, I figure Diamond's got to be a pro, what with the business he's doing at Caesars. I hear he's got a rep for being some kind of maniac with a death wish, but that's just part of his act, right? I mean, I know the entertainment brass at Caesars, all veteran guys, levelheaded as they come. No way they're gonna take on a loose cannon like Diamond if the hype around him is really true. Just doesn't add up. So I hold my ground, ignoring an ache in my gut that tells me things are about to go sideways. I never ignore that ache, angel. Never. But I did then."

"So what happened?"

Ponti started to speak but the words died on his lips. He coughed and took a deep breath.

"Maybe I'll tell you some other time."

"OK," Luna said softly. "Am I leaving first or you?"

"Go ahead. I gotta make a few calls."

Rising from the bed, she leaned in for a goodbye kiss but he was already busy checking his messages.

• • •

Charlotte hung back at least three car lengths as she followed Luna's Audi down Industrial. Traffic was light, lighter than she would have preferred. Her trusty Lincoln Continental wasn't the most inconspicuous tail car imaginable, but if she kept her distance the girl driving the Audi would most likely remain oblivious.

Charlotte had been staked out in the Honeydew's parking lot for the whole hour, having followed Ponti there from his office at City Center. She didn't have any direct contacts with the parking office from whom to pull a favor, so she relied on her handicapped pass to secure a spot where she could monitor Ponti's noontime egress from the building. A creature of habit who enjoyed being recognized by as wide a base of LV's citizenry as possible, he was a remarkably easy man to follow.

When Luna stepped out of the motel room at five minutes past one, Charlotte had to make a snap call: follow her or see where Ponti went after his inevitable emergence. She chose the former option on a hunch.

Now, idling at a red light two vehicles behind her quarry, it came to her. The bartender Rusty had described meeting at Unterwelt. Wasn't the girl in the Audi a perfect match?

She was. Charlotte congratulated herself for trusting the old fail-safe intuition that had served so well at Caesars.

She was enjoying this assignment immensely. Being out

in the field doing covert work brought a surge of adrenaline as precious as oxygen. It had been a long time since she'd performed any kind of surveillance that didn't involve the use of stationary cameras. Before joining the security unit at Caesars, she'd worked as a digital forensics investigator. The job was dreary in most aspects—untold hours sifting through data records and court documents—but every so often a case would require some honest-to-goodness field work, and she'd savored every second of that. All-night stakeouts in front of residential buildings to confirm a person never came home…mobile surveillance of a target's progress from massage parlor to keno lounge when said target was officially being paid to be on duty elsewhere…those were golden moments that Charlotte had come to covet more and more the higher she'd risen within the closeted confines of the Caesars security department.

So today was fun. Swept up in the low-speed chase, she'd blissfully lost track of any physical discomfort. Her knees weren't even bothering her.

The Audi turned southbound onto Spring Mountain Road, moving into Chinatown. Five blocks later it pulled into a strip mall and took a shady spot in front of a dim sum restaurant. Charlotte parked four spaces down, a pickup creating some visual obstruction. She quickly reached into the bag below her seat and pulled out a Nikon 16-MP camera.

The spiky-haired girl walked right past the Continental's grill, gabbing on her phone. Couldn't ask for a cleaner angle. Charlotte snapped four quick shots, watching as the girl stepped into a nail salon.

Charlotte grabbed her iPhone and used a USB cable to connect it to the camera. She scrolled through a bank of images, selecting the clearest of the shots she'd just taken. It captured the Audi's driver in perfect profile, the phone fortuitously held against the opposite side of her face.

Charlotte transferred the image to her phone and hit *Send*.

Then she sent a follow-up message:

ANYONE YOU KNOW?

Charlotte saw no need to sit here while the girl got a mani-pedi, but she wanted a few minutes to think while she waited for Rusty to reply. Pulling a pack of Kools from the glove box, she muttered a curse at finding it empty.

Her mind was operating in full-tilt forensics mode, assessing the data and looking for strands of connectivity.

Paul Ponti owned the building that housed Unterwelt. While not entirely out of line with other recent acquisitions by Allied Interests, something about that felt off. Rusty received a package from "The Underworld" that lured him out to Vegas. He payed a visit to Unterwelt and got a tip from the bartender about starting the search for Nossa Morte where Vegas began. The same bartender who, if Charlotte's instincts proved sound, just spent the last hour fucking Mr. Ponti.

The clue about where Vegas began turned out not to be a blind alley, as it had first looked, because it led Rusty to Cashman Park, where he learned of the existence of another underworld, laid out in two hundred miles of flood tunnels beneath the Strip. A trail of bread crumbs started to emerge in Charlotte's mind, scattered and incomplete but with an undeniable shape.

A message popped up on her phone. From Rusty.

THAT'S THE BARTENDER FROM UNTERWELT. WHERE ARE YOU?

Charlotte smiled, satisfied at finding her hunch verified. She typed a reply:

GETTING SOME FRESH AIR AROUND TOWN. YOU TOLD ME TO GET OUT OF THE HOUSE MORE, REMEMBER?

Another message came almost instantly.

DISENGAGE. LEAVE THE FIELD WORK TO ME.

Charlotte toyed with the idea of not sending another reply. Let him stew for a little bit, so he could see how it felt to be on the other side of the equation. Let him know what it was like to worry about someone you care for more than you want to admit, and who takes just a little too much advantage of that knowledge.

Discarding the temptation, she wrote:

MEET ME AT THOSE FANCY NEW GARDENS AT MGM. 30 MINUTES. DON'T MAKE ME WAIT.

Charlotte put the phone in the glove box. She jammed the Lincoln in gear and laid some rubber pulling out onto Spring Mountain Road.

She hadn't felt this good in weeks. So good that she let her guard slip, just a bit. Staying too focused on the road and not sufficiently on the rearview mirror, she never noticed the van that followed her all the way back to the Strip.

Her lapse of attention was understandable. From the bright blue logo painted on both sides, there was no reason to think the van contained anything more lethal than some pool-cleaning equipment.

18.

Forty-five minutes later, Charlotte was impatiently rolling an unlit cigarette around the corner of her mouth. A security guard posted at the south entrance to the Park at MGM Grand studied her with a baleful eye. He could see how badly she wanted to spark that Kool in flagrant defiance of the many signs.

The Park was in full bloom. Two city blocks of exquisitely manicured greenery, right in the middle of the Strip. Charlotte hairy eyeballed the guard from her perch on a bench. It had become a kind of telepathic game of chicken, the guard silently begging her to light the smoke so he could swoop into action and break up the monotony of his daily routine.

Charlotte didn't intend to the give him the satisfaction, no matter how keenly her system craved a jolt of nicotine. It wouldn't do to be escorted from the premises. Rusty was due to meet her any time now.

Checking her watch, she realized he was almost twenty minutes late. Surprise, surprise. Prima donna magician keeps his minder waiting without so much as a revised ETA text. Some things never changed.

Just as Charlotte was ready to test the guard's nerve by whipping out a lighter, Rusty appeared and sat next to her. She raised a brow at hearing about the delivery of the bouquet, but was more interested in telling him about the larger pattern her own efforts had unveiled.

"Try to follow this," she said. "Paul Ponti owns the building that houses Unterwelt. Bought it for a song last year. An unusual acquisition for someone with his public profile—"

"And one he clearly wasn't looking to advertise," Rusty broke in. "So he uses the shadow holding company."

"Correct. Unusual, but not necessarily dubious considering he's snapping up that whole part of town. Long odds it'll all be trendy condos and Whole Foods six months from now."

"He's also getting some action from this bartender chick. The one who rather blatantly tipped me off about looking for Nossa Morte where Vegas began."

"She has a name."

"Most people do."

Charlotte shot him a crooked grin.

"Think I don't have contacts at the DMV? People owe me favors all over town."

"OK, I'm waiting."

"Daniels, Luna."

"Luna?"

"You heard me. Parents must be druggies or into some New Age bullshit. DOB August 12, 1995. Lives in a condo in Sinatra Cove, one of those new gated communities off Desert Inn Road. I bet you'll never guess—"

"Who owns the property? Allied Interests."

"Hell, no. Ponti owns this one outright. It's the kind of overbaked eyesore he's proud to stamp his name all over."

"I wouldn't call this a cohesive theory, Charlotte. I see the trail you're pointing to, but it's all so goddamned roundabout."

"I don't think that's the salient question, do you?"

Rusty tried giving her a blank expression, like he wasn't following. It probably felt as phony as it looked. Charlotte gave him a bemused shake of her head.

"OK, I'll come out and say it. If Paul Ponti is behind this whole scheme, the only question that matters is why. When I mentioned his name yesterday in the loft, your face went three shades of white. You used to be pretty good at controlling tells when I put you on the spot. Maybe you've lost your edge, or maybe this guy's name just rattled you *that* much. Which is it?"

Rusty glanced around, as if the manicured expanse surrounding him might offer some escape from what he'd been trying not to admit since reconnecting with Charlotte. There was no way out.

"Never got around to telling you why I left Vegas, did I? Why I walked out on a solid gold contract, the kind of gig I'd busted my ass more than a decade to land?"

He stood, looking too wired to remain seated. Charlotte followed after a pause and they strolled along a pebble pathway shaded by lush poplars.

"Well, you probably surmised things went a little off track. The drugs, I mean. No one kept as close an eye on me back then as you did, but I was damn good at concealing the damage. Even from myself. I knew it couldn't last. Just wanted to get through my commitment with Caesars. After that, my plan was to fade away for a few months, dry out at some clinic in Idaho. Let a little bit of mystery build up about why I went off the radar, then come back and book another contract once I got my head straight. Brilliant plan, huh?"

"So what happened?"

"I got an invitation," he said, "the kind you don't turn down. Private party up in Summerlin, some girl's sixteenth birthday. God knows I didn't want any part of it. But like I said, this was a command performance. So I showed up at the party, twice as loaded as usual, and things went bad."

Charlotte waited for Rusty to formulate the words needed to make a full confession.

"A trick went wrong. One I never should have tried, way too risky. It involved gunpowder and a neodesim magnet. Someone…the guest of honor, in fact, got hurt. Badly. I brought her out to help me with the trick. She didn't have to do anything difficult, just hold the magnets and hand them over one at a time.

"I hadn't practiced nearly enough, and being coked to the gills didn't help matters. The gunpowder ignited, there was a small explosion…this sixteen-year-old kid's down on the ground. Hands over her face, blood pouring through her fingers. It was…

"Don't ask me how I got out of that house in one piece because I don't remember. Next twenty-four hours, total blackout. When I finally came to my senses, I knew I was finished. Not just in Vegas, but anywhere in the limelight. I could never bring myself to perform again, but that was the least of my worries. When you hurt Paul Ponti's daughter, in his own fucking house, in front of a hundred of his big-shot friends, you're done. You're just done. So I bolted. Loaded up my car and drove east. I didn't stop driving for almost six months, stayed in shitty motels all across the country. Finally landed back in the same East Coast beach town I grew up in. Been hiding out there ever since. Doing a good job of it, until a week ago."

"You never found out what happened to the girl?" Charlotte asked. "Never even bothered to see if she survived?"

Rusty could hear the disbelief in her voice, and the contempt.

"I kept an eye on the news for weeks. Never so much as a ripple. Ponti must've decided it was a private matter that could only embarrass him."

"Christ, when it comes to making enemies you don't play small ball. I guess it explains a few things."

"Not really," Rusty muttered. "If Ponti's looking to settle the score, he's picked a fucking bizarre way to do it. I mean, he obviously found where I was living back East. Could've just sent some guys to my house."

Charlotte shook her head.

"Maybe this suits his personality better. Power trip, drag you back onto his turf. Scene of the crime, you might say."

They walked in stilted silence for a bit, into the most secluded section of the park.

Rusty glanced at his watch. "Feel like making a run over to UNLV with me?"

"No thanks. Got some more snooping to do."

Rusty laid a hand on her shoulder.

"No, Charlotte. I told you already, no more tails. It's too dangerous. Leave the field work to me."

"Relax. Few calls I want to make, all from the luxurious safety of my house. Had enough excitement for one day."

Rusty didn't quite buy that.

"Got a leaf in your hair," he said, reaching with his left hand to pluck something out that wasn't there. The momentary misdirection gave him an opening to lightly press his right hand against the small of her back. So lightly she never felt it, and had no awareness of the tiny EverTrac GPS device he'd just planted into the fabric of her sweater.

Rusty had executed thousands of such crosshand placements in his career. Back in the early street magic days, he would often make cold approaches on passersby and ask them to reach into their hip or breast pocket. Stunned reactions uniformly arose when they would pull out a live gerbil, a burning smoke pellet or some other object that most certainly had not been on their person only moments before.

Rusty felt a little creepy placing the GPS on Charlotte without her consent. And he knew it was a half-assed measure at best. As soon as she took off the sweater and donned another garment in its place the device would be rendered useless. But it made him feel just a little more secure knowing he could at least potentially track her movements. He didn't trust her bland assurances she would stay away from more field work; she clearly enjoyed it too much.

"Got it," he said, pretending to flick the invisible leaf away.

"Sir Galahad all of a sudden," she murmured, giving him a look in which her true feelings for him surfaced for barely the blink of an eye. Then the gruff veneer snapped back into place and she turned away.

Rusty watched as she walked toward the nearest exit. The drain on her energy following today's excitement was evident in how heavily she leaned on the cane. He couldn't help but smile watching her pace accelerate the nearer she drew to open air and the chance to spark up a fresh smoke.

Still got the touch, he thought with wry satisfaction. *She never felt it.*

19.

The meeting at Wright Hall got off to a rocky start. The fact that Rusty showed up fifteen minutes late didn't help. He had no idea the UNLV Campus was so vast, nor laid out in what struck him as a highly illogical fashion. It took much longer than he'd anticipated to find the right building, having to ask for directions three times along the way.

Dr. Lima gave a curt handshake, drilling him with deep brown eyes just a shade darker than her complexion. She offered him an uncomfortable metal chair across from her desk, which was piled high with folders and files.

"I thought most students did their exams online these days," Rusty said, nodding at the stack.

"Many professors encourage that, but the department allows some leeway. I find a certain benefit comes with the added time required for my students to turn in their work the old-fashioned way."

Dr. Lima was looking at Rusty with what appeared to be a mix of curiosity and amusement. Even before she spoke the thought forming in her mind, Rusty knew he was cooked.

"Rusty Diamond. Your name struck me as familiar over the phone."

"It's a little uncommon."

"You used to be a performer, yes? I saw you, I think at Caesars. Why are you looking at me like that?"

"Just kind of funny. I've been wondering how long it would take till someone called me out. Been in town three days and you're the first."

"Were you hoping to be recognized, or dreading it? Judging from your expression, I'd guess the latter."

"It's a little odd. Three years ago, I couldn't walk half a block on the Strip without drawing notice. I really don't miss that, but part of my brain keeps expecting it to happen."

"You've changed your look considerably. I seem to recall a lot more hair."

Rusty smiled and ran a hand over his cropped skull, finding it slightly more familiar to the touch now.

"Figure I'm doing my part for the environment. My showers are a lot shorter now."

"Saving money on conditioner too, I'd guess."

She matched his smile but Rusty found the vibe a little odd. After emphasizing her time was in short supply, why bother with this friendly chitchat?

If I didn't know better, I'd say she was a fan.

Dr. Lima put that notion to bed with a brisk change of tone.

"I've made my reservations about your project clear, and that was before I knew who you were. They've doubled in the past few minutes."

"Why's that?"

"Strip magician turns documentary filmmaker with an interest in indigenous cultures of the rainforest. An odd vocational shift, if you'll forgive my saying so."

Rusty shrugged.

"Spend enough time in the spotlight, you start wondering what it feels like to be behind the camera. A refreshing change, I must say. And the Payocu strike me as a fascinating culture."

He watched Dr. Lima's face as he spun that web of bullshit, hastily concocted and delivered with not nearly as much conviction as he would've liked. He detected no cocking of the brows or tightening around the corner of the mouth, and she kept her shoulders square to his without rotating away.

Maybe she bought it.

"Here's the real issue I'd like to get a handle on," he said. "Is there any evidence suggesting the Nossa Morte ritual may have migrated to the U.S.? Whatever its legitimacy, have you heard of any instances where Americans have engaged in the practice? Maybe right here in Las Vegas?"

Dr. Lima replied with a slightly more vehement version of the harangue she'd given over the phone. She emphasized the provable falsehood of the Nossa Morte legend, and the lack of credible research indicating the Payocu had practiced any kind of death rituals for the past hundred years or more.

Rusty could see the meeting was going nowhere fast. And it seemed increasingly clear that whatever awaited him at the end of this line of inquiry was bound to be a dead end.

"Maybe we can try another tack," he interrupted. "Wonder if you might tell me what this means."

He pulled a sheet of the Skyloft's bedside notepad from his pocket and handed it to her. She read it aloud:

"*A chegada de que mês informa o Payocu há apenas dois meses no período chuvoso?*"

Dr. Lima set the paper down like it might leave a stain on her fingertips.

"I'm getting *déjà vu* here, Mr. Diamond. When we spoke on the phone, you asked me to translate some Portuguese, a task easily accomplished by thirty seconds spent online."

"Indulge me, Doctor. Out of nostalgia for whatever enjoyment you got from my show at Caesars, if nothing else."

She smiled slightly at that.

"It says: 'The arrival of what month tells the Payocu there are only two months left in the rainy season?'"

"OK. Mean anything special?"

Her smile faded, quick as it had appeared.

"No. It's a trick question. Where did it come from?"

"One of my interview subjects for the documentary. Potential interview subjects, anyway. Some Frenchman, claims to be an anthropologist with years of hands-on contact with the Payocu."

"What's his name?"

"Prosper Lavalle," Rusty provided.

"Never heard of him, and if he's legitimate I would have. He sounds like a fraud, Mr. Diamond. I'd take any information he has to share with the greatest suspicion."

"Good advice. But can you tell me the answer?"

"Like I said, it's a trick. There is no answer. The Payocu don't conceive of time as we know it. No watches or calendars. Just day and night, and the rainy and dry seasons."

"So no months."

"Correct. They do, however, need to plan ahead for upcoming seasonal changes before they occur."

"How do they do that, without keeping track of time?"

"They observe the world around them, Mr. Diamond. With a keenness few of us can even imagine. They use plants to track the Earth's revolution around the sun."

"A plant tells them that?"

Dr. Lima opened the web browser on her laptop. She typed nine keys and hit Enter, then swiveled the computer around so Rusty could see the screen. A Wikipedia page showed the image of a tall flowering plant with red petals as bright as any neon on the Strip.

"This plant, to be precise. It's called Heliconia."

"Very pretty. And it has significance to the Payocu?"

"It blooms at the start of April every year in their region. The rainy season ends in June."

Rusty leaned close to study the plant name.

"Heliconia." Nine letters, just right for the second prompt to get me into the message boards.

Dr. Lima started to turn her laptop away.

"Could you hold it for a sec?" he asked, pulling his phone out. "I want to make sure I have the spelling right."

20.

From his comfortable seat on the leather couch, Paul Ponti spun the cap off a fifth of Johnnie Walker Blue. He'd instructed Trent to have a bottle waiting for him. It was the only way he was going to sit through this impromptu meeting peacefully.

Ponti started to pour a healthy three fingers over ice into a crystal tumbler but stopped himself halfway. Not a good idea to lose control during the conversation about to unfold. This red-haired freak had an ability to needle him that few other people possessed, or would even dare to flirt with.

Not even Paula at her brattiest…God, would she really refuse to come to the party?

No, to hell with it. Ponti forced himself to derail that unproductive train of thought. Better to focus on the guy sitting across the room, typing away on two keyboards and making some serious coin in the process.

Ponti stared up at the bank of computer screens above Trent's desk. He had to admit some unspoken admiration for what he saw. For the last several minutes, Trent had steadily racked up fresh rows of alphanumeric codes and monetary figures, each representing a transaction. A boatload of them, coming in nonstop.

Business was clearly booming here in room 706 of the Charleston Arms, which suggested to Ponti maybe Trent wasn't as unbalanced as he came across. Could the whole thing be an act? Who could say, given the kid's wild-eyed ambitions of opening some avant garde performance space in the midst of the hottest real estate property to sprout up in Vegas since City Center Complex. Ponti wasn't sure if Trent was truly nuts or only showbiz nuts, and he didn't possess sufficient interest to probe for the truth.

"Saturdays are always the busiest," Trent said over his shoulder without stilling the movement of his fingers on the keys. "Right about two o'clock, when the rubes finish drinking lunch and their harpy wives start complaining about not having tickets for a show. Half drunk and henpecked is the ideal mental state for any customer of mine."

"Wrap it up. I gave you a ten minute window."

Trent didn't reply, just kept typing.

At first Ponti was surprised he'd been invited to witness the inner workings of this illicit setup. Figured Trent would prefer to meet out in the open at some neutral location. But the rationale became clear soon after entering the room. Ponti sensed the twitchy kid was trying hard to instill a sense of camaraderie and shared trust between them as partners. Equals, even. He no doubt wanted to impress Ponti with the sophistication of his ticket scam operation.

And it was impressive, at least in terms of income, if the figures scrolling down the monitor were legit. So much so that Ponti had to wonder why the idea of bogus online scalping hadn't occurred to him during his long and active criminal career. Maybe Trent didn't realize the risk he'd potentially taken by inviting him here. At an earlier stage of his life, Ponti would have gladly dropped a pill in the kid's dome and made off with all these monitors and servers. Someone in his crew was bound to be able to figure it out.

Ponti was about to forcefully start the conversation when his daughter's face swam into his mental landscape. Christ, there it was again...another unbidden thought about the one person he hadn't yet found a way to control.

This was happening more often as the fiftieth-birthday party drew nearer. Ponti found himself stopped cold continuously throughout the day, Paula's memory arresting any forward movement as surely as quicksand. He couldn't help hoping that, once his conscience was cleared regarding this business with Diamond, he might find a way to reconcile with her. Or at least convince her to drop whatever grievances she held against him and simply be his daughter again.

"Who told you to put a tail on Luna?" he barked gruffly, causing Trent to flinch.

"No one. I made the decision independently, Paul."

Trent stopped typing and spun his chair around.

"It's not like I was trying to conceal it," he continued. "I just thought Soren might keep an eye on her as a way of reciprocation. I know for a fact she's been secretly reporting to you on our progress."

Ponti gave a bored shrug: *So what?*

"Why?" Trent pressed. "Have I failed to provide updates, just as we agreed? It's your lack of faith I find distressing."

"Look, kid. I have a right to some—"

"Let me be clear," Trent broke in. "Don't make the error of thinking this is somehow personal. Luna's sex life couldn't be of less interest to me. It's just that I entered into this partnership under the hopeful assumption that we were operating on a level of mutual trust."

"Get this straight. It's not a fucking partnership. You're working for me. Deliver what you promised, and you'll get what you want."

"Understood. I'm just having a hard time understanding why you wouldn't be pleased with my progress up to this point."

"I keep telling you, there's a clock on this thing."

"Right. Still waiting for my invitation, by the way."

"That's funny."

"You've made the timetable quite clear, Paul. The target needs to be snared and dispatched before the clock strikes twelve on the day heralding the fiftieth year this planet's been graced with your presence."

"Tomorrow, in other words."

"I have a calendar. And I'm glad you're satisfied, considering what I've accomplished in just a few—"

"You're drawing it out too much," Ponti snapped. "Could've wrapped this shit up last night."

"I told you, he'll bolt if he thinks it's a setup. Besides, it's more fun to see him sweat a little."

"Fun's got no part in this. Not for me."

"A little more patience, that's all I ask. The Raven's back in town, and he's on the hunt. Have faith. If he fails to piece it together soon, I'll take more proactive measures."

"That's all I want. Proactive."

"How about a little trust, Paul. In return for what I've delivered up to this point."

Ponti rubbed his brow, feeling sapped by Trent's repetitive pleas for validation. Probably the product of neglectful parents, which went a long way toward explaining his warped fixation on Diamond.

"What's your beef with him, kid? It's not just a jilted fanboy's worship gone sour, is it?"

Trent recoiled, almost imperceptibly, but Ponti's eye caught it.

"Oh yeah, I've got juice with the security people at Caesars. I heard about you, playing Stagedoor Johnny night after night. Taking a job as a goddamned janitor, bugging the guy till he told you to beat it. Pretty pathetic. But hey, if it gets you out of bed in the morning, who am I to judge?"

Ponti smiled at the reaction his words were producing. Trent was sinking into his chair like a tortoise into its shell. His jaws had welded together tightly enough to damage his molars. One hand reached into the pocket of his leather jacket, too causally to catch Ponti's eye.

"Seriously, what happened? Can't be as simple as him refusing an autograph request. Did you ask to be his apprentice, to learn at the foot of the master only to get spurned? Christ, it's like some chick hung up on the guy who popped her cherry years after the fact."

No reply from Trent, who was now past the point of speech. Ponti figured maybe it was time to lay off. He could see the kid's lean frame constricting beneath the leather jacket as a flush of embarrassment stole across that callow face.

But Ponti couldn't see what Trent's right hand was clutching in his jacket pocket. Couldn't know that the small red ball in his grip had the power to kill both of them in a blinding flash—and that every fresh taunt brought that possibility closer to fruition.

Ponti finished his drink and stood. He buttoned his jacket without any conscious appreciation of how close to death he'd just come.

"Tell that scarred freak to back off," he said, turning for the door. "Where Luna goes and who she sees is none of your concern."

Trent took great care in formulating a response, his tongue bleeding from where he'd bitten it in an effort to stop himself from detonating the grenade.

"You should be thanking Soren. He found something interesting I haven't told you about yet."

Trent let that hang for a moment.

"Turns out he wasn't the only one doing some surveillance at the Honeydew."

"Who else?" Ponti asked.

"Haven't locked down a name yet, but it looks to be a

friend of our mutual friend. I'll have more information for you tonight."

Ponti yanked the door open and strode out of the bedroom. He shot a noxious glance at Soren, who was lounging on a sofa in the front room. They didn't share a word as Ponti stepped out of the apartment.

Soren rose and walked into the bedroom. Trent was back at the keypad, robotically processing a new order. All traces of the homicidal mania that gripped him moments before were gone.

"How much longer?" Soren asked.

No answer from the desk.

"Soon as this is wrapped up and the lease is signed," Soren continued, "we cut ties with that fucker. Other than paying rent, we never see him again, right?"

"You can relax. It won't be our call to make. I'm quite certain Mr. Ponti won't want to continue our association after another twenty-four hours have passed."

Soren processed those words with a furrowed brow.

"So…wait. If you think he'll cut us loose, how's he gonna come through on the lease?"

Trent swiveled around to drill Soren with his unevenly tinted eyes.

"You don't really think we're giving him the Raven, do you?"

21.

"Pause it there, Mike."

The bearded technician at the control desk followed that instruction. He froze the security camera footage with a click of the keypad. Rusty leaned forward to get a better look.

It was a lightly pixilated image. A high-angle view of the Skylofts' valet parking lot, with some palm trees filling out the right edge of the frame.

"No, that's too far," the woman seated to Rusty's left said with a trace of irritation. "Roll it back, Mike."

The technician grunted under his breath and toggled the footage on the monitor in reverse one frame at a time.

"What are we looking for here?" Rusty asked.

Janet Raleigh, Guest Relations Director for the MGM Grand Skylofts, turned to face him with a painted-on smile.

"We've isolated the intruder on four separate cameras, Mr. Diamond. Each angle gives a clearer shot than the previous, but I wanted to show you all of it so you appreciate just how seriously we're taking this matter."

Rusty just nodded.

Upon returning to the loft from UNLV an hour ago, Gustave had passed him a message from Ms. Raleigh, apologizing for last night's "hiccup" and asking when he might be able to spare a few minutes. The MGM Grand's security department was extending the unprecedented offer of inviting a guest into their inner sanctum, in the hope that he might be able to assist with their investigation.

Now here he was, inwardly smiling at the irony of being ushered past a set of barred doors similar to those he'd failed to talk his way through at Caesars two days before.

The footage kept reversing until Janet Raleigh snapped her manicured fingers.

"Stop there, Mike."

The image froze, showing a male figure approaching the valet entrance. Dressed in a gray custodial uniform, a baseball cap covered his face from the camera's view.

"That's who left it on my bed?" Rusty asked.

"Beyond doubt."

"Got an ID on him?"

"Not yet. I was hoping you might be able to help in that regard."

"When was this captured?"

"Yesterday, 6:13 P.M. Right after the early evening shift change."

"Can't really see much."

"There's a better view from the interior cameras. We've got him crossing the lobby about two minutes after this was recorded. It offers scant more detail than this angle, but there's more."

Janet Raleigh turned back to the technician.

"Cue up the floor fourteen footage."

Mike tapped away at the keypad.

A new image came up. Overhead angle of the hallway outside Rusty's loft. Empty, no movement visible whatsoever. A time stamp at the top of the monitor read 8:29 P.M.

Must've been halfway to Summerlin around then.

"There," Janet Raleigh exclaimed, jabbing a finger at the monitor. "That's him."

The same male figure stepped into view from the bottom

of the frame. His baseball cap was off, revealing an unruly tangle of long reddish hair. A dark blue bellman's jacket was worn over the custodial uniform. He wheeled a room service tray down the hall, stopping at the door to 1418.

From the footage, Rusty pegged him to be a lanky six-footer, somewhere in the 175-pound range. A dark blotch on his left hand could have indicated a tattoo.

The figure appeared to knock on the loft's door. A lack of audio made it impossible to tell if the knock was genuine or simply performed for the benefit of the camera.

After a pause, the bellman reached into his pocket and pulled out an access key. He swiped it and pushed the cart inside.

"Is it standard practice for your staff to let themselves into a loft when a guest doesn't answer the door?"

"None of this is standard practice, Mr. Diamond. Fast forward, Mike."

Rusty watched the time stamp accelerate as the monitor sped through three minutes of static footage. It resumed normal speed when the bellman emerged from the loft with his cart.

"Here's where it gets interesting," Janet Raleigh said.

The bellman moved back down the hallway in the direction from which he'd appeared. Just before stepping out of the frame, he stopped and looked directly into the security camera's lens. A smile broke out on his face. Then the bellman disappeared from the screen.

"Back up and push in on him, Mike."

The technician toggled back a dozen frames and magnified the image 200 percent. That pale grinning rictus filled the monitor.

Jesus. Is that…I know him!

Janet Raleigh was giving him an expectant look.

"Do you recognize the man, Mr. Diamond?"

"Not sure," he said tentatively, his initial sense of recognition fading. "Thought I might, but I'm not sure."

"Unfortunate. A direct ID was our most hoped-for outcome."

"He's deliberately showing his face," Rusty uttered. "He wants you guys…or me, to know his identity."

"So it would seem. That's why we thought it was important for you to see this."

Now Mike the technician was glaring at Rusty with the same intense scrutiny coming from the guest relations director. He felt like he was expected to say more, but that was bullshit. How was this *his* responsibility?

"Mr. Diamond, the man who entered your loft is not an employee of this hotel. Nor has he even been."

"You're sure about that?"

She nodded.

"The bellman slated for last night's shift on floors twelve through fourteen didn't show up for work. We took no notice of his absence, because someone logged in under his name. It was only after you reported the breach that we ran a staff review and found the discrepancy."

"Christ. I'm surprised it's that easy for someone to clock in with someone else's name."

"We all share your surprise. To be candid, it's a shock I'm having a hard time processing."

Rusty noticed her cheeks redden with what looked like a mixture of embarrassment and fury.

"So what happened to your guy?"

"He turned up in an urgent care facility. A good Samaritan delivered him last night, a little past seven. He'd been badly beaten, but the doctors expect a full recovery."

"Is he talking?"

"I spoke with him briefly, he's still under sedation. Last thing he remembers is parking his car in the employee lot.

Whoever assaulted him must have done it somewhere between the lot and the south staff entrance."

"Then it's probably on tape," Rusty said. "Don't you guys have cameras monitoring the whole property?"

The guest relations manager cleared her throat.

"With over a thousand people employed at this resort, there's simply not enough room to provide onsite parking for the entire staff. Lower-tier employees use a satellite lot, three blocks south on Paradise."

"So it could've happened anywhere along the way. Lot of foot traffic, but I guess if the attacker got lucky he could have avoided notice."

"LV Metro is reviewing their own surveillance video in the immediate area. We're waiting to hear from them."

After a pause, Janet Raleigh added, "Our best chance of identifying this man lies in footage from the fourth camera."

On cue, Mike dialed up a new angle on the monitor. It showed the loft's intruder walking swiftly through a pair of swinging doors. Bellman jacket discarded, the baseball cap was back on his head.

"This was shot just outside the kitchen at Crush, less than ten minutes after he left your loft. As you can see, he's cutting a rather brisk path to the south service entrance. But again, he pauses directly beneath the camera to favor us in profile."

Rusty squinted, not listening to her. His eyes focused on something. He could feel, almost like a physical expansion, a sense of comprehension falling into place.

I know I've seen you before, fucker.

"Look at his uniform," he said, pointing at the monitor. "See that on the shoulder?"

"What is it?"

"It's a patch found on the custodial uniform at Caesars. Everyone who services the areas used by long-term residents wears it."

Raleigh gave a dubious squint. "It doesn't look clear to me."

"I'm positive. Spent a lot of time in the Palace Tower, and I saw that patch on a daily basis."

"Does it suggest anything to you?"

"I don't know," he said, then rose from his chair in a way that communicated this meeting was over. He needed some time to think, alone.

Janet Raleigh produced a thin cream-colored envelope and offered it tentatively. Rusty paused before accepting it, wondering if she actually had the nerve to hand him a nondisclosure agreement right now.

"A token of our profound embarrassment. I hope it helps to make up for the inconvenience."

Curiosity got the better of him. He opened the envelope and had to suppress a laugh. Inside were two tickets to the David Copperfield show.

"Front row, huh?"

"Those have a street value of a thousand dollars. Just a small gesture of how much we appreciate your discretion."

Rusty slid the tickets back in the envelope and glared at her. He thought his silence was worth considerably more than a grand.

"Of course," the hotel manager added quickly, "we've arranged to upgrade you to another loft. Two bedrooms with a jacuzzi deck. No added fee, naturally."

Rusty shook his head and pocketed the tickets.

"I'll stay where I am. Just change out the bedding."

"Surely you'd feel more comfortable relocating—"

"No need."

That was true—there really was no need. He'd briefly considered accepting the room upgrade when Gustave mentioned it this morning, but rejected the idea. Nossa Morte had gotten that close to him once. Why assume they couldn't do it again?

More to the point, why try to hide? Making contact had been his sole reason for coming here.

Mike the technician walked him from the monitor room down a hallway to a staff elevator. Rusty emerged two stories up and was led by a security guard down a hallway that deposited him into the main lobby of the Grand. The whole area was bustling with activity, and it felt good to get caught up in the flow of it.

He strolled westward, through the casino and into the entertainment complex. His feet formed a path on their own without taking any direction from his conscious thoughts. It occurred to him he was walking to the one place in this vast hotel he'd managed to avoid since checking in. He was drawn in by the tickets in his pocket.

The David Copperfield Theater.

There it was, big as life. And try as he might, there was no way Rusty could look at the blazing marquee over the theater's front doors and not feel a certain sting.

Could've been mine. This, or something better.

He knew that was no idle speculation. The entertainment brass at Caesars had virtually guaranteed him as much. His audience was rapidly outgrowing the five-hundred-seat Etruscan Room, just as his name recognition was making the leap from local cult figure to a more prominent level of notoriety. He never got anywhere near household status, but the flight path was clear enough. Caesars had made it clear, when his contract was to be renegotiated at the end of the eighteen-month run, the option of building a larger dedicated venue onsite bearing his name was very much in play.

Yeah. Everything was in play, and I burned it all to the ground.

Trying to shake away these thoughts, Rusty walked over to look at a bronze bust depicting Copperfield in larger than life dimensions. Nearby was a plaque dedicated by the Society of American Magicians, officially naming him "King of Magic."

You deserve it, Dave.

Rusty spotted a woman and a young boy turning away from the box office. The boy's crestfallen look said everything. Whether it was sold-out or too expensive: either way, they wouldn't be seeing the King in action on this trip.

He approached them, circling around so as not to surprise the woman from behind.

"Excuse me. None of my business, but I'm guessing you had no luck."

"Sold out," she said. "Stupid mistake, waiting until we got here."

She gave her son a chuck on the shoulder, which didn't seem particularly effective in cheering him up.

"We'll do it next time."

Rusty produced the envelope from his pocket.

"Two front row seats right here. All yours."

The boy's face lit up like a pinball machine but his mother looked dubious.

"How much?"

"Free of charge. I can't use them."

"Seriously," she pressed, unsmiling. "What's the catch?"

"No catch. You'd be doing me a favor, actually. My girl-friend's under the weather, ate a bad oyster. She'd never forgive me for going without her. I really don't feel like trying to sell these on Craigslist, so they're yours if you want them."

Rusty could see the boy restraining himself from reaching for the envelope.

"You're being straight with me?" the woman asked, her tone sounding slightly more hopeful than skeptical.

"Absolutely," he said, handing her son the envelope. The boy opened them and pulled out the tickets. His eyes went saucer and he shoved them in his mother's face.

"Wow," she said. "This is really generous. Thank you so much."

He just nodded and walked away, feeling good about the transaction but unwilling to be thanked for it. He was never going to use the goddamned tickets anyway, and his reasons for that were less than noble.

He stopped cold in his tracks. Something clicked in his head, the sense of connection he'd felt but could not pinpoint in the security office.

That face, the stringy red hair and off-kilter grin.

And the custodial patch from Caesars! Christ, yes...

Rusty started running for the Skylofts.

22.

Rusty was speed dialing Charlotte's number as his left foot kicked the loft's door shut. He'd required significant willpower to refrain from placing the call until he had some privacy.

It rang three times. Rusty paced the floor, willing her to answer and grunting with frustration when he got voice mail.

"Call me soon as you get this. I know who it is. I saw his goddamned face."

He pocketed the phone and went straight to his laptop, ignoring the need to take a monster piss. The screen was frozen, keyboard non responsive. Rusty couldn't get it to reboot even when attempting to force-quit all open applications. Renewed fears of a virus implanted by the message boards flooded his mind.

No, not now!

Digging a coin from his pants, he extracted the battery, jammed it back in and pressed the power button. To his immense relief, the laptop booted up normally. He opened up the Tor browser and was surprised not to be prompted with the same initial password question about the knife turning to steel.

They must have logged my IP, he thought. Not a very comforting notion, his personal computer's address being stored in the Nossa Morte database, but he didn't dwell on it. Instead he started entering the nine-character response to the second question in Portuguese.

_Hel_____

Rusty couldn't remember the complete spelling of the flower Dr. Lima had provided for him. He pulled out his phone and it started ringing the moment his fingertips made contact.

"Charlotte," he half shouted. "I saw his face!"

"So I heard. Calm down."

Rusty gave a concise account of his session in the security office. Charlotte cackled when he mentioned the Copperfield tickets he'd been offered as a bribe for his silence. Her tone sobered when Rusty told her about the bellman who'd been attacked.

"Christ, this is a coordinated operation. They must've done some legwork in isolating the right employee and figuring out when to make their move."

"He showed his face. Deliberately. Fucker looked right at the camera, and smiled. He _wants_ me to know."

"And you do, apparently. How long are you gonna keep me in suspense?"

"Couldn't remember the name at first, then it hit me. Trent."

He waited to see if that sparked any recognition.

"I have no idea who you're talking about, Rusty."

"Think back. Weird kid, worked on the custodial crew in the Palace Tower. You recognized him, remember? Said he used to wait at the stage door with the rest of the autograph hounds. After he got the custodial gig he was always loitering outside my suite, trying to buttonhole me. Every time I came back from a dinner or a rehearsal he'd be there, pretending to vacuum the hallway. I ignored it at first until he started badgering me."

Charlotte let out a long contemplative sigh.

"Right, right…it's coming to me. He was some kind of überfan. Took the job just to get near you, correct?"

"Yeah. Wanted to become my apprentice, or something crazy like that. Drilled me with all kinds of detailed questions about the performance. At first I was impressed, because he seemed to know his shit. Then I pegged him for a spy, hired by another performer to swipe some of my secrets. Then it dawns on him: he sees himself as my protégé. And he's at least half psycho to boot. So I finally bitch about it to you, and that's the last I saw of him."

"Yep," Charlotte said. "I can picture the creepy bastard. Tall skinny kid, red hair. We brought him in for a Q&A. He was twitchy as a hamster on speed."

"Did you have him fired?"

"Can't recall. Fired outright? Doubtful. Reassigned to another wing, most likely. Reprimanded for pestering a valued guest, et cetera."

Rusty grabbed a bottle of water from the fridge. He downed three big gulps.

"So this Trent kid," Charlotte said. "Did you ever give him a reason to hate you? I mean really hate you?"

"Other than blow him off and possibly get him canned, nothing I can recall. You know I was loaded half the time back then."

"That's a conservative estimation."

"Point is, I have no clue what I might've said to him. All I remember is he wanted to learn magic from me."

Charlotte grumbled into the phone, chewing the information over.

"Anyway," Rusty continued, "I guess the next step is clear enough."

"Way ahead of you. I'll contact HR at Caesars, see what they have on file."

"That's what I was hoping you'd say. Call me with whatever you find out. If there's a current address on him I'll end this shit tonight."

"Oh, by the way," Charlotte said, "I unearthed another piece of info you might want to hear about."

"Yeah," Rusty said absently, sitting down at the computer, his mind already racing toward getting into the message boards.

"Paula Ponti. You'll be glad to hear she's alive and well."

Rusty almost dropped the phone. His mouth felt too dry to speak.

"What? Tell me…"

"More than that, seems she's had a major falling out with Daddy. Made some good fodder for SinCityConfidential.com a year or so ago. I guess once Paula got old enough to get curious about her old man's past. You know, the dirty old days, before he became a beacon of civic pride. What she discovered must've been a little too much for her. There was a big blowup at the Cactus Club, apparently. She called him a crook right to his face in front of half the town's upper crust. He grabbed her hard; she stormed out—very ugly scene. I'll send you the gossip rag's link so you can pore over the details. Bottom line? By all accounts she hasn't spoken with Big Paul since then. Cut him out of her life since she became a legal adult. Takes his money I'm guessing, but shuns all contact."

"But she's alive," Rusty said stupidly, as if that were the only fact that had lodged itself in his mind. And indeed it was.

"Alive as you or me. And from what I've read about her, no signs of any injury or disfigurement. Whatever happened at the house that night, I think you might've built it up in your mind way beyond the reality."

"It's possible, I guess."

"Like you said, clear and sober thinking wasn't exactly your strong suit back then."

"Charlotte, I can't begin to thank you…"

"Don't start with that shit now, we're hardly out of the woods here."

She ended the call on that cautionary note.

Rusty just sat there for several long minutes, staring at the computer screen without really seeing it. Was it possible? Could he allow himself to believe what she'd just shared with him—that the most shameful act of his life, from which he'd spent the last three years hiding—never really happened? Or at least not on the scale he'd imagined?

No. Obviously he'd injured Paula Ponti to some degree. Otherwise why would her father be behind some twisted scheme to lure him back out to Vegas? And why in God's name would someone with Ponti's standing connect with a nutcase like Trent the custodial stalker?

Pondering it all made Rusty's head throb, so he turned on the phone again and found the flower name Professor Lima had given him.

Clicking on the computer screen's prompt box, he finished typing all nine digits.

Heliconia

Rusty hit Enter, and the hidden world of Nossa Morte opened up to him.

At first glance, it resembled every other online message board he'd ever seen. All text, no graphics. Just a scroll of different topics in a basic grid, with notations of how many replies the original post had received.

The boards were scarcely populated, with a total of thirteen members. Currently, he appeared to be one of four online, including a moderator with the handle death_trip.

Pretty lame, Rusty thought. *Not much traffic here, Trent.* He found that to be a cheering discovery.

Less cheering was the fact that almost every single thread on the board was about *him*. With a few exceptions that seemed to cover more general topics of magic, the majority related to specific aspects of Rusty's career and speculation about what had become of him since his last public appearance.

He scanned a sample of the discussion categories:

Performance Art:
    Top Five Nossa Morte Principles
    Who Carries the Raven's Abdicated Torch?

Blurring the Lines:
    Death as the Ultimate Performance

Confederates and Participants:
    The Nature of Willingness and the Subconscious Acceptance of Sacrifice

Sacred Sources:
    Historical Antecedents from Around the Globe
    Magic in Amazonian Death Rites

The Raven:
    False Promises and Empty Magic—A Legacy of Shame
    Where Did YOU See the Raven Perform?
    Live from the Loge Section: Footage of the Raven's Breakthrough at Caesars Palace
    Poll: The Raven: Dead or Alive?
    Raven Sightings, Post them here—He STILL lives!

Video Links:
    The Raven's Closest Brushes with Death
    Nossa Morte in the Underworld

With a clear shot of insight, Rusty knew the next step to take. He clicked on a link reading: _Start a New Thread_.

In the subject box, he wrote: _It Worked!_

Underneath, in a larger box enclosing the body of his message, he typed the following:

> _That's right, fuckers. Congratulations, your little plan worked. The Raven's back in LV, but why am I bother-_

ing to tell you that? At least one of you knows it already. Thanks for the delivery, by the way. Next time, don't wait till I'm out of the loft to drop by. Ring the god-damned bell and face me. That's right, I haven't checked out. Room 1418 and I'll be here as long as it takes to finish this.

It might sound like I'm speaking to the whole sick crew but I'm directing these words to one sniveling little shit in particular. Yes, Trent. I remember you. And you know what? I applaud you. Took a respectable amount of vision and initiative to orchestrate your scheme, and it paid off. I'd have gladly sprung for a plane ticket if you wanted to just come visit me back East after tracking down my address. We could've hashed out your grievances face to face, but that wouldn't satisfy you, would it? You needed to bring the Raven back to where it all went down, I get it.

So let's do this, Trent. No more cat and mouse. Let's meet tonight, face to face. Just say when and where. Don't back down now, I'm counting on you.

Rusty hit Enter and the new thread appeared at the top of the board. He felt like he'd gone a little overboard in baiting his target, but it felt kind of good to write anyway.

Nothing to do now but wait. Either Trent would respond or Charlotte would get back to him with more information from Human Resources at Caesars. Whichever happened first, he'd react to it.

Feeling antsy, Rusty went back to the Video Links section and clicked on a link titled: *Nossa Morte In the Underworld.*

A new page opened up, containing nine video links. All were dated, starting from roughly three months prior with the most recent being yesterday. The names of the links were familiar to Rusty. They were all tricks from his old act, and he noted they were among the most dangerous he performed on a nightly basis.

He clicked on the top link, dated April 13. _The Deadly Pendulum_. Always a crowd-pleaser.

Rusty felt a grim smile come to his lips.

OK, Trent. Let's see how good you are.

He sat there watching some grainy, low-resolution footage in the video box. The robed, hooded figure stood on a low stage, the resemblance as jarringly accurate as ever. Rusty's biggest fan, reborn as a deranged doppelganger.

Strapped down to a table in front of Trent, the smaller figure of a young woman. Swinging from a rope above manipulated in his hands, a large crescent-shaped blade. Similar setup to the way Rusty did the gag, but a poor-man's version of it.

Trent spoke to what appeared to be a small audience outside the frame, or perhaps simply the suggestion of one. The audio was weak and tinny. Rusty had a hard time making out the words.

But audio wasn't required to see what Trent did with that crescent blade as the trick reached its conclusion. The camera didn't cut out early on this video. Rusty saw it all happen, and the grin on his face turned into a rictus of numb horror as the footage went to black.

He didn't want to watch any of the other Nossa Morte videos. But he knew he had to.

23.

Charlotte reached for a pack of Kools on her living room coffee table. She let a hearty expletive fly at finding it empty. Jesus Christ, the second empty pack in one day.

Maybe it was a sign she should quit, but she didn't want to believe that. Crumpling the pack in her hand, she hurled it to some dark corner behind the sofa.

And immediately regretted it. Rusty's comment about the house being in need of a cleaning crew rang in her ears. She couldn't dismiss the truth in his words.

There was no denying she'd let the place go to seed in the past three months, along with herself. At first, during those hellish weeks following her dismissal from Caesars, it was so easy to wallow in self-pity. Do nothing but smoke and brood all day long.

Dismissed: the ugly reality. Quite a stretch from taking a voluntary leave of absence. No one at the casino other than her direct superior knew the real deal. She'd been allowed to let that cover story fly for the sake of her dignity.

Well, enough of the self-pity bullshit. That all ended today. The notion of making her home more clean and livable brought a smile to her face.

In truth, she'd smiled more in the past three days than in the previous three months. It annoyed her to consider the source of this guarded happiness, all the more so because the son of a bitch probably knew it himself. But in her solitude, she could admit that being in Rusty's orbit again boosted her vitality more than a fistful of the most potent meds ever could. She'd always loved the selfish bastard, an obvious fact they'd treated as the third rail of their professional relationship.

And yet, he never missed a show. Not until the day he vanished altogether. The matinee at two thirty was canceled. Then the eight o'clock dinner show.

It wasn't until late that night that a valet admitted under intense questioning that he'd claimed Mr. Diamond's car just past dawn. Said Mr. Diamond loaded three large bags into the vehicle and handed him a five-hundred-dollar tip. Which direction was he headed in? Mr. Diamond didn't say.

For the Caesars entertainment brass, it was a private outrage and a huge public embarrassment. Their rising star entertainer, with more than three months left on his seven-figure contact, had vanished just like one of his acts. Only Rusty wouldn't be reappearing from some hidden trap door to wild applause. He was gone for good, and no one could guess where. Not even Charlotte Raines, his closest confidante in the Caesars hierarchy.

She dismissed the unpleasant memory and leaned over the coffee table, frowning at the pain in her knees. The rough checkerboard pattern of paperwork laid out before her might look utterly haphazard to an untrained eye, but to Charlotte it was as readable as a map of the Strip.

A map was exactly what it was, of sorts. A map of connectivity linking Paul Ponti to the package that had arrived on the doorstep of Rusty's rented home three time zones East. Her contact at the city planning office had come through, almost too well. There was more data in front of her than she could hope to process in any kind of expeditious manner.

It was in there, somewhere. The link she'd been putting together in her mind. Ponti's secretly acquired property holdings along the Homeless Corridor. All the paperwork related to that spree was now in her hands. Plus a cherry on top—a recent zoning ordinance required for a wholesale transformation of that part of town, one that barely got shoehorned through city council on the back of some massive lobbying. Not by Ponti directly, rather a firm with connections to the governor's office in Carson City. Charlotte knew with a little digging she'd be able to establish Ponti as a client. The guy was buying up the Homeless Corridor and at the same time backing some kind of scheme involving Rusty's old stalker.

Charlotte knew the Daniels girl was the key. Tending bar at Unterwelt and tending to Paul Ponti's bedroom needs at a slummy motel. Feeding Rusty the line that led him, indirectly, to the flood tunnels running underneath much of Ponti's newly purchased holdings. The same tunnels that just might lie at the center of Nossa Morte's twisted—and quite possibly lethal—"tributes" to the late great Raven.

Ponti. The girl. Trent. The Underworld.

So engrossed in her thoughts, Charlotte barely heard the knock at the door. It was soft, tentative. Almost like the person outside didn't want to raise the attention of any neighbors.

She paused before rising. The last time someone had appeared on her stoop was two nights ago, when Rusty resurfaced from oblivion. The last time before that…she couldn't remember. No one came knocking in Henderson anymore, not since the crazed epoch of mass evictions.

The knock sounded again. Three short taps. An urge to ignore it, coming from some cautionary place in the pit of her stomach, only irritated her. Since when was she the kind of woman afraid to look through a damn peephole?

Standing with a grunt, she shuffled over to grab the Remington 870 from where it leaned into a corner. She approached the door and laid an eye to the glass circle.

Nothing. No one on the stoop. She stood on tiptoe to gain a higher angle, see if someone might be crouching below the peephole's level. Impossible to be sure but it didn't look like anyone was down there.

The sound of breaking glass caused her to jerk her head away from the door. It came from the back of the house, most likely the kitchen.

Charlotte pumped the Remington and steadied the stock under the crook of her left arm. She looked around wildly for her cane. No idea where she'd left it after coming through the front door on her return from the MGM Gardens.

A small squeak emanated from the rear of the house, and she recognized its source. Someone had just pushed open the mason window to the left of the broom closet. Obviously. First they needed to break the glass so they could reach in and push back the lock.

Charlotte half expected to hear the next sound before it reached her ears. The heavy tread of two feet lowering onto the linoleum floor.

She could feel herself start to freeze, and the momentary inaction infuriated her. Her mind was busy recreating the afternoon drive and trying to calculate if anyone could have followed her here from her tailing of the Daniels girl from the motel to the nail place to the MGM.

Seemed eminently possible; she'd been so consumed with tracking the Audi it never dawned on her to keep a weather eye on her own rearview. Just went to show how much her intuitive faculties had atrophied during this long convalescence.

A boot scraped across the kitchen floor. With three painful steps, Charlotte flattened herself against the wall. She had to bite her tongue to suppress a yelp, but managed to remain silent.

Standing hidden behind a tall bookcase, she craned her head a few inches forward to monitor the hallway entrance leading to the kitchen. With the shotgun raised at waist height, she needed the wall for support. The angle was no good from this position. Whoever was in the kitchen could easily get within a few feet of her before she had time to train the barrels. From that distance, the possibility of having the gun stripped from her damnably feeble grasp was all too likely.

Goddamnit, where was that fucking cane?

Charlotte realized she'd stopped breathing when she heard the voice.

"This thing's only going one way, lady. Question you want to be asking yourself right now is, how much is it gonna hurt? That part's pretty much in your hands. To a degree."

Another five seconds of silence passed. Charlotte's eyes fell on her cell phone. It sat on a pile of papers on the coffee table, three interminable steps away. Far too dangerous to make a lunge for it, and it would be a pointless effort anyway. The odds of emergency responders making it to the house in time to do any good were too slim to bother considering.

Oh, well. At least she had Mr. Remington in her hands. Maybe she'd have to stay here all night, wedged between the bookcase and the wall. Waiting for the intruder to make his move. Charlotte knew he wouldn't wait that long. He'd either go on the offensive or hit the eject button and try some other time.

This line of thinking soothed her slightly. She felt like John Wayne in the final reel of *Rio Bravo*, carving out a safe nook from which to make a stand against the bad guys. All she needed was a pack of smokes to make it slightly more endurable.

A loud crash near the front door caused Charlotte to swivel ninety degrees to he right, her finger tightening on the trigger. She realized a fraction of a second too late that it was a deliberate distraction. The intruder had hurled a lamp from the kitchen hallway, shattering it against the door.

She jerked back around, wincing at the pain in her knees. It was too late. The big man was moving at her like a wrecking ball, his movements too rapid to track. Charlotte's vision honed in on the scars on his face even as both brawny hands grabbed the barrel end of the Remington. With a brisk tug the gun flew from her grip.

Moving on instinctive panic, she tried to burrow farther into the wedge between the bookcase and the wall. A small field animal wildly digging for cover as a predator approached, only to find flinty ground offering no purchase for safety.

When the scarred man spoke, his voice was improbably soft. Even gentle.

"Stop that and calm down. We need to talk."

"Get the fuck out of my house! Cops'll be here any second, scumbag!"

"Nah. Out here in Henderson? I'd say we got plenty of time to get cozy before anyone rolls up."

Seeing no alternative, Charlotte made a tentative step away from the wall.

"At first," the man said contemplatively, "I couldn't figure the tail. I knew why *I* was following the little snatch. Trent wants me to, even though it's a waste of time. So she's meeting with the big man, probably feeding him updates on Project Raven in between rides. So what? It's his party. But what the hell's *your* interest in little Luna? I think about it, and it becomes clear as glass. Or should I say a Diamond. Talk about sad. I knew the bastard lost any balls he ever might've had, but bringing in an old lady to do his recon work?"

Charlotte reached a hand out to the bookcase for support. She feared her knees might buckle any second. The fear welling inside her was like a wave of icy water.

"Got a little gimp there, huh?"

"Last warning, asshole. Get the fu—"

Soren smashed the Remington's thick wooden stock into her left kneecap. Charlotte couldn't even cry out, the pain robbing all the breath from her lungs. She staggered forward, flailing to prop herself up with one hand on a small table. Soren delivered another blow with the stock to the base of her skull. Her whole body jerked forward, knocking over the table. It shattered underneath her weight as both collided with the floor.

Soren stood above her, listening to her weak moans for a minute. That second tap was probably excessive—wouldn't be getting much out of her for a while. But he didn't intend to stay in this house very long either. Just long enough to call Trent with a piece of helpful news.

• • •

Eight miles northwest of Charlotte's house, Rusty carried a fresh cup of coffee from the kitchen over to his laptop to give it another check. It had been a frustrating few hours. No update from Charlotte, and no response to his post on the message boards.

He'd forced himself to do more than just sit around and wait, even making a brief trip down to the casino for the exercise. Every time he checked the computer and saw no reply, his frustration grew.

But not this time.

One new comment had been posted in the thread he started. It was short and to the point.

Took you long enough, Raven. I was starting to lose faith.
Diner at the White Cross, 2:00 A.M. Get us a booth.

24.

The White Cross Pharmacy crouched over a desolate corner of Las Vegas Boulevard not found in any tourist maps. The closest establishment of any repute was the giant needle of the Stratosphere three blocks away, just barely clinging to the northern edge of the Strip before urban squalor took over.

Rusty pulled into the lot facing the pharmacy and parked well out of sight of the entry. He killed the engine and the lights, thinking what a dumb move he'd made by bringing such a flashy ride to this place at this hour.

Should've Ubered it. Let's make that the last tactical error of the night.

His watch told him he was fifteen minutes early. That was good; he was in no rush to move. Fact was, he needed a few minutes to ground himself before stepping through that nauseatingly familiar doorway.

Of all the places to be summoned within the city limits of Las Vegas, none had the power to spike his sense of stepping into quicksand as much the White Cross. Trent must surely have known that, or intuited it somehow.

Rusty was all too familiar with the pharmacy and the small diner wedged against its southern flank. Open twenty-four hours, this place had long served as a hub for all kinds of sketchy activity. Not even the presence of a security guard armed with Mace and a billy club could dissuade some of LV's more desperate citizens from venturing to the White Cross in the wee hours, in search of whatever they required to hold on until sunrise came.

Drugs, check. Prostitution, check. High interest loans with a tight repayment window, check. Last-minute bookmaking on the early race at Saratoga, check. All that and more could be procured in and around the White Cross, for a price.

Rusty had paid more late-night visits here back in the bad old days than he cared to recall. And in truth, many of those addled missions were permanently obscured in the mists of chemical blackouts. It was always his last resort when the usual sources turned up dry. On the rare occasion when no groupie or hanger-on was backstage with a gram to spare…when it was too late for even Dr. Fred Schneider to pick up the phone… Rusty found himself here.

And here I am again, he thought, stepping out of the car and dodging mounds of papery debris that bounced across the lot like tumbleweed.

But this time, I've got all my faculties. What's left of them.

Steeling himself with that reminder, he walked past the main entrance to the pharmacy and toward a smaller door facing the street corner. A hand-painted sign on the stucco read *Vickie's Diner*.

He pushed through the door and stepped into a vivid slice of memory come to life. Rusty smiled with nostalgia despite himself. The first thing to hit him was a rich texture of smells— fried grease, maple syrup, freshly brewed coffee, and a dash of Lysol.

He lowered himself into a red faux-leather booth, hands resting on the Formica tabletop. Facing the entrance.

The diner was as empty as he'd expected. Two old men in matching flannel slouched over their plates at the counter. A waitress stood by the register, barking an order at a fry cook Rusty couldn't see from his vantage point.

The waitress ambled over, order pad in hand.

"Coffee?" she said in a declarative tone.

"Sure thing."

"What else? The eggs florentine have been getting raves lately. New cook."

"Just the coffee, thanks."

The waitress rolled her eyes, displeased to have walked all of ten paces for a two-dollar tab.

"Someone's joining me. He might eat."

"I'll try not to let my hopes run wild." She turned away.

Rusty waited, keeping his eye on the front door. A memory came to him of an early-morning breakfast he had here once with a trio of topless dancers from Zumanity. They'd spent a long expensive night drinking Cristal in a private nook at Tao, and the girls insisted on some greasy food before deciding where things went from there. To the best of his recollection, one of them ended up staying with him at Caesars for a week or so.

Entombed in the memory, he never saw Trent coming.

The lanky, dark-eyed figure slid into the seat across from him like a wraith conjured from thin air. Rusty's breath got caught somewhere in his sternum. A sense of disorientation flooded strong.

Then he remembered:

Back door to the parking lot. Of course. Used to slip out that way sometimes, when a customer looked too much like a narc.

Trent was decked out in full Raven regalia; wig, goatee, black leather jacket. The resemblance was even more unnerving in person than on a computer screen.

Rusty felt like he was looking into a cracked mirror, despite having altered his own appearance. He refused to speak first. The two men held eye contact for so long it began to resemble some childish game.

"It's a bit much," Trent said in a voice that quavered slightly, "Not just being in the presence of greatness, after all this time. But a dead man come to life. I imagine the bystanders at Golgotha felt much the same."

"Cut the shit. There's no need to start brownnosing me now, is there?"

"Fair enough," Trent replied, after flinching. "I'll be more candid. You're not looking well, Raven. I've heard firsthand reports, but I wasn't quite prepared for the…diminishment, that's all I can call it. You look much smaller without all that hair. Odd. And the goatee. I never realized how much you needed that to make the whole getup work. "

"Found out for yourself though, didn't you?"

The waitress appeared at the table, looking at Trent like he was exactly the kind of lowlife she'd expected to join Rusty. Trent asked for ice water and she walked away muttering audible obscenities.

"Sorry, that was rude. That's not how I want this to go. I'll *always* be a fan, no matter how badly you let us down."

"Not a fan. A pathetic wannabe. There's a difference."

Rusty saw Trent's Adam's apple bob like he was trying to swallow a tablespoon of cinnamon.

"Why the Payocu?" he continued, looking to control the flow of conversation.

"Come again?"

"Well, most of what you put in those boxes makes sense as a trail of breadcrumbs. From a lunatic's point of view, anyway."

"Exactly," Trent smiled. "That's why I was confident you'd piece it together."

"What if I hadn't?"

"Don't worry. I had a more direct approach in mind as a backup. I knew I wouldn't need it."

"OK, but the stuff about the Payocu. Linking your sick little act with some obscure tribe from the Amazonian rainforest, that part escapes me."

"Just an added wrinkle," Trent shrugged. "No significance,

really. I'd seen some TV show about death rituals among indigenous peoples, the term Nossa Morte stuck in my head. Catchy, huh? I thought it would give you something to sink your teeth into."

"So then the textbook page from UNLV. Figured that was enough to point me toward Vegas, just in case the box's return address didn't get it done."

"I'll say this much, Raven. For someone who looks to have suffered serious physical deterioration, your mental capacities haven't dimmed. It's almost unfair—"

"Where'd you get the dice?" Rusty broke in. "I'm assuming you actually have the other one."

"That's not what you really want to know, is it?"

"Humor me."

"Piece of cake. After you bailed on Caesars I bribed a bellman to give me five minutes in your suite. You left behind all kinds of shit. Must've been in a hurry to make tracks. I wonder why?"

Seeing an opening, Rusty almost spoke Paul Ponti's name but stopped himself. Let Trent divulge the connection, if he chose to.

"Back to my point, Raven. I was saying before it's almost not fair picking on you in your weakened state. But there I go, being rude again. Nerves, that's all. It's not every day you meet your hero. Even less often when he's come back from the dead."

"I was never dead, Trent. You can knock that shit off. I left Vegas, that's all."

Trent slammed a fist on the table, making the cutlery jump.

"And who said you could do that?"

Barely spoken over a whisper, it had the impact of a scream. Rusty took a glance at the counter. The two elderly diners kept their backs turned, either not hearing the conversation or pretending not to.

"I was supposed to check with you first? Why?"

"Because you owed us. Where would you be without us?"

"If you're talking about my fans, you're the only one who seems to have taken it so hard. Maybe that's because you're crazy as a goddamn loon. I don't care. I just want this to stop."

The waitress walked over and set down Trent's water glass. She turned away without bothering to ask if he wanted anything else.

"Midnight tonight," Trent said, leaning over the table. "Nossa Morte's last performance, with a special guest star. Check the message boards for detailed instructions, and don't be late. You want it to stop? This is the price you pay."

"Sure, I'll come. And why wouldn't I bring a dozen cops with me?"

"Two reasons, aside from what should be a very obvious fact that the police in this town don't concern themselves with what happens to the kinds of gutter waste we use. Each performance just means one less vagrant for them to roust."

"Whose goddamn fingers and teeth were those?"

"Doesn't matter, that's what I'm trying to tell you."

"Is he still alive?"

Trent batted away the question.

"A disposable volunteer, nameless. No one of any concern to you or the cops or anyone else."

"You're kidding yourself, Trent. Just 'cause they crack down hard on transients doesn't mean they'll turn a blind eye to a goddamn killing spree."

"Sure about that? Homelessness is about as welcome around here as an Ebola outbreak. What city's more about optics than Vegas? Bad for business, all those filthy bodies crowding the walkways and sidewalks. Christ, you see them right on the Strip these days."

Rusty finished his coffee, wondering if he should just try to lure Trent outside and kill him with his bare hands. If he could.

"This is all academic, Raven. You *will* be there at midnight, and you won't be bringing any cops."

"What makes you so confident?"

"Like I said, two reasons. First, you're going to commit a crime, a serious one. In fact, just the kind of crime you claim the law would be likely to frown upon. That's the only way you get in, and your only prayer for altering the course of what's already underway."

"OK, I'll bite. What kind of crime?"

"Felony kidnapping, what else? We need a volunteer for the performance, and you're going to supply one. Starting to get the picture?"

"Yeah. You want to implicate me in your sick game like—"

"You *are* implicated! You're the source of everything we do, understand?"

"What's the second reason?"

Trent giggled, and the sound made Rusty's teeth grind.

"Check the message boards when you get back to your fancy loft. There's a new thread up, I think you'll find it interesting. Make sure to download the Periscope app if you watch it on your phone."

"You know what? Fuck you. I'm not doing a goddamn thing."

Trent leaned back in his seat, one hand reaching into his jacket.

"Well, if that's how you feel...I guess we could end it right here. "

He produced a spherical object the size of a baseball in his hand. Protruding from the top and clenched between his thumb and index finger was a metallic square resembling a small Zippo lighter. A brass hoop ran through the center.

"Recognize this?"

Trent peeled his fingers away from the sphere. A combination of letters and numbers were stenciled on the side. Rusty didn't need to bother reading them. He slowly pulled his hands back off the table.

It was a military-issue hand grenade. Identical to hundreds of grenades he'd used in one of his most dangerous stunts onstage at Caesars. The stunt began with Rusty's two assistants trying him up with a length of steel chain—one around the ankle and the other around his wrists. He then positioned himself into a steel box standing upright in the center of the stage.

One of his assistants secured a padlock on the box's lid and closed it. The other climbed up on a ladder, pulled the pin on the grenade and dropped it into the box through an opening on the top. Both assistants then ran offstage as if their lives depended on it.

The Etruscan Room fell utterly silent at that moment, show after show. People in the audience leaned forward in their seats. Some cupped hands nervously over their ears, others looked away entirely.

The gag's payoff was a simple one—Rusty didn't make it out in time. The grenade detonated with a thunderous boom before he could free himself of the chains. The box's door flew off its hinges and clattered to the stage amid huge plumes of gray smoke.

When the smoke cleared, the standing walls of the box stood empty. No trace of its shackled occupant. Some of the more gullible ticket buyers indulged in a moment of breathless speculation—was it possible Caesars' rising star had been killed performing a stunt that was just *too* dangerous?

A spotlight on the rear of the stage dispelled any such notions. Rusty, free of his binds and changed into a clean set of clothes, came casually strolling onto the stage from the orchestra pit. Back to the crowd, he let the applause reach a fever pitch before turning to take a bow.

Trent looked over at the two old men and the waitress.

"We'd have some witnesses, assuming they live. What a

tale they could tell. Master and pupil, blown to bits by one of the Raven's favorite props."

"Nah, I don't think you want to do that. It would only spoil your fun."

Trent inched the grenade just a bit closer to Rusty's side of the table.

"It's not the M37. Not the training model, like you used. That's a genuine M67, the kind soldiers kill people with in the field."

Rusty took a moment to confirm that statement by reading the numbers printed on the red surface.

"Can I have it?" he asked calmly. "You made your point."

"Does that mean you agree to my demands?"

"I'll be there, just like you said."

"Terrific."

Trent extended his hand so Rusty could grab the grenade. He performed a small misdirectional cue with his other hand. Expertly performed it. So much so that Rusty couldn't respond in time even though he saw it happen.

Oh, shit.

At the moment Rusty's fingers wrapped around the grenade, Trent pulled the pin.

25.

Rusty's thumb snapped down on the detonator. Preventing an explosion, for the moment.

"I must be in as poor shape as you claim," he said, "not to see that coming."

"Don't be too hard on yourself," Trent replied, sliding out of the booth. "Nobody stays at their prime forever."

Before Rusty could master the use of practice grenades, he'd immersed himself in the fatal specifications of their combat counterparts. Thus he knew the spherical object clenched in his sweating palm offered a minimum of four seconds for him to get safely away before it detonated. If he was lucky, maybe as much as six.

Trent smiled like he'd just read his thoughts.

"That's a defective unit, I should mention. They're a lot cheaper to come by on the deep web. I mean, who wants a grenade with an unpredictable fuse, right? You might have less than two seconds to deploy it, or as many as ten. Then again, it might be a dud."

Trent gave Rusty a last appraising glance, and nodded.

"It's been an honor, believe me when I say that. I'll see you real soon."

He turned and walked out the front door.

Rusty lowered his hand carefully, holding the grenade out of sight beneath the table. He used his free hand to fish his wallet from his back pocket. He extracted a ten-dollar bill and placed it next to his empty coffee cup.

No reason to dine and dash just because I'm holding live ordnance.

Moving at a measured pace, he slid out of the booth. He nodded to the waitress. She turned away without smiling, making Rusty think the look on his face was considerably less relaxed than what he was attempting to convey.

He saw no reason to follow Trent out the front door. The back exit was closer.

Twenty paces carried Rusty out of the diner. He found himself in a small, darkened parking lot behind the building. He whipped his head in a 360-degree pan, looking for the most desirable place to ditch the grenade. If not optimal, then at least not catastrophic.

The other businesses that shared this lot with the pharmacy and diner were closed. The nearest residential buildings were a block away, separated from the lot by an alley.

Rusty walked toward a dumpster in the far corner of the lot. Its plastic lid hung open like a grimy mouth. On the ground next to it sat an old Panasonic tube television with a shattered screen.

Christ, what a dinosaur. Good twenty pounds, easy. Might just help with shrapnel containment.

He did another visual sweep of the lot to ensure no one was within the immediate area. He lowered himself into a crouch and struggled to lift the TV set with his free right hand, pressing it against the side of his body. The damn thing was even heavier than it looked.

Ready?

Inhale.

Exhale.

Go.

Rusty lobbed the grenade into the dumpster's wide maw.

One second.

He stood to full height and used his left hand to grab the dumper's dangling lid. Giving it a shove, he flipped it over. The lid slammed down, sealing the dumpster.

Two seconds.

Gripping the bulky TV set with both hands now, he placed it on top of the lid. He spun on one heel, wincing at a stab of fiery pain in his calf. His other leg shot forward.

Three...

The explosion knocked him to the ground before his ears registered its concussive aural force. The dumpster launched five feet upward, somersaulting, its boxy metal frame transformed into a five-hundred-pound projectile.

Feeling gravel scrape his chin, Rusty rolled away from the blast site. Torqued his body as hard as he could, trying to distance himself and the airborne dumpster before it rejoined the earth.

Four seconds.

Why am I still counting?

The dumpster came crashing down several feet away. Too close. Ears still ringing from the grenade blast, he heard this second combustion clearly. He kept rolling away, then stopped.

Fuck. The TV. Why did I think it would do anything except turn into an airborne weapon?

Even as that thought bloomed in his mind, a blur in the air above caught his eye. Not knowing which direction to move, he blindly scrambled a few feet to the left.

The Panasonic smashed onto the gravel in the precise spot his head had been occupying less than a second before. A small dusting of glass particles covered his face. None found his eyes, by the force of dumb luck.

Rusty lay there, heart hammering, vaguely aware of doors opening and lights coming on in the general vicinity. He knew he needed to get up and get the hell away from here. His mind issued that command to his legs and his legs agreed in theory, but some kind of delayed shock kept them motionless.

Then he heard the laughter. Coming from just a few feet behind him. Before he even turned to look, he knew who it was.

"Goddamn, Raven. You've really gotten old. And slow. I didn't expect you to be in top form, but this is just sad."

Rusty lunged at him but his rubbery legs didn't support the sudden movement. He staggered to a standstill, leaning against the back wall of the diner.

Trent turned and moved into the darkness.

"Don't forget to check the message boards."

• • •

Rusty was still trembling slightly when he stepped out of the car at the Skylofts' valet stand. Just how close that television had landed from his skull was a realization that didn't fully kick in until he was pulling the Barracuda out of the White Cross parking lot. He scarcely recalled the drive back to MGM.

It was more than a delayed panic response that had his whole body feeling like it was connected to electrified cables. A rush of anger came over him with just as much power. Still in a partial haze, he barely registered the presence of the valet, the concierge, or the elevator operator.

Only after locking the door to the loft behind him did he begin to feel somewhat calm. Trent's words about receiving further instructions rang in his ears. He opened the laptop and the Tor browser. No more prompts required; he was directed straight to the message boards page.

As Trent promised, a new thread appeared at the top of the Videos section. The title was blunt:

Motivation to Follow Orders

Clicking the thread, Rusty found himself looking at

another video screen. But this one was different than the ones he'd screened before. There was no Play button to click, rather the low-resolution footage ran on a stream. A small circular logo revealed it to be uploaded from the Periscope mobile app, capable of transmitting live footage from wherever the camera was placed.

A box of text above the video player read:

> *You inquired about your second reason for cooperating. Take a look. Click the Instructions link after you've gotten an eyeful.*

Rusty focused on the footage. It was dim, murky. Looked to be shot from an overhead angle in some dingy basement room. Puddles on the floor, exposed piping in the unpainted brick walls. No more illumination than that provided by a bare bulb hanging from a cord. A digital clock perched on a sink showed the current time.

In the center of the room, a hardback chair. In the chair, a woman, seemingly unconscious. Head drooping forward onto her chest, long tangles of hair obscuring her face.

A small groan escaped Rusty's lips even before his mind consciously processed the image.

She was wearing the same clothes he'd seen her in at the MGM Park. Light sweater over a cotton shirt, dark slacks. Both her hands were tied behind her back to the chair's sturdy frame. Ankles bound in similar fashion.

It was the angle of her legs that made Rusty clench his fists hard enough to leave red crescents on his palms. Her left knee appeared to be shattered, calf jerked at a horribly unnatural angle. Rusty thought he could see a spur of white bone protruding from a rip in the slacks.

A wave of self-reproach hammered him as he recalled deliberately concealing the extracted teeth and severed finger from Charlotte. Had she known of their inclusion in the third package, she might have tread with greater caution. A full understanding of the threat presented by Nossa Morte may have kept her from venturing into the field and inadvertently drawing the notice of whoever had taken her captive.

Not Trent himself, I'd guess. Big motherfucker with the scars probably snatched her.

Time passed, Rusty didn't know how long. All he could do was stare at the footage, watching the minutes on the clock tick by. Muttering curses and prayers under his breath with no awareness of the words.

He finally forced himself to scroll down to the Instructions link. Clicking it, a new text box appeared below the video player.

> *Open the attached PDF file. It's a map of the flood tunnel system. Download it onto your phone and use it for guidance tonight. It will lead you to the performance area. I don't need to tell you what will happen to your friend if you fail to show on time. Do as you're told and she'll live. I don't expect you to believe that, but what choice do you have?*
>
> *As I told you already: don't come alone. You're going to take full responsibility for what happens tonight, and that includes bringing along a participant so we can complete the ritual together.*
>
> *You know where to go fishing; you've been there already. I'm not overly choosy, just make sure it's a young specimen, easily manageable. Sedation comes in handy for this kind of work. I have no doubt you'll be able to get your hands on the kind of chemicals required for that.*
>
> *Study the map. Make a careful review of the entry point—it's highlighted. That's where you leave your car and proceed on foot. If you find it necessary to put the participant in a state that makes walking impossible,*

use the wheelbarrow outside the tunnel entrance. Allow at least thirty minutes from the time you enter the tunnel to when you're expected. Speak to no one you may encounter along the way, and keep the participant well covered at all times.

DO NOT BE LATE.
DO NOT COME ALONE.
DO NOT ALERT THE COPS.
YOU KNOW THE CONSEQUENCES
OF FAILURE.
SEE YOU IN THE UNDERWORLD.

26.

"Are you fucking kidding me?"

Those were Jim Biddison's first words as he stepped into the Skyloft. Rusty had to grin at his friend's awestruck expression.

"I mean, this is unreal," Jim walked over to slide open the door to the patio.

"Not bad for a few nights," Rusty conceded.

Biddison stepped back into the loft, clearly not prepared to face the morning sun. It was a little past 9:00 A.M. and Rusty could tell from his crimson eyes he'd made the most of his first night in Vegas.

"What's it run you?"

"More than I should be spending."

"Christ. I know you've been sitting on a fat nest egg, but this is too much."

"Harrah's is nice."

"It's alright. Got a sweet deal on the room, just about everything comped. I'm on their rewards program."

Rusty raised a brow.

"Really? When do you find time to gamble? And where, in Ocean City?"

"I don't do a lot of it these days, ever since the baby. Hell, ever since the wedding. I used to sneak up to AC when me and Kim were still dating. Racked up a ton of membership points, and those never expire."

"Of course not. They know a sucker when they see one. So what'd you get into last night?"

"Nothing too crazy," Jim lowered himself onto the couch. "Don't have the stamina to burn the streets down anymore. I started drinking on the plane, half in the bag by the time we landed. You blew off my text—no surprise there—so I was flying solo. Dice didn't do shit for me but I had a good time anyway."

Rusty was enjoying listening to his old friend talk, hearing the familiar but forgotten cadences. It was a massive relief just to see his face at this tense hour. But Rusty was still feeling ill at ease. A nagging, guilty suspicion that contacting Jim would prove to be a mistake would not leave him be.

The decision had came just before dawn. He'd retreated to bed after watching the Periscope feed for more than an hour, eyes welded to the screen, praying to see some sign of life from Charlotte.

A few minutes past three o'clock she lifted her chin briefly before it slumped back down on her chest. She was under some kind of sedation, which Rusty took as a blessing. While likely intended to keep her docile, the drugs must also be doing some work to dull the pain.

But she was still alive. For now. He carried that knowledge to the bed and collapsed, knowing sleep would not come. Ideas and speculations about what he could do tormented him as the minutes ticked away.

Trent had lined it up perfectly. As promised, he'd provided Rusty with ironclad motivation to show up at the subterranean performance stage, and bring a "participant" with him. If he showed up late, or alone, Charlotte was dead. If he tried to find and free her, either alone or with police assistance, she was dead.

Turned out he was wrong in not expecting to sleep, because his head jerked up from the mattress at 7:04 AM. One thought rang clear.

Jim. If I ever needed a friend, I need one now.

He'd waited a few hours before making the call, knowing damn well Biddison would not be waking early. On the fourth attempt Jim picked up with a groggy epithet. Rusty asked how soon he could get over to the Skylofts.

Now he was here. And Rusty was struggling with how to broach the topic at hand.

Jim helped him get there by asking, "So how's your top-secret business going?"

"It's a fucking disaster. That's why I called."

"What a shock. I knew it wasn't something simple like wanting to hang out. Never is, with you."

"Well, I figure a whole week of R & R's got you feeling antsy. Probably miss the white-knuckle excitement of the Ocean City Police Department."

"Please. I'm a goddamned desk jockey these days and you know it. Haven't fielded a hot call in months."

Rusty poured himself another cup of coffee. He offered one to Jim, adding a nip of Jameson at his request.

"Hair of the pooch," Jim uttered, taking a sip. "I'm guessing you're gonna buy me breakfast in compensation for dragging me out of bed at this ungodly hour."

"Sure. We'll hit the Bacchanal Buffet at Caesars, but let's talk first."

"Fine. Out with it."

"Gotta promise me something. The rest of this conversation, it's between two guys who were tight back in the day. You're not a cop now, understand?"

"That's an intriguing open," Jim said with a twinkle in one bloodshot eye. "Sounds like you're mixed up in some heavy shit. Again."

"I'm serious. This requires total discretion. I'm not looking for Lieutenant Jim. I need Bulldozer Biddison, the maniac who tore up Tidal's receiving corps back in '98."

Rusty saw a grin that told him he'd struck the right chord.

Nothing got Jim Biddison in a peppier mood—the kind of mood in which he best expressed himself by cracking skulls with or without the protection of a badge—than mentioning his former gridiron glory at OC High.

"Just how far is my discretion supposed to go?" Jim asked. "Into the realm of criminal activity?"

"Most definitely."

"There's a body in that closet and I'm supposed to help you dig a hole?"

"Friend of mine needs help in the most desperate way. You're the only one I can turn to."

Jim took another sip, then raised his hands in a bogus posture of submission.

"OK, you've got my word. Unless you're about to confess something on the lines of rape or murder, I'll hit the off switch on my cop meter."

Rusty gave an appreciative smile and took it from the top. One step at a time he spoke about the three packages arriving at his house in Maryland and everything that had happened since he arrived in Vegas. He focused solely on Trent and Nossa Morte, leaving Paul Ponti out of the scenario.

Jim listened intently, processing what he'd heard.

"I'm sure you can guess my first question," he said after Rusty stopped talking.

"Why didn't I go to the cops as soon as the packages starting arriving? Couldn't, Jim. Not without presenting evidence that could implicate me. They had that part all figured out, even threatened to send another box to the OCPD if I didn't follow orders."

"I don't see a frame sticking here. You haven't set foot in Nevada in almost—"

"Can you prove that? I can't. Living like a hermit—your words, remember?—has some drawbacks when it comes to coughing up a good alibi. Even *you* don't know for sure where I've been and what I've been up to the past few months."

Biddison looked ready to argue but changed tack.

"OK, this Trent freak wants you to take part in one of his…uh, ritual performances, whatever. Which you seem to be convinced entails homicide. I'm having a hard time believing that last part."

When Rusty started to protest, Jim stopped him.

"A string of killings underneath the city and no one knows about it? No bodies? No evidence of a crime? No missing persons reports?"

"These aren't the kind of people whose disappearance generates a report, Jim. They're street vagrants, runaways. Most likely recent transplants to Vegas. If anything, their parents may have filed a report months or years ago, whenever they left home. I can show you the goddamn video clips if you want."

"Rusty, you should know better than anyone how easily shit can be faked. It's too implausible. Even if this guy has been offing street kids for some kind of sick entertainment, how could he force you to take part in that? What's his leverage against you just turning him in?"

Rusty pulled out his phone. He opened the Periscope feed, flinching again at the same image it showed. Charlotte was still gagged and bound to the chair. Nothing appeared to have changed other than the time on the digital clock. It read 10:13 A.M., matching the clock on his phone.

He handed it over for Jim to see.

"Either I do what Trent says or she dies. Simple as that."

Jim examined the phone silently for more than a minute. Then he handed it back and walked out onto the patio. Rusty followed, waiting for him to speak.

"Jesus Christ. Being friends with you's a risky proposition."

"I owe her, Jim. She watched out for me when I was at my absolute worst, then I bailed on her without so much as a thank you."

Jim glanced over, drilling Rusty with a glare.

"Oh, you pulled something *like* that on a friend? Hard to believe."

"Bust my balls all you want. Take a swing if that's an itch that needs scratching. I'm begging for your help here."

"Got a lead on where she's being held?"

"More than a lead."

Rusty opened the phone's GPS tracking app. The small red dot hovered at the same location as when he'd first checked last night, roughly ninety miles to the northwest.

"Where is that?" Biddison asked.

"Rhyolite. Tiny ghost town in Death Valley, about an hour and a half from here. Used to be a low-level tourist draw, now it's pretty much abandoned. Good place to hold someone hostage, or worse."

"Surprised you haven't gone out there, just to check."

"Can't risk it. First sight of me, she's gone."

Jim peeled his eyes away from the phone's screen.

"Back up a little. How were you able to find her with this?"

"Dumb luck. I planted the tracker on her yesterday afternoon. Just did it on instinct for my own peace of mind, knowing it was probably futile."

A throb of techno music wafted in from an adjacent lot. Rusty followed Jim inside and pushed the door shut, muting the noise.

"You realize she could be anywhere right now. What are the odds whoever snatched her didn't find the device? If they did, what are the odds of them planting it someplace miles from where she is, just in case you decide to go looking?"

Rusty opened up Periscope again, having anticipated those questions.

"It's still on her. This thing's tiny, hard to detect. She's wearing the same sweater I hooked it into. Is that a guarantee? No, but it's all I fucking got."

"Look, I know this isn't what you want to hear, but you

gotta understand it's the right thing. Let's get the cops involved, now. I got a pretty high-ranking contact at LV Metro, met her at a ballistics convention last time I was out here. I'll call, they'll round up a small tactical force—"

"No!" Rusty half shouted, slamming a palm on the countertop. "That's a fucking death sentence for Charlotte. First sign of cops, that motherfucker slits her throat."

"And then what? He's gonna just disappear into the desert? No, if you're right about all this, you've got a very workable situation with a good hostage negotiator."

"These guys are fucking insane. No way I can count on a negotiator getting her out alive. It's a solo deal, you or me. I'll do it if I have to, but that'll put her in twice as much danger if I don't show at the Underworld on time."

"Yeah? And what are you gonna do when you get there?"

"I'm gonna end it. You don't really want to know any more, do you?"

Rusty left it at that. He hadn't mentioned anything about the need to bring a participant with him, knowing that bit of intel would evaporate whatever slim chance he had of enlisting Jim in this plan.

A crazy plan. Half-assed at best and dangerous as hell. But it's the only one I got.

"You realize they won't let her live," Jim said softly. "Whether you go along with them or not."

Rusty smiled, just barely.

"That's where the Bulldozer comes in."

There, he'd laid it on the table. Banking on knowing his friend maybe better than Jim knew himself. All that pent-up aggression, the bottled need for confrontation that wasn't being satisfied the higher he moved up the OCPD ranks into the realm of desk work. Jim was a field man, always had been. Built for action. In high school that field was the gridiron, where he'd played with a ferocity that scared his own coaches and hospitalized more than a couple players on opposing teams.

Jim's football prowess only grew in college, but it wasn't until he strapped on gun and badge that he really found his natural arena. And he'd managed to walk the thinnest of lines. There had been numerous excessive force complaints, but nothing serious enough to derail his career. To his fellow officers, Jim was broadly loved and only slightly feared. Exactly the guy you wanted riding shotgun in your prowler on a domestic abuse or home invasion call.

The guy I need right now.

"Sure," Biddison said with a shake of the head. "Makes sense. I get to play commando, help your friend walk away from this and maybe take out a few deserving pieces of shit in the bargain."

"Only one, I'm guessing. But he'll be a handful."

Rusty knew what was coming next but he let Jim get there on his own.

"Ten years ago, I wouldn't think twice. You know that. Things are different for me now."

"I haven't forgotten you've got a wife and daughter back home, not to mention a pretty comfy life. If this shit's too crazy—hell, I know it is—then just walk away. Don't think I'll hold it against you. It's not your fight, anyway."

Biddison paced the floor. Rusty could feel energy vibrating within that muscled frame, but he couldn't quite read its intention. He had the feeling Jim was either going to ask for directions to Rhyolite or take the poke at Rusty's jaw he'd somehow managed to suppress all these years.

"Christ. All I wanted to do is kick back in Sin City. Blow off some steam for a few days."

"That's not an answer, Jim."

"I'll let you know when I have one."

27.

Rusty pulled the Barracuda into the fenced lot of the Public Storage Facility on Valley View Road. Along with Dr. Fred's house and the White Cross, this was the one place in town he'd really hoped to avoid visiting. Way too many memories contained in Unit 2711, but he'd need to call on some of them before tonight was over.

The storage facility's lot lay more or less deserted as early dusk took hold. Rusty had banked on that being the case. The last thing he wanted to deal with was a nosy employee or even a customer of an adjacent unit.

If pressed, how exactly would he explain his ownership of the items he'd be loading into the Barracuda's trunk—not to mention the purposes he had in mind for them tonight? Any casual witness might reasonably assume that what Rusty was transporting to his car resembled less a collection of performance devices than a small arsenal. His own identity as retired magician might seem distinctly less likely than a wild-eye militia member.

Throwing knives. Smoke pellets. Handcuffs. Blindfolds. Flash paper, cotton and rope. Those were among the more innocuous items inside the unit. And they were the first things he saw as he removed the padlock and raised the rolling door.

The knives were all housed in a beautifully crafted wooden case with a hinged glass face. Well over three dozen in total, with blades ranging from two inches to more than a foot. Throwing knives had been Rusty's stock in trade before he could afford more expensive devices to make audiences gasp at what looked like very real brushes with disaster.

Rusty figured he'd only take one blade with him into the Underworld, folded behind his belt. He couldn't decide which knife best fit his purpose after a quick scan, so he carried the whole case from the storage unit to the Barracuda's trunk. So far, no one had spotted or harassed him.

Keep going.

The next items he hauled out were even more likely to raise some eyebrows. Two heavy crates marked with stenciled warnings of DANGER: HIGH EXPLOSIVES looked real enough to give any bypassers pause. And those warnings were not only for effect. Each crate Rusty gingerly laid in the trunk and buttressed with thick rolls of bubble wrap carried enough gunpowder to bring down a small building.

He only planned on carrying maybe two small charges with him on tonight's mission, and sorely hoped deployment of neither would become a necessity. Still, he adhered to the viewpoint that it was always better to have something and not need it than to need it and not have it.

Anyway, it wasn't the gunpowder he really wanted. Rather the thick mesh netting, cables, and pulley contained within the two crates. Those rare tools were essential to his plan.

He knew smoke pellets were a no-brainer, and tossed a half dozen into the car. Figuring a pair of sterling-silver handcuffs were a good choice if restricting someone's movement became a priority, he pocketed those as well.

Back in the unit, Rusty laid eyes on an old friend. The Glock 9mm he'd used nightly for his initial closing act, a slightly revamped take on a traditional bullet catch. Unfortunately the bullet housing mechanism had jammed during a botched performance (one of the few of his whole career, other than at Ponti's house) and he'd never gotten around to fixing it. So there was no point in bringing the Glock to the Underworld.

Not a problem. It really wasn't his intention to use any loaded firearms tonight—at least not of the lethal variety. With that thought in mind, he reached for his very favorite relic in the whole unit. A propulsion gun designed by his own meticulous hand, made of solid brass and the only one of its kind in the world.

We meet again, stranger. Ready for some action?

The propulsion gun felt heavier than he remembered, its thick brass handle cool against his palm. Opening the chamber, he confirmed six darts lay waiting to be discharged. All it would take was activation of the trigger built to his precise specifications: made of pure Ivory, with a five-pound pull weight. Just right to ensure deadly accuracy.

Classifying the propulsion gun as strictly nonlethal was taking it a bit far. Fired at a human target from a distance of up to ten yards, one of the darts could cause death depending on which part of the body it pierced. Fired at point-blank range, the chances of a fatal injury grew exponentially.

Rusty didn't intend to put his hand-crafted gun to such dire work tonight, not if he could help it. But he sure as hell wanted to have the option available. Assuming his aim was still reasonably close to what it had been back at his performing peak, he could plant a dart in someone's leg or torso from a healthy distance, effecting instant incapacitation.

Of course, he didn't know what complications might arise from all that polymeric dust swimming into a target's bloodstream. Nor did the question give him pause right now. The propulsion gun was intended as a last resort. He'd only turn the barrel on someone if no other recourse presented itself.

Once all the gear was loaded, he slammed the trunk shut and glanced up with a start. An elderly man in soiled dungarees stood three parking spaces away, staring at him with an unfriendly scowl.

"Evening," Rusty said casually, walking around to the driver's side of the car.

"That's some strange cargo, mister."

The old man stepped quickly forward, his gait both aggressively inquisitive and a bit nervous. He stood right in front of the Barracuda's grill like a traffic cone not to be driven around.

"You work here?" Rusty asked.

"Night watchman," the old man said, jabbing a gnarled finger at a small badge Rusty had failed to notice on his shirt pocket. "My job to keep an eye on any kind of funny business might be going down on the premises."

"Funny business?" Rusty echoed in a pantomime of confused innocence. "Not around here?"

"Oh, yessir. You'd be surprised—I might go so far as to say shocked—to know what kind of purposes some folks think they've a right to put these storage units to. I'm talking about flat-out criminality in some cases."

"Huh. Bet you got a few tales to tell."

"Make your toes curl, some of 'em. Probably the worst was back in the summer of '09 when the bottom dropped out of the housing market. Certain people took to living in these units out of sheer desperation, for short times anyhow. You don't want to hear about some of the things we found. Few of them unfortunate souls, you might say they checked in and never checked out. Rotters. Don't take long for a body to decompose in a compressed space with a desert sun heating it. I can't even begin to think of the stench without my stomach turning."

Rusty opened the car door, hoping this would be a sufficient signal to move the man from his spot. No dice.

"Gotta tell you," the security guard continued with a cold squint. "Some of them items I saw you loading up, they made me mighty curious."

"Don't worry about me. Got some unusual hobbies, that's all."

"Hobbies, huh? Looks more like an interest in guerrilla warfare."

"Looks can be deceiving, friend."

"Not in my experience."

Rusty didn't have time for this. He got behind the wheel and started the engine. He flipped on the highbeams, bathing the security guard in eight hundred watts of sodium glow. The old bastard just narrowed his eyes a few more degrees, didn't even raise a hand to block the light.

Rusty revved the engine a couple of times, to no effect, then stuck his head out the window.

"Don't believe everything you see, old timer. Anyway, I'm closing out my lease here tomorrow. Whatever it is you think you saw ain't your problem anymore."

A pause followed, one lasting so long that Rusty found himself starting to admire the old man's salt.

Then the security guard jerked his head and spat out a fat oyster of phlegm, right over the hood. It missed by inches, hitting the dirty gravel next to the tire.

Before Rusty could say anything more, the old man turned on a heel and marched away. Gunning the engine, Rusty tore out of the parking lot with a screech, leaving plenty of rubber on the ground as a souvenir.

He glanced into the rearview mirror and was surprised to see a grim smile welded onto his face. Then again, maybe it wasn't so surprising. Felt good having all that familiar gear at his disposal once again.

Rusty banged a hard right onto Valley View Road. The night was about to get interesting.

28.

The private parking lot behind Luna's condo fell into early evening darkness. A pair of overhead sodium lamps that usually clicked on an hour before sundown were both out. That struck her as odd as she pulled her Audi to a stop. It had never happened in the year and a half she'd lived here.

One of the many perks of residing in Sinatra Cove was that most routine maintenance issues were attended to in an efficient, automatic manner. When her garbage disposal had crapped out a few months ago, a repairman showed up at Luna's door before she'd had a chance to notify the manager. Everything was connected via fiber optics across the whole twelve-acre property, and when something stopped functioning correctly the central computer snapped into action.

All of which made the darkened lamps an oddity, but Luna didn't think much of it as she opened the garage door with a clicker mounted on the Audi's sun visor. She inched the car inside and killed the engine.

Luna occupied a two-bedroom unit in the My Way complex. Her one complaint was the lack of a direct entrance from the garage, which would have made carrying in groceries a lot easier than having to walk outside and along a flagstone path to her front door. She didn't have any groceries tonight, but after two hours at the gym she was eager to get out of her sweat-soaked clothes.

A thumbprint scan opened the front door. Her condo was located in the Cove's most remote enclave, and thus considered primo real estate. Luna liked the sprawling quiet of the place, but the isolation bugged her at times. Her closest neighbors were almost half a block away, their unit shrouded by a tall stand of palms.

It wasn't that she felt unsafe. That was impossible, given the twenty-four-hour security presence that manifested itself in countless hidden cameras and armed guards patrolling the grounds in golf carts.

Despite those reassurances, Luna sometimes wished Ponti had installed her in one of the less elite units, closer to the development's more populated front end. She would have been perfectly satisfied with a one-bedroom in the Blue Eyes building right off the entrance.

But Paul wouldn't hear of it. She was something special to him, and he insisted on giving her the very best home available in his most recent high-end development. At first she'd assumed his own privacy was the motivating factor, but he'd only come to see her here a handful of times in eighteen months. He much preferred the seedy anonymity of the Honeydew Inn for their trysts, and for reasons Luna didn't want to ponder too closely. She doubted they would point to any great level of respect in the eyes of her silver-haired lover and benefactor.

She entered the marble-floored foyer and bolted the door behind her. Two handclaps induced a golden curtain of light from recessed bulbs. Her stomach was growling; she hadn't eaten anything since some egg whites for breakfast and it was now almost eight o'clock in the evening. Though desperate to strip off her gym togs and draw a hot bath, the need for food took primacy.

She was halfway across the marble floor, heading for the kitchen, when she lost her balance. The floor appeared spotless but a wide patch of tiles was slicker than if someone had spilled a bucket of olive oil on them.

Falling backwards, both arms windmilling helplessly, Luna saw the ceiling swim into view. Something was wrong. Instead of the cream-colored dome she expected to see, a large black mass hung from two thick cables. In the brief instant Luna saw it, the thing looked like a massive tarantula held aloft by twin strands of webbing.

She braced for the impact of her skull on the marble, but it didn't happen.

With a loud snap, a hydraulic pulley made the two cables go taut and the spidery net swooped down to ensnare her. Just as she was about the collide with the floor, another snap of the pulley yanked the net up. It tightened around her like a cocoon, rising until it swung back and forth five feet in the air.

Squirming in panic, too shocked to scream, Luna just barely registered the presence of another person in the foyer. She heard the thud of boots approaching and saw a tall dark shape from the corner of one eye.

"We need to talk," Rusty said, his voice calm. "First question before we get started, can I count on you to keep your cool?"

"Get me out of this thing and get the fuck out of here!" she screamed. "Do you know how dead you are?"

"Yeah, but I figure I got a few hours left. Don't worry, I'm going along with the plan. But I need some information first."

Luna said nothing, just continued to squirm against the netting.

"Don't waste your time. That mesh has a tensile strength of three hundred pounds. It used to keep a pile of cinderblocks from crushing me onstage. Great gag. I called it the Satanic Spiderweb."

Her wriggling continued, a bit less frantic.

"No chance in hell of freeing yourself," Rusty said, "but

you don't have to. I'll let you out if I feel like I can count on your cooperation."

It took several minutes of back and forth for Luna to regain sufficient composure to agree with him. He adjusted the pulley mounted to the east wall and gently lowered the net to the floor. She immediately began to claw her way out but he barked at her to lay still and let him do it. Ten seconds later she rose unsteadily to her feet, backing away toward the staircase.

"How did you get in here?" she asked in a raw voice.

"If you mean the front door, don't delude yourself into thinking a thumb scan's impenetrable. Just getting onto the property took a little effort, I'll admit. Guards at the gate made a climb over the rear berm my only option."

"And you turned off the garage lights?"

"Figured we could use some privacy. I expect someone will be coming by to repair the wire anytime now, so let's get down to cases."

"You're a goddamn fool. Don't you know about a dozen cameras have spotted you by now? Cops are on the way, believe it."

"Nah. They'd have kicked in the door an hour ago if they knew I was here."

To her surprised look, he added, "Oh yeah, I've made myself comfortable in here since about six. Didn't know when you'd be coming back, and I couldn't afford to miss you."

Luna maintained eye contact, but she was inching away from the staircase toward the front door.

"Try to bolt, I'll break your goddamn neck. Could've done that already, in case you're wondering. If I'd rigged the net at a slightly lower tension…"

He let her finish that sentence in her imagination.

"So why didn't you?"

"Because I'm not sure how deep you're involved in this shit."

"Look," she began, her tone calmer. "I don't know what they want from you. It's just a big mindfuck, as far as I can tell. Trent's got some ax to grind, whatever. I try not to get caught up in his neurosis."

"But you *are* caught up in it. I guess it's your boyfriend who makes you play along."

Luna didn't respond to that, having no clue how he might have connected her with Paul.

"I know why Ponti wants my head on a plate," Rusty continued. "Don't even blame him, but this has gotten way out of hand."

"Don't take all that Nossa Morte stuff too seriously. Trent likes to spook people. It's mainly bluff."

She could see Rusty studying her eyes to tell if she really believed those words.

Apparently not.

"A bluff, huh?" he said through gritted teeth.

His right hand snaked out to grab her wrist firmly. His other hand held up a mobile phone inches from her face.

"Look at it!"

Shuddering, Luna forced her eyes to focus on the screen. It showed the Periscope feed. Same image of Charlotte in the chair, except the bulky figure of Soren was visible again. He was pacing the floor behind his captive.

Luna gasped, and it was a sincere reaction. She started to say something but never got the chance. Rusty's free hand moved from her wrist to grip her by the throat.

"That's a good friend of mine, understand? She was following *you* before she got snatched. Still want to tell me this is all a mindfuck?"

His grip tightened. Luna's pupils went wide, her face darkening.

Rusty released her and she sank to her knees.

"I don't know anything about that," she said, still kneeling. "I've never seen that person before."

"But you know the fucker with the scars. Don't you?"

Rusty's right foot launched out in a kick. It missed Luna's ribcage by inches and smashed into a brass lamp. The lamp fell and clattered onto the floor.

She forced herself to a standing position, unsure if he'd missed her intentionally or not.

"What do you want?" she asked.

"Information, like I said. You might recall our last conversation got cut a little short. Not that it wasn't productive. You did alright, feeding me that bit about where it all began. Then Scarface shows up, right on cue."

As Luna listened to him speak in calm, precise tones, she grew increasingly convinced his surge of aggressive anger moments before had been calculated. That he'd been in full control of himself the whole time, in a sense performing to create an effect. It had worked.

"Let's talk about our mutual friend," he said.

"We don't have any mutual friends."

"Sure we do. Your boyfriend, Mr. Big. The one making all this possible. I'd like the whole story."

"I don't know the whole story. I follow orders, that's it."

"From Trent or Ponti?"

"Who do you think?"

"OK, I'll get the ball rolling. Ponti has a beef with me, that's not exactly news. Somehow he connects with Trent. I can't imagine two less similar guys, but they share one common hatred. Call it a confluence of shared interest. Ponti figures Trent knows how to bait me better than anyone. Trent knows Ponti's got the pockets to bankroll any kind of operation he dreams up, no matter how insane. I'm warm, right?

"In the meantime, Trent starts getting rid of the homeless trash that Ponti can't have fouling the part of town he's about to beautify. One corpse at a time, that problem diminishes. Word gets around that people are being lured from Cashman Park to a nasty end under the streets, maybe they figure Vegas isn't such a friendly town to camp out in. They move on to some other place. Problem starts to solve itself even quicker. Win-win."

Luna shook her head.

"I don't know about any of that. All I know is the first part. Paul wants to see you and he's using Trent to make it happen, that's true. The rest of that stuff about the homeless, I don't believe it."

Rusty smiled grimly.

"Come on, I want to show you a neat video."

"Look, I told you. I had no idea they took your friend."

"This is something different. Just so you know exactly what your playmates have been up to during this whole…what'd you call it, a mindfuck?"

She followed him into the kitchen, knowing it was futile to run. Rusty's MacBook was open on the onyx countertop. He clicked the first of the nine Nossa Morte videos and rotated the computer so she could get a clear view of the screen.

"Trent's idea of a good time, made possible by your lover."

He hit Play and opened the video window to a full-screen view. The hooded figure standing behind the table with the crescent-shaped blade swinging overhead. The young woman strapped down underneath, rendered immobile.

"I've seen this one," Luna whispered. "Couple times on the stage at Unterwelt. Good trick. Trent created it himself."

Rusty paused the video player.

"Actually, it's been around since the Renaissance. Lucretti's Deadly Pendulum. It fell out of fashion when the Grand Guignol craze died down in Paris in the '30s, which is why you don't see it performed much anymore."

Luna gave a *who-cares* roll of the eyes.

"I'm sure Trent told you it was all his. Seems he's got a little inferiority complex when it comes to magic."

"Whatever. I've seen it before. When the blade gets close to the girl's neck there's a little blast of smoke—Trent sets it off with his foot behind the table—and three parakeets come flapping out of nowhere. From the crowd's perspective it looks like they're flying out of her mouth."

"You sure about that?"

Rusty clicked the Play button.

"This wasn't shot at Unterwelt," he said quietly. "It was shot in the real underworld, and it's got a different ending."

Luna gave him a sideways glance that told him she picked up his implication and wasn't buying it. Then she turned to watch the screen.

The crescent blade was now swinging in wide arcs, faster and faster. Trent manipulated the rope with his hands, guiding its descent. It was a quicksilver blur in the grainy video window, impossible to track with the eye.

"Now," Trent proclaimed to unseen audience, "we summon the Raven to see the true power of what he unleashed. With this tribute, we call him out from hiding!"

The girl on the table either saw something in Trent's body language or picked up a note of finality in his voice. Whatever it was, it triggered a violent reaction. She attempted to sit upright on the table, her torso wriggly wildly in a futile effort to free herself from the bonds.

A voice off camera, male and husky, yelled, "Do it!"

Trent jerked the rope laterally; the blade dropped two or three feet even as it knifed through the empty air with the speed of a helicopter's rotor. The slicing of the girl's jugular happened so fast there was no way to see it on camera. Her head jerked back, eyes wide and sightless for a protracted moment before the blood came.

Someone screamed off camera, but whether in terror

or ecstasy was impossible to tell. A dozen other voices over-lapped the scream. Then came the applause, prompting a deep bow from Trent followed by a hasty disappearance behind the curtain.

The video went black.

Luna stayed hunched over the laptop, eyes boring into the screen as if to resume the footage or force out some explanation of what she'd just seen. Rusty waited for her to look up at him.

"You're going to tell me that was real?"

"You know it's real. This is what you've been a part of, for months now."

"I've never been down in the tunnels. I never really believed…"

Rusty moved the cursor to the next video clip.

"Want to see more? I could only stand about four or five till I started to get sick."

"No. Don't make me watch any more of that."

It came out as barely a whisper. Then she gave him a glance he couldn't quite read.

"You're really going down there tonight?"

The question caught Rusty off guard. He thought that maybe he'd actually been getting through to this person—that she understood the position she'd helped to put him in, wittingly or not.

Maybe she doesn't understand a goddamned thing.

"Got no choice," he answered. "But I need to go some-where else first."

"Where?"

"Cashman Park. Got some hunting to do. And you're gonna help."

29.

Jim Biddison merged into the right-hand exit lane to get off Route 374, turning onto a narrow two-lane road that led into Rhyolite. The dying sun was an orange-peach blur in the windshield. Off to his right, a series of craggy cliffs rose from the desert floor like some giant crooked staircase.

Jim downshifted to third, smiling at the purr of four hundred horses under the Infiniti's hood. He was enjoying the experience of driving a vehicle he couldn't even afford to dream about owning on his cop salary. Rusty had given him a platinum American Express card and told him to rent whatever felt right from the Hertz connection at the Sklyofts' concierge desk. Jim went with a black Q60, and after only an hour and a half of driving it he was already forming an attachment.

Not that he had the luxury of appreciating the car's novelty factor right now. Jim kept one eye on the wheel as he rolled toward Rhyolite and the other on his cell phone mounted on the dash. The EverTrac app was running on the screen, leading him with a series of directional cues toward the blinking red dot.

After leaving the MGM Grand in his newly acquired ride, Jim had driven straight back to Harrah's and spent the next several hours unsuccessfully trying to nap. A little after two o'clock, he tried calling his wife but got her voice mail. Kim was most likely at the beach with her mother and the baby.

Jim left a long, rambling message, the gist of which was he was having a good time in Vegas—but not *too* good, haha. Then he took a quick shower, dressed himself in jeans, a t-shirt, and track shoes, and drove the Infiniti to a gun shop on Industrial Road. Hell if he was going to make this mission unarmed.

The shop was called Northeast Weapons, and Jim was familiar with it. He'd made an undercover visit when last visiting Vegas for the ballistics symposium. His contact with the LV Metro Firearms Task Force had taken him along on a standard recon run to make sure the store's background check practices were up to snuff.

Everything went fine. When Jim and the plainclothes officer tried to purchase a pair of handguns without offering the proper ID, the clerk turned them down cold. Whether the guy caught a whiff of cop or was simply doing business in strict accordance with the law, Jim couldn't say for sure. He didn't particularly like how the clerk eye-fucked them during the aborted sale.

Well, that was almost five years ago and Jim didn't expect to be recognized, even if the same surly bastard was on duty today. Besides, he had all the documentation necessary to make a legal purchase. And he was more than willing to pay the added cost of an expedited background check.

A different clerk was behind the counter, and the transaction went smoothly. A few minutes past four o'clock, Jim walked out of the store with the weight of a Ruger SR40 pistol pressing against his thigh, a box of rounds in hand, and a ProMAX Premium Kevlar vest over his shirt. One of the vest's twin pockets held a nine-inch leather blackjack with a hand strap.

Jim caught himself whistling a tune as he left Northeast Weapons. Not something he did with any great regularity, and usually restricted to the shower after a particularly nice round in bed with Kim.

The truth was clear, even if he didn't like admitting it. Jim was feeling jazzed by being in possession of all this gear. He'd have to ditch it before leaving town (dismantling the Ruger's firing mechanism first), and with any luck he wouldn't need any of it. But he couldn't deny the rush of being suited up after a long boring stint of desk work back in Ocean City.

Rhyolite's low skyline came into view, highlighted by a last bloom of sunlight to the west. Jim had done some googling on this miniscule Old West ghost town, once a semipopular attraction for tourists looking for something off the beaten path. In recent years, as the number and variety of experiences available to guests in Vegas mushroomed, interest in Rhyolite had fallen off a cliff. It was, once again, a genuine ghost town.

A booth near the entrance of the parking lot was empty. From its ramshackle appearance, no one had stood inside to collect the posted five-dollar fee for quite some time. Jim backed into a spot near the parking lot's entrance, nose pointed out for a fast getaway if that proved necessary.

He stepped out of the car and surveyed all directions. Not a soul in sight.

Jim entered the town with a light tread, moving down the center of its dusty main drag. The GPS indicated Charlotte—or at least the tracking device—was located roughly a hundred yards to the northwest. That would lead Jim down the main drag for a block or so before branching off.

Empty husks of formerly thriving businesses sprouted from the sunbaked soil on both sides of the street. Bank, general store, livery. At the south end of town, a well-preserved train station overlooked rust-covered tracks barely visible through tall shoots of desert grass.

Jim kept using the phone for guidance, turning right at a small intersection leading down a narrower side street. One abandoned colossus stood at the end. From his online research

Jim knew this to be a bottle house formerly used by Adolphus Busch in the early days of his beer empire.

A piece of deadwood snapped under Jim's foot, startling him. He kept to the right of the street, using the awning of what looked like an old stable to offer as much obstruction from the bottle house as possible.

All those windows overlooking the street from the building's front face, many of them broken. No way of telling who might be clocking his progress from inside.

Or how many might be in there, for that matter. Jim had paid close attention to Rusty's description of the scarred man he'd encountered at Unterwelt. The Periscope feed seemed to show that this person had been assigned the task of guarding the hostage. And then almost certainly disposing of her, when the time came.

All clear enough, but that didn't rule out the possibility of backup. Even armed with the pistol, Jim didn't feel prepared to handle multiple attackers. His hope, dim as it rang in his mind, was to find the woman alone and exit the scene in one unimpeded swoop.

Wishful thinking perhaps, but there was no reason to rule it out entirely. The scarred man might have been summoned to the flood tunnels for Rusty's arrival. With Charlotte injured, drugged, and physically incapacitated to begin with, was it really necessary to keep an eye on her? Her chances of escaping on her own were pretty much nil. Maybe they'd decided to let her die of starvation and exposure rather than choose a more direct method of dispatch.

The front door of the bottle shop was secured with a padlock on a rusty chain. It didn't appear to have been opened in many years. Even if Jim could somehow loosen the chain—an act impossible to accomplish without making a huge amount of noise—the appearance of a thick bolt in the gap between to door and the wall proved that task would be pointless.

He circled around the right side of the building, which was obscured entirely in shadow. A row of low windows stretched along the brick flank. Any of them would do for entry, assuming Jim could achieve that without slicing himself to ribbons on all the broken glass. He cursed at having neglected to pick up a pair of thick work gloves. Thinking twice, he realized gloves would make efficient operation of the gun an impossibility.

Jim chose the third window to enter, as an overturned barrel lay on its side beneath, allowing for easy elevation. He slashed his left palm on a shard of glass and banged his right knee against the steel window frame, but hoisted himself up and through and into the warehouse.

30.

The entrance to the flood tunnels opened up beneath Las Vegas Boulevard a quarter mile south of the city limits, exactly as Trent's map indicated. Rusty pulled the Barracuda into the narrow culvert and killed the lights. The dashboard clock read 11:42 P.M. He got out into the chilled night air.

Less than fifty yards away, but elevated beyond his view, cars whooshed by in both directions. Only the low angle and the culvert's steep walls offered Rusty any sense of concealment from the road. It still seemed a wildly unlikely place to perform the task assigned him, until he reminded himself that Trent and his cohorts had done the same thing numerous times without attracting notice.

Or so I've been led to believe. And why would I doubt anything he has to say?

Rusty took a few steps down toward the tunnel's yawning mouth. A sign to the right prohibited unauthorized entry in bold letters. The sign was pockmarked with bullet holes.

A chain-link fence guarded the perimeter, its bent and bowed wires revealing a steady stream of human traffic into and out of the restricted area. Off to one side, partially concealed by a clump of chaparral, was a wheelbarrow. Again, everything matched Trent's instructions.

Rusty walked back to the car and popped the trunk. The sight inside made him almost physically sick.

He's already won. No matter what happens from here on out, look what he's made me do.

Rusty checked the zipper to make sure the bag hadn't rolled over during the drive. As gingerly as possible, he snaked one arm beneath the legs and another under the back, and unsteadily hoisted the bag over his shoulder. A hundred and ten pounds, he estimated, and every bit as unwieldy as when he'd loaded it.

That's why they call it deadweight, he mused grimly.

It sickened him to think of having transported this cargo all the way across town. As if that journey represented the worst of what would happen to the person inside the bag tonight.

Fifteen hurried footsteps carried him down to the barrow, into which he gently deposited the duffel. Tonight's tribute to Nossa Morte, served up to Trent's precise specifications. Young. Pliable. Willing. At least willing enough to get in the Barracuda and pop a pair of pills offered in Rusty's palm.

Dr. Schneider had come through for him after all. Two five-hundred-milligram tablets of hydrocodone. Just the right amount to induce blackout for a couple of hours, especially in someone so light.

Checking his watch again, Rusty figured the drugs would start wearing off within thirty to forty-five minutes.

Right on schedule. And no time to dick around out here in the open.

He hurried back to close the Barracuda's trunk and lock the doors, then back down the culvert to take the wheelbarrow in hand. He'd affixed his cell phone to his wrist with a velcro strap so he could consult the map PDF without holding it. He had the screen's brightness cranked to the highest level, which drained the battery but would allow the phone to double as a flashlight.

With a last look behind him to make sure no one was monitoring his progress, Rusty stepped into the Underworld.

It was surprisingly easy going for the first hundred yards. Rusty used the flashlight sparingly, stopping every few minutes or so to sweep the beam in front of him and determine no hazards lay in his immediate path.

The obstacles he had to move around were unchallenging: some abandoned shopping carts, a worm-eaten dresser laying on its side with empty drawers like eye sockets, several mattresses so filthy he gave them the widest berth possible as he moved past them.

The map indicated he'd reach an intersection 125 yards from the entrance. Rusty was relieved to find that accurate, giving him hope the remainder of the route would prove equally reliable. He turned left at the cross, entering a narrower tunnel that took him on a northward course.

A thin trickle of filthy water ran down the middle of the concrete path, sluicing downhill from the mountain range twenty miles outside the city. Rusty kept to the sides as much as he could. The barrow's thick tires were well-suited to handle uneven ground.

Moving faster than wisdom dictated, he almost went face-first into the muck when his right foot landed on a rat grown to a size he'd thought only native to Manhattan. The rat's screech, unnervingly like that of a startled infant, rung in his ears as he stumbled forward, barely remaining upright.

The tunnel opened up once more to the left. Rusty could hear a massive whooshing sound, the sewer system carrying untold gallons of water directly above his head toward a treatment center two miles out of town.

After another thirty yards, he detected a small reddish glow in the distance. Getting closer, Rusty could hear a low murmur of voices. He set the barrow down and approached without it.

It was a tiny encampment of the type he'd seen on news reports, back when the exodus to the flood tunnels among those recently dispossessed in the wake of the housing crash generated widespread coverage.

Three people huddled around a small gas heater. Rusty could only make out basic human shapes, no details. The largest shape stood and flicked on a high-intensity flashlight.

Rusty stopped approaching, allowing the beam to sweep over his face.

"I'm friendly," he said. "Can you maybe lower that thing a little?"

The beam stayed on his face for a brief interval before moving down to focus on his chest. Searching for any weapons, clearly.

"Nothing to share tonight," a gravelly voice said from somewhere behind the flashlight's glare. "Dinner roundup closed hours ago."

"That's OK. Just looking to make my way past, didn't want to startle anyone."

The flashlight clicked off. As his eyes adjusted to the sepulchral darkness, Rusty got a better read on the three people in front of him. The person wielding the light was a bearded man whose leathery face could have expressed an age range anywhere from late forties to early seventies. He crouched on a plastic milk crate, clad in only a pair of blue jeans and ratty high tops.

A much younger woman sat in a beach chair to his left. Standing next to her, a boy of about twelve. Behind them was a makeshift hut complete with a double bed, a chest of drawers and a bookshelf holding dozens of paperbacks.

"We try to accommodate," the bearded man said. "Code of the Underworld, help out a stranger and it'll come back on the karmic loop. But we got nothing to spare tonight and that's just the truth."

"Like I said, not looking to partake of anything you got,"

Rusty answered in the mildest voice he could muster. "I'll just be passing by."

The bearded man drilled him with a penetrating look Rusty had no problem seeing in the dim light.

"Oh, no. You ain't passing by. You're one of them."

"One of who?" Rusty asked, not liking the audibly hostile tone coming from the man.

"One of them freaks. You're going to see the…fuckin' show, whatever."

"Wait a minute…"

The man stood, his voice going hoarse. "Think we don't know what goes on? Sick, it's goddamn sick!"

"Got me wrong, pal. I'm just looking for a place to set down my load for the night. I'm no threat to you."

"Fuckin' A right you're not!"

Rusty heard a click after those words, sounding very much like a switchblade opening.

One of the bearded man's sinewy arms jerked out with the knife, pointing down the tunnel in the opposite direction from which Rusty had approached.

"Walk!" he sputtered. "Goddamn vultures is what you are. Go, and make peace with your own soul for taking part in that sickness. It'll all come back on the karmic loop, you can count on that! Fuckin' A!"

Rusty backed away slowly, hands up.

"I'm going. You won't see me again."

He retreated to reclaim the wheelbarrow and started pushing it forward as quietly as possible. He tried keeping to the opposite wall of the tunnel to avoid having the barrow spotted by the threesome.

He knew it was futile. Even from twenty feet across the murky tunnel, Rusty could feel the bearded man's recriminating gaze on him as he passed the encampment. He was grateful when the dim reddish glow was just a tiny dot in the distance behind him.

Another hundred paces and two turns took him deeper into the warren of tunnels. Rusty had never experienced such looming darkness before. It was similar and yet totally different from the darkness in which he'd become accustomed to performing at Caesars, when he'd allow himself to be locked in a steel coffin and submerged into a massive tank of water. This vast concrete abyss, emitting sounds and echoes that found his ears from all directions, felt less like a place than some monolithic entity. Breathing him into its core with each step he took.

Rusty had no choice but to use his phone as a flashlight. He was stunned to discover huge tracts of intricate graffiti art on the walls. Some stretched for what must have been entire city blocks. The quality ran from crude tagging to some exquisite murals depicting the hellish existence of the Underworld in strokes that brought Hieronymus Bosch to Rusty's mind. He thought he discerned the words "nossa morte" scrawled into some of the more grotesque tableaux but didn't pause long enough to confirm it.

He was getting closer. He could feel it, even without consulting the digital map for more guidance on when to make the next turn. A malignant funk hung in the low, compressed air, much stronger than in the stretches of tunnels closer to the entrance. Rusty guessed himself to be somewhere more or less under the midpoint of the Strip, though it was impossible to know. With a flash of morbid humor, he considered the irony of finding Trent directly beneath the Palace Tower at Caesars.

Maybe it was destined to end down here. Maybe I just never knew how far I could fall. And who's to say this isn't where the Raven belonged from the start?

He saw an opening in the near distance. The tunnel widened until it was a boxy, contained space, roughly fifty feet in diameter. Rusty guessed it had formerly been used to store clearance utilities during the construction of the flood tunnels. And he had to admit, it served fairly well as a performance area.

He pushed the wheelbarrow deeper into the space, passing two rows of benches. They faced a stage elevated several feet above the ground. Rusty recognized the layout from the videos on the Tor browser.

A trace of movement in the darkness caught his eye, followed by a scuffle of feet.

"Come on out, Trent. No point hiding now, is there?"

From the darkness, somewhere behind him:

"You're punctual, Raven. That's good. Seems you decided to take this seriously."

A silent beat, then Rusty was blinded by an overhead spotlight. It shone down from behind the stage, sending a thousand lumens into his retinas. He covered his face with one hand, lowering it when the light panned across the stage. It came to a stop directly on a long narrow table covered with a black velvet sheet. To the table's left was a video camera on a tripod. On the opposite side, a twenty-inch monitor similarly mounted next to a second camera. At the back of the stage was a work bench holding various tools.

Trent emerged onto the stage from a set of stairs Rusty couldn't see. He looked down on Rusty from within the folds of his cloak, cowl pulled loosely over his head.

How the hell did he get in front of me so fast?

"The master bows at the foot of the student," Trent uttered. "A cliche, but accurate."

Rusty grabbed the handle of the wheelbarrow and pushed it toward the stage.

"I'd rather not spend any more time here than necessary. Let's get this going."

"No, no. Your total cooperation is what's on tap tonight. Don't try to set the pace."

Trent turned the monitor on. Rusty flinched at seeing the

same image that had scarred his mind for the past twenty-four hours. Charlotte, still gagged and tied to the chair in that filthy room. She was awake, twisting weakly against the binds. The digital clock ran the current time.

"That's live, not a recording. And it's a two-way feed, through the second camera. My associate is watching us right now, believe it."

"I get the picture, Trent. I do your fucking trick, give you the satisfaction of watching me descend to your sick level. Then you let her go, right?"

Rusty parked the wheelbarrow at the foot of the stage.

"Excellent," Trent said. "Come a long way from the old days, haven't we?"

"Yeah, you've really flipped the power dynamic. Hope it compensates for all those lonely nights trying to get my attention for five seconds. Christ, I had twelve-year-old girls sending me love letters nowhere near as needy as you."

"Insults won't generate the reaction you're looking for, Raven. I won't be goaded. You've lost, isn't that clear?"

Trent glanced down at the wheelbarrow and gave an approving nod.

"Looks like you followed my advice about sedation. Soren only had to use that tactic one or twice. Most of them were all too willing to come here on their own two feet."

"It should be wearing off any time. All the more reason to get moving."

"I told you, don't try to set the pace! That's not how this works."

Trent jumped off the stage, dropping and landing with a lightness of footing Rusty had to admire.

"I'll need to frisk you, of course. You won't resist because you know exactly what resistance will buy you."

"Knock yourself out."

Rusty held both hands above his head. He'd anticipated this step.

Trent performed a thorough pat-down. He removed the throwing knives and the handcuffs, tossing them onto the stage with a shake of the head.

"Enjoying this, aren't you?" Rusty said. "Probably dreamt about it for years."

Trent started to reply but stopped when his hands reached the small of Rusty's back. He pulled out the brass propulsion gun and gave an appreciative whistle.

"Well, look at this. Quite a relic. Designed it yourself, if memory serves."

"That's right. You're holding both the prototype and the only working model."

Trent ran a finger over the brass barrel and the razor-sharp tip of a four-inch dart loaded in the chamber.

"This is primo, Raven. I really appreciate you bringing it tonight. Can't imagine what you thought you'd do with it."

"Force of habit," Rusty said with a shrug. "I never like to leave the house unarmed."

He realized the smile on his face was probably too broad and killed it. It wouldn't do to communicate his pleasure over the fact that Trent had failed to properly pat down the hidden pocket in his jeans.

"You put this to strong effect onstage," Trent said, still admiring the gun. "Interesting hybrid. Part bullet catch, part vanishing gag, right?"

Rusty nodded, warily impressed as he'd always been with the intensity of Trent's focus on his work.

"Shot it at one of your assistants, point blank. Great tension; it always got some gasps from the rubes when you aimed this thing right at her face."

Mimicking the words he'd just spoken, Trent lifted the gun and pointed it at Rusty.

"I never figured out the timing of it, not exactly. You pulled the trigger and a cloud of polymeric dust came flying out in a dozen different colors. Took maybe three seconds to dissipate. When the dust cleared, your bimbo assistant was nowhere in sight and the dart was buried two inches into the plywood set. Right where her head was, just seconds before."

Rusty swallowed dryly as Trent trained the gun on his left eye.

"Do you think we could pull it off tonight? I doubt it."

Rusty saw Trent's finger tighten on the trigger. Could almost feel the pressure of the dart's tip against his pupil.

Trent jerked the gun three inches to the left and fired it. Rusty's eyes filled with noxious dust and his ear sang in pain as the dart flew past, opening a hole above the lobe and taking a small chunk of flesh with it.

Gasping for breath in the clouded air, he rubbed his eyes furiously. The dust was only an irritant and not toxic, but it stung like a bitch. He used his other hand to staunch the bloodflow from his wounded ear.

Trent laughed and carried the gun to the work bench, along with the knives and handcuffs.

"You really have lost your nerve. Thought I'd do it, didn't you?"

"Where would I get an idea like that?" Rusty said, his voice chalky.

"Don't you know I need you alive for tonight to be any fun? Speaking of which, time's wasting. Bring your cargo up and lay it on the table. Face up, but don't unzip it yet."

"Want to give me a hand?" Rusty asked.

"You can manage."

Rusty walked to the wheelbarrow and hoisted the duffel over his shoulder. He mounted the stage and laid it down as gingerly as possible. The bag stirred slightly and a meek human sound came from within.

"Wearing off like I said," Rusty uttered. "It's been two hours so she ought to be fully conscious any minute."

"Perfect timing. We're just about ready to start."

"No audience?"

"Not tonight. Don't worry, the camera will capture it for posterity."

"So what's the gag?"

"One of my favorites, a timeless classic. Torn and Restored."

"Not very imaginative, Trent. Straight off the shelf."

"My twist on it is unique. I remember the first time I saw you pull this gag, out on Fremont. This was long before you got signed at Caesars. You pulled off the best Torn and Restored gag I ever saw. Took a whole fistful of cash from some tourist, marked the corner of each bill with a red Sharpie and proceeded to tear them into little pieces. Not just the usual cross-tear and fold job, I mean you *shredded* those bills. Tossed them into the air like confetti, I thought that cow was going to faint and her husband looked ready to lay you out. Then you asked her to reach in your hip pocket—hubby didn't like that either—but she did it and lo and behold. She pulled out all those marked bills, every one of them in perfect condition. It was impressive, Raven. That's when I knew you were the one, and this was before I saw you doing the really crazy shit. Like driving that bike through the plate glass window and disappearing in a cloud of red smoke."

"Jesus, Trent. You couldn't have been more than…"

"A child. Exactly."

"That's why you hate them?" Rusty asked, jerking a thumb toward the shrouded body on the table.

Trent shrugged mildly.

"I'm grateful to them. They serve their purpose well enough."

"So what are we waiting for?"

"I wasn't entirely truthful when I said there would be no

audience. This is actually a command performance, for one set of eyes only. Our benefactor insists on seeing it live. What he has in mind once we're done, I wouldn't want to guess."

At those words, Rusty heard footsteps coming from the darkness beyond the last row of seats. The heavy tread announced itself clearly, and it was with relief that he saw Paul Ponti step into the light near the foot of the stage. No matter what happened from here on out, he'd achieved his main objective by using intuition and a gut sense of how this was supposed to play out.

Bingo. Two in the barrel.

"There he is," Ponti rumbled. "The great disappearing act, back in town. In the sewer where you belong."

"Hello, Paul. Been wondering when you and I might get a little face time."

31.

The dank mustiness of the room penetrated Jim's lungs with each cautious inhalation. He stood utterly still, waiting for his eyes to adjust to the dim light coming in through the window. It smelled like something had died in here and decomposed long ago. He wanted to get out of this goddamned building as soon as humanly possible.

Stepping onto a cement floor covered with dust and glittery debris, Jim took care to move at a measured pace and keep his pulse at a manageable rate. He could just barely make out his immediate surroundings. A small room, fifteen feet square, each wall covered with empty shelves. At his feet sprawled a small beach of shattered glass, the remnants of hundreds of bottles once lining the shelves. One narrow door led to a deeper darkness.

Jim checked his phone. The map showed the red dot to be located less than a hundred feet from him. He dimmed the screen and kept the phone in his hand as he gingerly advanced across the broken glass toward the door.

In the hallway he turned left. Sixteen paces brought him to the entrance of a massive front room. Most likely the main bottling area during the old productive days.

Following the dot to the room's far side, he found himself at the head of a wide stairway leading down to the subterranean level. He descended slowly, counting all twenty stairs on the way down.

A faint glow came from down the hallway to the left. Jim felt his heart start to jackhammer. The adrenaline was flowing and nothing would stop it. He'd felt this way many times as a cop, before career advancement took him off the streets. All those hot emergency calls. Biddison thrived on the high preceding the action, and he was juicing hard now even as a sense of impending danger swelled up in the darkness around him.

He approached the glow slowly. It gained in intensity as he moved closer, coming from an open doorway. Jim flattened himself against the wall and put the phone in his pocket. He withdrew the Ruger from his parka and switched off the manual safety. With one last fortifying breath, he raised the gun and swung around into the doorway.

The image greeting his eyes was a life-sized version of what he'd seen on the Periscope feed. A small, cramped room, most likely used as a storage area when the bottling company was still active. One bare bulb hung from the ceiling, emitting a sickly greenish light at a hundred watts. Perched on a tripod was a video camera, pointed toward the center of the room. Above and behind it, a twenty-inch monitor showed a low-resolution and heavily pixilated image: a hooded figure standing behind a table in a darkened area.

Jim didn't bother looking at the monitor for more than a second. All his attention was on the center of the room, where a woman was bound to a heavy wooden chair.

From Jim's vantage point, it was impossible to tell if he was looking at someone alive or dead. His initial impression leaned toward the latter option. Charlotte's head was not slumped forward as he'd seen before, but jerked over the back of the chair. Her long graying tresses trailed down like some kind of burial shroud. Even a quick glance revealed the great amount of abuse her wracked frame had endured before or after being transported to this room.

Jim's stomach tightened with a sickened sense of outrage that had nothing to do with the fact that this person was close to a friend of his. He stepped into the room, almost afraid to lay a hand on her shoulder.

His first touch invoked no response. He shook her as gently as he could muster. A groan came forth and Jim emitted a small prayer of thanks. Using his free hand, he lifted her head to a neutral position. He was gratified to see she possessed enough strength to keep it upright, blinking at him in misty confusion.

"Charlotte. My name is Jim Biddison. I'm a friend of Rusty's. I'm taking you out of here."

More blinking, followed by a small nod of the head that may or may not have been voluntary. No use trying to get her to speak until they were safely away.

Jim kneeled down and examined the binds keeping her legs affixed to the chair legs. Nothing but some quarter-inch nylon rope, carelessly tied. The same binds kept her wrists secured behind the chair's back.

He inserted the gun into a vest pocket and started working at the rope around her ankles. He leaned close to whisper in her hear.

"Charlotte. Stay with me, OK? We're out of here in no time, and I'm taking you straight to the hospital. Get you all fixed up, alright?"

He couldn't tell if the noise that followed was a response to his voice or simply an expression of pain.

Jim kept working on the leg ties. The knots were loose but thick, slowing his progress.

"I'm carrying you out, so you don't need to worry about moving. You don't have to say anything either. I'll just keep talking so you know I'm here."

He loosened the rope from the chair's legs. Only another minute was needed to untie her wrists.

Jim repositioned himself and tried one more time to get her to focus on his face. Understanding that she was in safe hands might be critical to maintaining whatever strength was left within her.

"Look at me, Charlotte. I'm Rusty's friend. This is all over, understand?"

For a brief moment, Jim thought he detected a glimmer of comprehension in her eyes. A small hint that indicated a response from her beyond simple oblivion.

Only at the last second did Jim realize she was trying to warn him, and by then it was too late. He barely registered the impact of the lead pipe against the back of his skull.

32.

The first thing that struck Rusty as Ponti approached the stage was the man's size. Though a solid six feet with a barrel chest for ballast, he didn't loom nearly as large in the flesh as he did in Rusty's imagination. He was really quite average looking.

Funny, the way the mind can fuck with you.

Rusty studied Ponti closely as he climbed the small set of stairs onto the stage. It was disorienting. Over the past three years, whenever he'd lost control and allowed himself to wallow in mentally recreating that awful night at Ponti's house, it was usually the daughter who claimed the majority of his attention. Seeing her down there on the tile next to the pool, blood seeping through fingers covering her face.

But as clear as Paula remained in his mind, he'd held onto a vivid recollection of her father as well. Beholding him now, not nearly the giant of his haunted memories, Rusty wondered what other tricks his mind had been playing on him all this time.

The man's voice, however, was exactly as he recalled. Cigars and cognac poured over a cracked glass.

"I'll say this much, Diamond. Some things are worth waiting for."

"That's kind of you, Paul. I have to tip my hat. You've gone to some pretty impressive lengths to bring me down here. I'm just surprised a man of your stature would set foot in such a vile place."

"Where better to dispose of a hunk of trash? Didn't think I'd be inviting you back to the house, did you?"

"Speaking of that, how's your pup?"

Ponti didn't have a reply, thrown off guard.

"Hope I didn't injure his eye too badly," Rusty continued. "Dumb brute was just doing what you trained him to do. I don't hold a grudge for giving my leg a taste."

Ponti's look of surprise quickly faded.

"Should've figured. Most guys, they'd know better than to come back to the scene of their misdeeds. But not you."

Rusty stepped closer, sensing the more he could needle this man the better his odds of rerouting the course of events to follow.

"I was just hoping to get a look at her, Paul. Figured she might still be living there, keeping those family ties nice and tight."

Ponti's large frame shuddered slightly. Another nudge or two and he would explode, creating the kind of chaos that was Rusty's only possibility for changing the odds here.

Trent stepped around the table, inserting himself between the two men.

"Don't let him rattle you, Paul. This thing's been scripted down to the last detail, remember?"

Ponti just shrugged and glanced at the table. The bulge of a shoulder holster was brazenly visible beneath his jacket.

Another slight movement came from within the duffel bag. Along with the murmur of someone emerging from deep sleep.

"I think," Rusty said, "that's our cue."

"I concur, Raven. You're going to love this."

Trent walked over to the work bench and picked up a sheathed sword, three feet in length. He removed the sheath with one hand while the other clutched the gilded hilt. The blade gleamed in the dark light, tip raised upward.

"A suitable tool for the task at hand, I think you'll agree? It's a perfect replica of Houdini's famed bow cutter. I had it handcrafted at the Gallerie Versailles."

Rusty whistled.

"Looks expensive. You pay for that too, Paul?"

Ponti ignored him and glanced up, noticing the video camera.

"That fucking thing running?"

"Don't worry," Trent replied. "I won't turn it on till we get underway. You'll be well out of frame by then."

"No fucking cameras, period."

Trent raised a hand as if ready to argue, but said nothing.

"Christ," Ponti growled, his patience crumbling. "Just get this shit over with."

One more needle.

"To be honest," Rusty said to him in a low conspiratorial tone, "I didn't learn till just yesterday she'd shut you out of her life completely. Won't have a damn thing to do with her own father, I'm told. Smart girl."

It was hard to be sure, but Rusty could swear some of the color drained from the other man's face at those words. Only to come roaring back as rage overtook remorse, inflamed capillaries filling his cheeks.

Ponti's left hand twitched. Rusty knew he was forcing himself not to reach for the shoulder holster.

"You fucking son of a bitch. Think I'm not happy to waste you right here and now? I don't need all this weird crap Trent's got in mind. Just been humoring him 'cause he seems to have a good read on how you operate."

Trent again stepped around the performance table, his gait agitated. He was careful to keep the sword down by his side.

"Don't let him goad you, Paul!"

Rusty and Ponti held their ground for a moment, then Rusty turned and walked over to the table.

"Paul," Trent said quietly. "Why don't you take a seat in the front row? I'll walk our star through his paces."

"Don't fucking tell me to sit or stand or any goddamn thing. I waited a long time to lay eyes on this piece of shit and I'll do as I please."

"I only ask for a few minutes. You can have it out or do whatever after I'm done with him."

"That so, Trent? You're really gonna hand him over to me just like that? Coulda swore you had some trick up your psycho sleeve, won't allow yourself to be denied the satisfaction."

"Jesus," Rusty said. "You two want some privacy to hash this out? I can come back."

"Shut the fuck up, Diamond!"

Ponti visibly forced a measure of calm on himself. He backed away from the table a few paces.

"Fine, kid. A deal's a deal. Do what you gotta do to get this out of your system, but make it quick. Then he's mine."

Trent gave a small nod of his hooded head.

"Thank you, Paul."

Turning to Rusty, he continued, "Torn and Restored is, as you mentioned, a staple of the illusionist's handbook. But the trick, the *lie*, is only pretending to sever the item before magically revealing it to be whole. Tonight, you're going to make a tear that can't be restored."

He started to hand Rusty the sword but paused.

"And remember, if you get any smart ideas about maybe running this through *my* gut…"

He pointed the tip of the sword to the monitor showing the Periscope feed. Then he rotated the sword so that Rusty could grab it by the hilt.

A more vigorous movement came from the duffel bag, and a louder sound of awakening.

"Everything's happening right on schedule," Rusty said, reaching for the zipper of the duffel. "No fun pulling this kind of gag if the participant can't feel it happen, right?"

From opposite sides of the table, Trent and Ponti stepped closer. Rusty saw a wary disbelief in Ponti's eyes. Like he wasn't quite prepared to witness something he'd known about, but only as an abstraction. That real blood was about to spill from a total stranger, for no reason at all.

Rusty grabbed the zipper and yanked it down. He could sense Trent recoiling even as his hands parted the flaps to reveal the person inside.

"Wake up, Luna. Time for the show."

33.

Jim's face collided with the floor, his left cheek taking the brunt of the impact. It was jarring enough to jolt him from the brief unconscious state the three-foot pipe in Soren's hand had put him into. A moving shadow on the floor telegraphed the next swing, coming down in an arc like an executioner's ax.

Jim rolled over to the left. The pipe's end smashed into the cement where his cheek had lain a half second before.

Looming over him, Soren hefted the pipe for a third swing. Jim's left leg jerked up in a reflexive motion. The heel of his track shoe landed in Soren's groin. It struck hard enough to send the pipe's downward curve askew, but not hard enough to delay the next attack by more than a moment.

Pushing with both feet, Jim scrambled backward across a grimy puddle to buy himself some breathing room. He lurched upright, using the wall behind him for support. His right hand dug into the Kevlar vest, finding the Ruger's grip. It was out of the pocket in less than a breath, his arm rising to train the muzzle on Soren's chest even as his thumb flipped off the safety.

Too slow. The pipe flew at him in an overhead swing, knocking the gun loose. Jim heard it clatter across the floor and blocked another blow with his left forearm. The pipe struck the fleshy side rather than the bone, causing significantly less pain but still stunning him.

Jim spun around. He braced himself against the sink, eyes

darting frantically for something to use as either weapon or shield. Nothing presented itself. Soren swung again and Jim barely managed to duck. The pipe smashed into a mirror over the sink, sending a starburst of broken shards onto the floor.

Jim was now totally winded, and cornered. Nowhere to run, his only option was to launch himself in a forward attack before the next strike came. He aimed for the big man's knees, a flash of memory from his linebacker days roaring into his mind.

Still not fast enough. Bulldozer Biddison had lost too many years and packed on too many pounds to catch a younger assailant off guard. Soren saw what he was doing and swung again, this time at a lateral angle like a batter in the box.

The pipe smashed into Jim's outstretched left hand, shattering a dozen small bones. He howled and retracted the hand toward his body. His fingers were immobile, feeling like they were attached by threads.

Soren buried a kick in Jim's ribcage, doubling him over. The floor rose to meet him again as consciousness flickered in and out.

Through a filmy curtain he saw Charlotte writhing in her chair. Rocking it back and forth on its wooden legs.

Soren kneeled down and pressed the circular end of the lead pipe against Jim's throat.

"Diamond really wants this bitch to die, huh? He must not value your life much either."

Soren dug his free hand into Jim's vest, looking for another weapon. He pulled out the blackjack and chucked it across the room. Checking Jim's pants pockets, he came up empty.

"Not that I give a fuck about your name. Just curious who's stupid enough to show up here."

"James Biddison, Lieutenant with the Ocean City Police Department." The words came out with a coppery taste, and Jim realized his mouth was bleeding heavily. "There's a Clark

County Sheriff's task force outside. They'll be through the door in about thirty seconds, so do what you're gonna do."

"Nah. Diamond's not that stupid. Maybe he figured one suicidal moron might come in here and mix up the odds, but he wouldn't risk calling the cops."

He pointed to the monitor. The image had changed somewhat since Jim had entered the basement. The hooded figure was now standing at a different position on the stage, facing two other men with their backs to the camera. Jim recognized Rusty on the left, engaged in what looked like a tense exchange with a burly silver-haired man in a designer suit. Between them, a sliver of what looked like a slim female body was stretched out on the table.

"Want to watch the show?" Soren said. "See the Raven do what he never had the balls to do onstage? None of that rubber-knife bullshit tonight."

Jim stared at the monitor, then made a quick visual sweep of the floor. Where the fuck did the Ruger land?

A kick to the solar plexus halted his scan.

"Ocean City, huh? Must be one of Diamond's fuckhead friends. Long way from home now, asshole."

"Eat shit," Jim growled, wishing he could come up with something a little more original even as his eyes swept the floor again.

There. In the corner to his right, hidden in shadow beneath a blocky work table. The pistol's barrel was pointed right at him. Eight feet away, maybe ten. Jim estimated he'd need at least three full seconds to get a handle on it.

"That's a two-way feed," Soren muttered with a yawn, "in case you're wondering. They're a little too busy to check out our progress here, but as soon as it's done Diamond will have the pleasure of watching me kill *two* of his friends before Ponti puts a bullet in his head."

Jim's eyes flicked over to Charlotte. She was tipping the chair backward as far as she could, using her toes for traction.

Soren noticed Jim's averted gaze and jerked his head around just as Charlotte lifted her feet from the floor. The chair rocked forward, her body weight providing enough momentum for it to tip over.

It fell straight forward, toward Soren. He reached out with one hand and grabbed her before the chair could crash to the floor.

"Got some spunk, I'll give you that."

Soren shoved her backward and released his grip. The chair tilted over in the opposite direction, hard enough for the legs to get airborne before it splintered against the floor. Charlotte released a brief wail and lay still.

Jim gave a silent prayer of thanks for Charlotte's courage and moved. The distraction she'd created gave him the window he needed. He reached for a narrow shard of glass from the broken mirror, fingers clenching the wide end hard enough to draw blood. He heaved his arm forward, driving the tip deep into the back of Soren's thigh.

Soren bellowed, more surprised than hurt. He swung a reflexive elbow at Jim's head, but it was a glancing blow that only succeeded in moving Jim closer to his objective. The gun now lay less than five feet away.

Jim scrambled for it crablike across the pockmarked floor.

Soren yanked the embedded shard from his leg and hurled it away. He dove onto Jim's back with all his body weight, driving a fist into the base of his neck. Jim saw stars but his right arm sprang forward on sheer survival impulse.

His fingers grazed the barrel of the gun, but couldn't find purchase before Soren snaked an arm around his throat. He tightened the chokehold, screaming incoherently into Jim's ear.

Vision fading as consciousness started to leave him, Jim felt his outstretched right arm start to go numb. He heard a sound, weak and tinny as if transmitted through an old AM radio. It was a wail of pure animal pain. Jim could just barely discern its source through one blood-clotted eye.

Charlotte was lifting herself from the floor, using her shattered knees. Hurtling forward, she fell onto Soren's back and reached around to claw his face. Soren kept his chokehold in place while he swiveled around to shove her away. As she reeled back, a stray fingernail scraped across his eye. The pain caused Soren to loosen his hold on Jim by a tiny degree.

It made all the difference.

The momentary release allowed Jim to inch forward and grab the Ruger. Everything after that seemed to happen in strobing slow motion. Jim watched his fingers close on the barrel and pull it to his chest. With dreamlike ease he rotated the gun to grip it properly.

Soren was pressing one hand over his wounded eye as Jim rolled onto his back. The gun rose until the muzzle wavered in the air three inches from Soren's scarred left cheek.

Jim pulled the trigger. Barely saw a cloud of blood droplets emerge from the hole in his attacker's face. He kept pulling it till the chamber was empty and the dead man's body slumped down on him.

34.

"What the fuck…"

The words came from Ponti's lips as a strangled whisper.

The three men stood frozen for a moment around the performance table, gazing down at Luna as she emerged slowly from her drugged stupor.

Rusty turned to Trent with a broad smile.

"Just like you said, Trent. Piece of cake getting into her pad."

He rotated toward Ponti.

"You really need to beef up security at Sinatra Cove. I barely broke a sweat getting over the rear berm. And those thumbprint scanners are so overrated."

"What the fuck," Paul Ponti repeated, taking a half-staggered step toward the performance table. His glare rose from Luna to Trent.

"Another one of your sick gags? You two in this shit *together*?"

Trent raised both of his hands.

"Paul…no! This isn't…I had no idea."

"Fuck off. You really think I was gonna cut you in on my property?"

Ponti shoved Trent out of the way. He bent forward, laying a palm on Luna's chest.

"Don't worry," Rusty said. "She'll be right as rain in a

minute or two. Of course, by the time we're done she'll wish like hell I'd given her a lethal dose. Much easier way out than what Trent's got planned."

Trent spun around and lunged for the sword. Rusty pulled back a fraction of a second too late. Trent's thick gloves allowed him to grab the sharp end without slicing his hands open. He yanked with all his body's strength and pulled it free.

"I'll give you this much, Raven. You haven't lost the capacity for surprise, but you're still too slow!"

A small gasp came from Luna. One eyelid fluttered open, then the other. Rusty was reminded of the first time he'd seen her, tending bar at Unterwelt.

Ponti cradled Luna's head in his hands, lifting her from the table.

"Talk to me, baby. It's Paul. You're OK."

"Not for long," Rusty said. "Right, Trent? You doing the honors or me?"

Luna sputtered a few incoherent words in a dull voice. With Ponti's help, she dragged her legs off the table. She stood, a bit wobbly. He guided her across the stage and sat her down on the work bench.

"Don't try to stand, just relax. I'm taking you out of here."

Ponti opened his jacket and pulled a snub-nose .38 revolver from the shoulder holster.

"But first, this motherfucker dies."

"Don't get sore at me," Rusty said. "I know we got our beef from the old days, but this is all your boy's work. Gotta be careful who you partner up with. I figured with your experience, you'd know that."

As he spoke Rusty slid one hand into his hidden pants pocket, fingers closing around the smoke pellet that Trent's frisk didn't catch.

The revolver's muzzle tracked an upward arc until it drew a bead on Rusty's chest.

Rusty saw the motion, all of it happening in a simple flow. But the corner of one eye remained glued on Trent, who was running in a direct line toward the open space separating him from Ponti.

Rusty threw the pellet at the stage as hard as he could. It exploded in a plume of gray smoke, instantly obscuring his vision even as he dropped to the floor.

He took himself down hard. Not with any hope of escaping the first bullet to roar from Ponti's gun, but to buy Trent an additional half second to close the gap.

Ponti lowered the .38, following Rusty's descent.

"He's mine!" Trent shrieked, charging through the smoke with the sword gripped aloft.

Landing on his knees and rolling sideways, Rusty never saw the tip of Trent's sword pierce the big man's torso at the precise moment Ponti's finger closed on the trigger. An agonized scream was overwhelmed by the gun's report.

The impact jarred Ponti just enough to send his gun arm askew several inches. Even as Rusty hit the deck, he felt the bullet hum past his head with barely three inches to spare. His knees' impact with the stage shook him with greater force than he'd anticipated, and he failed to cushion the blow by rolling smoothly to one side.

Luna saw it all happen and her scream matched Ponti's.

Trent crouched and used all his leg strength to push the sword in deeper. It passed beneath Ponti's ribcage and entered his stomach. The revolver clattered to the floor as both Ponti's hands clutched the seeping red mass of his abdomen. He let out a final groan and all life left him.

The smoke plume was quickly clearing. Luna screamed again at the sight of her gutted lover.

Rusty scrambled to his feet. He'd intended to roll toward the table where the propulsion gun lay. Instead, his clumsy landing left him at least five paces away from putting it within arm's reach. Way too much time for Trent to get there first.

"No chance, Raven!"

Trent withdrew the sword from Ponti's body with a grunt of effort.

Rusty dove for the bench. His shoulder collided with a leg of the performance table, making it wobble. It rolled sideways, hitting the stand supporting the monitor. The monitor toppled over, screen smashing on the ground.

Losing his balance, Rusty knocked into the work bench, upsetting its contents. The propulsion gun skittered away from him, falling from the bench to the floor.

Trent bounded across the stage with one wild leap, clutching the sword like a war chief. He swung it down hard toward the base of Rusty's neck.

Rusty heard the propulsion gun's report just before he saw the cloud of polymeric dust blossom before his vision. The tip of the sword came slicing down through the air above him, but it was propelled by gravity alone. It missed him by a foot and fell to the floor.

Trent was already backpedaling toward the edge of the stage, his left eye blinded by the dart Luna had fired.

Both hands stretched outright, he rotated 180 degrees as his feet lost contact with the stage. Falling to the ground below, the impact drove the dart deeper into his orbital cavity. He never made a sound.

Rusty lay there, knees on fire, eyes misting in the hailstorm of multicolored dust raining down on him. He pushed himself to a seated position with one arm, using the table for support as he rose to stand.

Luna stood behind the work bench, both hands still gripping the propulsion gun.

She whirled on Rusty and aimed the brass barrel directly at his face.

"It's empty," he said. "One shot only."

He had no way of knowing if she recognized that as a total lie. Four more darts still lay in the chamber.

"You…" she said weakly. "This is all because of you…"

"Give me the gun, Luna. It's over. Nothing else is gonna happen."

Luna lifted this gun slightly as he drew closer, keeping it trained on his face.

"It's over. All of it. No one else is gonna die down here, thanks to you."

The eyelid twitching Rusty had first noticed at Unterwelt was back at full steam, both sides of her face vibrating like someone in the grips of an epileptic fit. He had the impression it might last for a long time, maybe never go away fully after what she'd seen and done tonight.

"Let me have it," he said, hand extended to accept the gun.

Staring numbly at him, her eyes flicked away to some darkened corner. Rusty saw an opportunity to forcefully go after the gun but that wasn't what he wanted to do.

"It really is over, I promise."

He stepped toward her slowly, hand still out. Luna unclenched her fingers from the brass grip and he quickly liberated it from her. He knew there was something else he should say but for the life of him he couldn't find the words. So he just reached for her hand and started leading her out of the Underworld.

35.

Sunlight poured through the window of Charlotte's hospital room, casting its drab features in a warm midmorning glow. Even with the blinds down, it was too bright for Rusty's weary eyes. The prospect of never seeing another dawn in the Mojave Desert cheered him, but not enough to make him smile.

He was grateful for a lot right now—simply being alive topped the list.

The black-haired nurse muttered with frustration and plucked an unlit cigarette from Charlotte's lips. Rusty could tell by her body language this was not the first time the nurse had performed this task. Charlotte grumbled like a bear in a cage too small.

Rusty had steeled himself before entering the room several minutes ago. Jim Biddison gave him a full briefing of her condition over the phone early this morning. He'd driven Charlotte to Valley Hospital Medical Center straight from Rhyolite, and waited until almost dawn to get a prognosis from the attending physician.

The good news was that no threat to Charlotte's immediate health presented itself in the face of her injuries. In other words, she'd live. There was no other good news. The damage she'd suffered would likely take months to heal, and partial recovery was expected in the most badly impacted areas. Both kneecaps, already brittle from the osteoarthritis, had been shattered to a degree that required the insertion of metal replacements. This procedure offered some small silver lining, as the implants would prove more durable than what she'd been working with lately, and such an operation would have been unavoidable in the long term anyway.

Beyond that, the grim toll continued. Two cracked ribs. A contused clavicle. Left orbital impacted with enough severity to require surgery and more corrective procedures to come. One tooth gone.

So Rusty knew of the damage before he stepped into the room. He'd noticed, with a swell of affection, the unusually gentle timbre in Jim's voice as he cataloged her injuries over the phone. Nothing came as a surprise, but the sight of Charlotte in that bed was enough to mist Rusty's eyes in a way he prayed wasn't noticeable.

He waited as the nurse replaced a bedpan and huffed out of the room with the snatched cigarette.

"Asinine, isn't it?" Charlotte finally rasped, the words coming out with a slight whistle through the gap between her teeth.

"What's that?" Rusty dragged a chair close to the bedside.

"An unlit tobacco product, perfectly harmless to any and all, verboten by hospital policy. Not for the health effect, but to protect any innocent children who might happen to pass by outside and glance at this fractured crone. The one thing that might offer me a little relief, snatched away by the PC brigade."

"How bad's the pain?" Rusty winced at the stupidity of the question.

Charlotte noticed his grimace and reached out to pat his arm. The effort clearly caused some discomfort.

"With all these pharmaceutical goodies in me, I'll manage. It's the fucking rehab I'm not looking forward to."

"Charlotte, I—"

"Knock it off. You told me to stay away from any field

work. Warned me in big neon letters. I chose to do it, for my own enjoyment as much as anything else."

"Yeah, but if I hadn't come out here, brought you in from the start—"

"I said can it, Rusty," she said firmly. "There's a whole lot of different emotions I can handle from you, but maudlin ain't on the list. It's done, and I'd do it all again the same way if I had the chance."

After a pause, she added, "I might be a little more vigilant about watching my rearview next time."

One hand reached for a phantom cigarette, moving on autopilot. Charlotte caught herself and laughed, bringing a small smile to Rusty's face.

"Christ, look what a good trained seal I am. Maybe this little stitch up is just the catalyst I needed to put the coffin nails away for good."

"That would make me happy."

"Sure it would. You wouldn't have to feel quite so guilty if something positive came out of this whole fucking mess."

They let a silence pass, looking neither at each other or away.

"I hope you realize," Rusty began, "I'm covering every medical expense all the way through rehab, and any refurbishments that you may need around the house."

"You say that like you expect me to resist. Of course you're paying for it, and I'll exercise some latitude in deciding how much home improvement is required to make the place habitable for a cripple."

"Just so long as we understand each other."

"Your buddy, Jim? He's good meat. Could've used him on the security detail. Or ten of him."

"Jim's rock solid. He's the best."

"How bad's the damage on him?"

"Manageable," Rusty said, not wanting to dwell on the

extent of injury Jim had described to his left hand. "He'll need a little medical vacation from the Ocean City cop shop. I think it's about time he slowed down, anyway."

"And he'll have to spin a good yarn for the wife about how he got dinged up."

"I'm sure he'll conjure something plausible that's not too incriminating. Vegas is a wild town, after all."

"Wilder than usual the past couple days," Charlotte paused. "I'm guessing you'll make tracks soon as you wave goodbye to me? By the way, you can do it anytime. No need to drag this out."

Rusty reached over to lay a hand on her shoulder, taking such excessive care Charlotte shot him a smirk.

"Truth is, I can't wait to get on a plane," he said. "But I've got to stick around for another couple days. So you'll probably see me again, whether you like it or not. I've got one more visit to make before I leave."

• • •

Two days passed before Rusty attended to the final item on his Vegas to-do list. He spent most of that time with Jim, poolside at the Grand. They didn't talk all that much, content to quietly sip drinks and watch the talent stroll by. Jim's hand was set in a cast, and he'd be needing at least one corrective procedure to regain full working capability, but the prognosis was good. His other injuries didn't seem to bother him much, not even the welt at the base of his skull from Soren's pipe.

Rusty tried to think of a thousand ways to thank his friend for what he'd done, but none of them came easily. He had a feeling Jim didn't want to hear it, anyway.

Their shared company had started to grow oppressive by the end of dinner last night, so Rusty was relieved they were flying back home separately today. Jim took an early cab to

McCarran. Rusty would be following his tracks shortly, after closing this final bit of business.

The Eden Vale Mortuary Home was without question the most opulent storehouse of the freshly deceased in all of LV. Built like a giant tabernacle of ivory and glass, it bounced complex patterns of light from the morning sun in a fashion not unlike the Luxor pyramid.

Rusty parked the Barracuda in the closest spot he could find and got out. Approaching the frosted entrance doors, he felt a flutter of nerves arise in the pit of his stomach.

News of Paul Ponti's death had dominated local media for the past thirty-six hours, and generated a fair amount of national coverage. Rusty was responsible for the quickness of the media storm—if he hadn't placed an anonymous pay phone call to LV Metro reporting two bodies in the flood tunnels, and giving precise directions to where they could be recovered, there was no telling how long it would have taken before Ponti's fate became known.

A respected pillar of the city found dead in such a squalid environment was bound to generate plenty of ripples. And it wasn't long before the inevitable speculations began. Despite having operated as a high-profile land developer for more than a decade, Ponti's early years on the circuit were well documented. A flood of old reports, many long suppressed, started to seep out. Unnamed informants spread like ants over a picnic basket.

Barely a day after the news of Ponti's death hit the wires, his shadow ownership of Allied Interests had come to light. Someone inside the holding company sold that bit of intel to local muckraking portal SinCityConfidential.com. Within hours of the first online report going live, print and television outlets were parroting the information. Much was made of Ponti's recent acquisition of derelict properties along the so-called Homeless Corridor. That he'd been found in a subterranean flood tunnel known to attract large clumps of the transient population struck some public voices as a connection too strange to be coincidental.

Far less speculation arose about the other body on the scene. It would take almost a week to identify the decedent as Trent Hanson, twenty-seven years of age. Police searched Trent's high-rise apartment on Paradise and discovered the robust ticket-selling apparatus. Security camera footage at the Charleston Arms showed Paul Ponti entering the building and leaving ten minutes later on the day before the bodies were found. This only served to fuel conjecture about the nature of the relationship between the two men, while offering no substantive clues.

The eventual discovery of a third corpse in an abandoned bottle house in Rhyolite would not occur for months. A British tourist seeking some off-the-beaten-path excitement made a solo journey to the tiny ghost town. Snapping photos inside the former Busch facility, a stench of decay drew him down to the basement. Police came up with no leads for the obvious case of homicide by firearm, and no one ever connected it to the Ponti-Hanson case. Just a strange unsolved death out in the valley of the same name. Probably some personal dispute or drug deal gone wrong. The victim, identified by dental records as Soren Stark, had no known family or associates. His remains were disposed of at the downtown forensics center, and that was the end of it.

Rusty had followed the news coverage obsessively since returning to the loft from the Underworld. Before going there, he'd insisted on getting Luna medical attention for a gash on her arm she'd sustained in the Underworld. The possibility of infection from the filthy tunnels was all too high. She put up some resistance before finally consenting, but refused his offer to wait at the clinic while she received attention so he could drive her home. She'd seen the last she wanted to see of Rusty Diamond, and would find her own way back to Sinatra Cove.

Luna gave him a wordless look outside the clinic, one that Rusty interpreted as holding a mixture of contempt and gratitude. Her cooperation had obviously proven to be the lynchpin in how it all played out. Agreeing to take those two capsules of oxycodone and trusting where she'd find herself when they wore off. Rusty had told her she needed to get in the duffel bag and inside the trunk before they arrived at the tunnel's entrance, in case that area was being monitored. She consented, willing to do anything that would ensure another video like the one she'd seen on his computer never got made.

Luna may have hated Rusty for what he'd made her realize about the people with whom she'd been associating, but it was better to know than continue along in blind cooperation. So maybe she was just a little grateful to him as well. He thought that might be what she was thinking as she turned away and entered the clinic—or maybe she just regretted ever having crossed paths with him.

That unreadable look on Luna's face hovered in Rusty's mind as he stepped into the Eden Vale Mortuary Home.

A frigid blast of air conditioning and soft fluted tones welcomed him. At the greeting desk, he inquired where the Ponti viewing would be taking place. The clerk gazed back with hooded suspicion, clearly doubting from Rusty's appearance that his name would be found on the ultra-exclusive guest list. Rusty assured him he was here only to make a brief observance from outside the private room restricted to family, friends, and local luminaries. Carrot Top was said to be among the honored inner circle.

Following a blood-red carpet down a narrow hallway, he paused at an open door on the left. It led into a spacious viewing room lined with rows of seating on either side. At the far end of the room stood a small stage, the centerpiece of which was a raised casket laden down with enough floral arrangements to fill a sizable greenhouse.

Rusty stood just outside the doorway, gazing in. Something about the scene struck a queasy chord within, and it took him a moment to identify the sense of recognition.

Just like the performance area in the Underworld, he thought. *Raised stage with a sacrificial altar, two rows of seating for the faithful.*

Of those, only a few were currently in attendance at this early hour. The main viewing event, complete with a benediction from Archbishop Thompson of the Guardian Angel Cathedral, was not scheduled to start until noon. Rusty intended to be eastbound in the air before any of that got underway. He had a seat on the 10:40 nonstop from McCarran to BWI.

All that mattered right now, all he'd come here to achieve, was a quick word with someone he'd been both hoping and scared to speak with for over three years. And he was banking on finding her at this quiet interval before the main event. A long shot, but one he had to take before getting on that plane.

The girl despises her old man, by all accounts.

Those words from Charlotte rang in his ears.

Cut him out of her life since she became a legal adult, takes his money but shuns all contact.

Of the half-dozen heads poking over the seating benches, none struck Rusty as likely to belong to Paula Ponti.

He knew it was highly suspicious to keep his sentinel here for more than a few minutes, on the dim hope his intuition about her arrival proved accurate. Any longer than that, and he'd probably be escorted from the premises. What kind of freak comes to a casket viewing and doesn't even enter the room?

Rusty figured he could always take a seat in the back bench and monitor the room for her appearance, but that idea unsettled him. He was hoping to catch her either leaving or entering the viewing room, so as not to draw the notice of any other observers.

A nervous glance at his watch told him six minutes had passed since he'd entered the mortuary. At the far end of the hall, an usher was looking at him with an expression halfway between curiosity and mistrust.

Damn it. Gonna have to take a seat or turn and walk.

Just as that thought entered his head, a young woman approached from the greeting desk. Even from thirty paces, he knew it was her.

She'd matured well since he'd last laid eyes on her. Lost most of her baby fat and looked to have gained an inch or two in height. She wore a conservative black dress, knee length, and clutched a designer purse to her chest like some kind of shield. Her hair, darker than he recalled, was worn in a trim bob much different than the shoulder length tresses of her teens.

She was less than five feet away when it occurred to him he really didn't know what to say. Eyes cast down toward the carpet, she didn't appear to notice him blocking the doorway.

Before she walked right into him, he spoke.

"Paula?"

She jerked her head up, a startled look in her large brown eyes. To Rusty's mind, her demeanor was that of a cat burglar caught in a floodlight. It struck him just how difficult it must be to attempt a surreptitious viewing of your father's remains, especially when he was a figure of broad public notice.

"Who are you?" she said, and even as the words left her mouth Rusty could see recognition bloom in her eyes.

"I think you know, maybe. Can we talk for a minute?"

The woman nervously glanced over her shoulder, as if expecting another phantom from the past to materialize out of thin air.

"What are you…I mean, this is just so bizarre. I only came to pay respects before this place turns into a zoo."

"I don't want to keep you." He pointed to a small bench on the opposite side of the hall. "Just a minute?"

After a pause, she nodded, and followed him over. They sat, keeping a healthy distance between them.

"I'm sorry for your loss," he said lamely.

"No, don't tell me that. I can't even begin to guess what you're doing here, but you were obviously involved somehow."

"Your father had a beef with me, that's true. I don't need to tell you what it was about. I came out here to resolve it, but I swear on my own life I didn't take his. Not that you have any reason to believe me, but it's true."

"I actually do believe you. It was that other guy they found him with, right? I'm not blind, Mr. Diamond. Something like this has been waiting to catch up with my father for years. Decades. I'm not shocked and I'm not as bereaved as you might think. That's why I don't want to be involved with the whole circus in there. I'll find my own way to mourn, in my own time."

She paused for a beat, looking abashed to have spoken so freely.

Rusty caught himself staring at her with great intent, and forced himself to stop. It was hard not to examine every inch of her face, peering for signs of the damage he knew he'd wrought.

Nothing. From chin to brow, ear to ear. Not the slightest scar or blemish.

"I guess you're wondering how bad you hurt me?"

"Yeah."

The word barely left Rusty's mouth, which felt dry as tumbleweed. All the suppressed shame and self-loathing came over him with enough force to induce vertigo. He was fortunate to be seated.

"I got lucky," she said, almost sounding amused. "Another inch higher and one of those fragments…what did you hand me, a magnet of some kind?"

Rusty could only nod.

"One of those pieces from the magnet would've blinded me in my left eye. Killed me, more likely. Doctor said it would have passed right through the eye socket into my brain."

"Jesus Christ…"

"Still a little scar here," she said, pointing to a spot of slightly mottled flesh beneath her eye. Rusty saw it, barely. It could have been a natural pattern of her skin.

"Nobody notices it. Dad flew in a plastic surgeon from Switzerland, best in the world he was supposed to be. I believe it."

Rusty cast a glance at the usher, who had managed to move closer over the past minute or so. He was doing some fairly obvious eavesdropping, or trying to.

"I can't begin to tell you how sorry—"

"Don't. I mean it, there's no need."

"Oh yeah, there's plenty of need. And an apology hardly starts to cover it. If there's any way I can pay—"

"Please, stop. You know what my father was worth? Money's the last thing I need. Besides, I really should thank you. You saved my life that day."

This stunned Rusty so much he couldn't formulate a response.

"It's true. If you hadn't done exactly what you did, I'd already be in the ground. Right out next to where they'll bury Dad this afternoon."

"But, what? I don't—"

"After the accident, they raced me to the emergency room at Central. I barely remember the drive. I was in so much pain, and I couldn't see anything with a towel covering my face. A series of towels. Dad kept having to change them in the back seat of the Escalade. There was so much blood coming from the wound."

Rusty could barely maintain eye contact, but he managed to do it.

"They put me under and went to work on the wound to my face. During the operation, my heart went crazy. Some kind of really intense arrhythmia. It was very unusual for someone my age, even considering the trauma of the injury and having surgery. After I was stitched up and somewhat recovered, they ran a battery of tests on my heart. Turns out I had a blocked artery. Freak occurrence for a sixteen-year-old, a hereditary thing. Apparently my great-grandfather died of the same thing in his twenties. They put in a stent and I get checked up four times a year. My prognosis is excellent, but the doctor said they never would have detected my condition if I hadn't gone under for the surgery to my face. That's what I mean when I say you saved my life."

Rusty realized he had to say something in response to that.

"Well, I had no idea what to expect from meeting you today, Paula. I can safely say that wasn't even on the list of remote possibilities."

She shrugged, as if there were nothing particularly consequential about meeting the man who had inadvertently steered her away from an early grave while standing outside a room that housed her father's corpse.

"Everything happens for a reason, right?"

"I never really believed that. Not sure I do now, but…"

The sentence trailed off. He had no idea how to finish it, and Paula stood before he mumbled something else that made little sense.

"Look, the rest of my family is gonna be here any minute. I've already told them we could meet up later, and grieve in private. I just can't tolerate being here for all the bullshit speeches and platitudes about what a great man we've lost. I know who my father was, Mr. Diamond. He'd do anything for me, and

I loved him for that. Hiring you for the party was my idea, not his."

"Yeah, he made that pretty clear to me at the time. Wasn't real happy about inviting a gothed-up freak like me into his house. Guess he had the right intuition."

"But I wanted you there. You were my absolute favorite. I made him take me to your show at Caesars I don't know how many times. After the third or fourth he refused to go again, sent a chaperone with me. When I told him all I wanted for my sweet sixteen was a private performance from Rusty Diamond in my own backyard, he barely blinked before saying yes."

"He loved you very much, obviously. Whatever else he might've been or done."

A slight grin curved the corners of Paula's mouth.

"You didn't come cheap either, or so I was told. Dad never let me know the full cost, but he said it was more than the average girl might ask her old man to spend on her wedding."

A glimmer of reflected light came from the front end of the hallway. Rusty and Paula turned their heads at the same time, seeing a small cluster of well-dressed people filing in.

"God, here they come. I need to duck in so I can get away from here before it gets nuts."

"Of course. Thanks for talking to me. It means more to me than you'll ever know."

Paula laid a hand on his arm, then quickly retracted it. "Take care, Mr. Diamond."

"Looks like there's a back exit," he said, pointing in the direction where the usher held his position monitoring their conversation. "Might want to go out that way; I expect there will be plenty of cameras out front by the time it's over."

She nodded wordlessly and walked into the viewing room. Rusty watched her go, then turned and made for the mortuary's front door as fast as he could without breaking into a run.

Outside, the sun blinded him and he regretted having

already packed his shades. As he'd cautioned Paula, the first of what would be many news vans was rolling into the parking lot. Rusty made a beeline for the Barracuda and got in, feeling foolish by his momentary impulse to avoid any cameras.

You're not the Raven anymore, asshole. You're no one in this town. Thank Christ for that.

He gunned it out of the parking lot and started on the most direct course for McCarran. Idling at a red light, he checked a new text on his phone from Jim.

THANKS FOR THE TICKET, I COULD GET USED TO 1ST CLASS. 2 BLOODIES IN AND WE HAVEN'T LEFT THE GROUND YET. SEE U IN OC.

Rusty grinned and thumbed a quick reply.

DINNER ON ME AT FAGERS ISLAND. WE STILL GOT SOME CATCHING UP TO DO BEFORE I LEAVE FOR NOLA.

He placed the phone in the glove box and closed it. Jim would most likely text back, giving him shit about his planned move to New Orleans. Rusty didn't want to hear any of that right now, especially from someone to whom he owed so much.

His mind was made up. After a lengthy epoch of hiding from the past in calm coastal Maryland, it was time to move on. He'd known that in his bones even before those grisly packages started appearing on his doorstep. If was almost as if Trent and Ponti—two restless ghosts from his former life in Vegas—had summoned him out to this desert not simply to settle unresolved scores but to give him the nudge he needed to come out of his overlong seclusion. Rusty was either meant to have died here in LV or to take his survival as unimpeachable evidence that the past was finally in the past.

The answer was pretty clear.

As for what awaited him in New Orleans, he couldn't say for sure. He had an old mentor in the conjuring arts down there with whom a tentative reunion might continue, and a possible romantic interest waiting to be rekindled. Even if both of those options proved to be dead ends, Rusty would always have the familiar streets of the French Quarter to soothe him. Those same streets where he'd first begun practicing magic more than twenty years ago, not for money but for the sheer thrill of it.

He had to smile at the prospect of setting up shop on those flagstone corners again. Just another anonymous street artist, wowing the liquored-up tourists with acts of mentalism and sleight of hand. He'd do it, too. He'd definitely do it.

Hell, Rusty thought, gunning it down Paradise Road to the airport. *Might just feel like starting all over.*